W9-BWV-142

Poised on the balls of his feet, Bolan listened intently

"Just stay calm," Grendel cautioned. "We have to keep a real low profile. Lower than ever, after what Loomis told me this afternoon."

"Is it a secret?"

Grendel hesitated. "What the hell. You'd find out in a few days anyway. The boss has a new job to do, the biggest damn job ever." He grinned. "Do you remember the greaser who was hot under the collar about the DEA?"

"What about him?"

"Well, he got himself whacked. His people are furious. They think the government is to blame. So they're paying Trask to come up with a foolproof way to hit another target. You wouldn't guess who it is in a million years."

"The CIA? The FBI?"

"Not quite. They want to blow away the President."

Other titles available in this series:

Stony Man Doctrine
Terminal Velocity
Resurrection Day
Dirty War
Flight 741
Dead Easy
Sudden Death
Rogue Force
Tropic Heat
Fire in the Sky
Anvil of Hell
Flash Point
Flesh and Blood
Moving Target
Tightrope
Blowout
Blood Fever
Knockdown
Assault
Backlash
Siege
Blockade
Evil Kingdom
Counterblow
Hardline
Firepower
Storm Burst
Intercept
Lethal Impact
Deadfall
Onslaught
Battle Force
Rampage
Takedown
Death's Head
Hellground
Inferno
Ambush
Blood Strike
Killpoint
Vendetta
Stalk Line
Omega Game
Shock Tactic
Showdown

DON PENDLETON's

MACK BOLAN®

PRECISION KILL

TORONTO • NEW YORK • LONDON
AMSTERDAM • PARIS • SYDNEY • HAMBURG
STOCKHOLM • ATHENS • TOKYO • MILAN
MADRID • WARSAW • BUDAPEST • AUCKLAND

If you purchased this book without a cover you should be aware that this book is stolen property. It was reported as "unsold and destroyed" to the publisher, and neither the author nor the publisher has received any payment for this "stripped book."

First edition February 1996

ISBN 0-373-61446-2

Special thanks and acknowledgment to
David Robbins for his contribution to this work.

PRECISION KILL

Copyright © 1996 by Worldwide Library.

All rights reserved. Except for use in any review, the reproduction or utilization of this work in whole or in part in any form by any electronic, mechanical or other means, now known or hereafter invented, including xerography, photocopying and recording, or in any information storage or retrieval system, is forbidden without the written permission of the publisher, Worldwide Library, 225 Duncan Mill Road, Don Mills, Ontario, Canada M3B 3K9.

All characters in this book have no existence outside the imagination of the author and have no relation whatsoever to anyone bearing the same name or names. They are not even distantly inspired by any individual known or unknown to the author, and all incidents are pure invention.

® and TM are trademarks of the publisher. Trademarks indicated with ® are registered in the United States Patent and Trademark Office, the Canadian Trade Marks Office and in other countries.

Printed in U.S.A.

...like fire he meets the foe,
And strikes him dead for thine and thee.

—Alfred, Lord Tennyson
1809–1892

For those who cannot act, who are the helpless victims of the ruthless, I will strike back.

—Mack Bolan

PROLOGUE

The Drug Enforcement Administration's world came crashing down at four o'clock in the afternoon.

Agent Bill Keating had just sat at his desk on the third floor and turned to stare out the tinted window. The previous hour had been spent in a heated meeting with his superiors regarding DEA policy south of the border.

Keating was from the old school of law enforcement, which favored the big-stick approach. In other words, when diplomacy failed, flex muscle. He was sick and tired of coddling corrupt officials who did all they could to hinder DEA efforts. If it was up to him, he'd sweep into Mexico with an army of agents behind him and bring the flow of drugs to a screeching stop in a week's time.

But no.

The powers higher up wanted it made clear that all DEA agents were to tread with care. The State Department didn't want any more "incidents" on its hands, and woe unto the agent foolish enough to disregard policy.

Keating rested an elbow on the arm of his chair and propped his chin in his hand. In his mind's eye he relived some of the early days of his career, when he had worked at the Justice Department. Back then, criminals weren't pampered instead of prosecuted. Back then, an agent who made a bust could count on it sticking in court, when the legal system of the good old U.S. of A. was based on ideals, not ideas.

A swirl of red in the sky drew Keating's gaze. Several children were flying kites in the park. One kite, bearing the emblem of an eagle, swirled and dipped, trying to get airborne. He saw a boy of twelve or so frantically run back and forth to increase the lift, but there didn't appear to be enough of a breeze to hold any of the kites aloft.

So Keating was all the more surprised when he raised his head from the fluttering eagle to see another kite much farther away holding steady in the sky. Then he realized that it wasn't a kite. It was a silver dot, growing bigger by the moment.

He decided the object was an aircraft, but if so, the pilot was flying in restricted space. It made him think of the time a stolen plane crashed into the White House, and he idly wondered if another nutcase was trying to commit suicide.

The dot took on new dimensions swiftly.

With a start, Keating recognized those dimensions. He wasn't looking at a kite or a plane or anything else normally found in the airspace above Washington, D.C. No, he was gaping at a slow-moving missile on a beeline to the very building in which he sat.

"Get down! Everyone hit the floor! We're under attack!"

More than a dozen heads swung toward him. Disbelief and confusion etched every face. Keating wanted to say more so they would understand the urgency, but he had run out of time.

The blast was tremendous. Keating was knocked forward by the explosion. A hot wind lifted him off his feet and flung him through the air as if he were a rag doll. People, furniture and shattered pieces of both flew along with him. Something stung him in the calf. He tumbled end over end, careened off a wall, a filing cabinet. His shoulder snapped with a resounding crack, and the resultant pain nearly blacked him out.

Keating was only dimly aware of landing on his shoulder, of rolling several feet. The entire headquarters building shook as if in the throes of an earthquake. He felt the floor buckle under him. The next thing he knew, he was in free-fall.

The din was earsplitting. Wood and plaster were rent like twigs, steel girders were wrenched out of place.

Vaguely Keating was conscious of jolting to a sudden stop, of his leg lancing with acute agony. Above him bedlam reigned. The world seemed to be coming to an end. He struggled to stay awake, to keep alert, but a clinging fog enveloped his mind and he drifted into limbo.

How long the senior agent was out, he couldn't say. One moment he was unconscious, the next his eyes snapped wide open and he found himself lying on his side in almost total darkness. The air was musty, and he was slick with sweat.

Puzzled, Keating extended his good arm. His fingertips brushed a smooth wall, or what passed for a wall, only it was at an angle and so close to his head that he had only to crane his neck to brush it with his brow. He went to shift position and was swamped by waves of sheer torment that coursed up his leg and through his body. The leg was broken, as was his clavicle. There could be no doubt.

Faintly to Keating's ear came a peculiar scratching sound. He listened, straining, and made out a series of dull thuds and scrapes. It took him all of a minute to put two and two together and deduce the truth.

Searchers were digging through the debris, seeking survivors.

Keating cupped a hand to his mouth and took a deep breath. "Help! Down here! I'm trapped! Can anyone hear me?" He thought he heard a voice respond but he couldn't be sure. The simple effort it took to yell had produced a wave of dizziness so intense that he teetered on the brink of unconsciousness again. Despite that, he shouted louder, using the last of his strength. "Help me! Please! Follow my voice!"

Once more the void claimed him. Keating drifted off, fearing the rescuers hadn't heard him, that he had been buried so deeply he would never see the light of day.

Fate dictated otherwise.

The DEA agent came awake slowly, aware of a tingling, pleasant sensation that filled him from head to toe. Blinking against the glare of sunlight, he looked around and discovered he was in a hospital bed. He also saw a big man with rugged features standing nearby, talking to a doctor. The man turned and smiled.

Keating mustered one of his own. Suddenly all was right with the world. He was in competent hands. "Why, if it isn't Hal Brognola. Long time no see."

CHAPTER ONE

Mexico

The Chihuahua Desert was an inferno, though the morning wasn't yet half over.

Mack Bolan ignored the beads of sweat that had formed on his brow and peered intently through the telescopic sight mounted on his M-16. Well hidden among a cluster of boulders 250 yards from a sprawling hacienda, he studied the layout closely. Once the sun set, he was going in.

Six hours earlier Bolan had been high in the sky in a McDonnell Douglas F-4E Phantom II piloted by his good friend Jack Grimaldi. The ace pilot was in a somber mood. Given the nature of their mission, Bolan had readily understand why.

Just before Grimaldi dipped a wing to zip in low over the mountains flanking the desert, he had broken the silence by saying "The last I heard, the death toll stood at fourteen. And they expect to find more bodies in the rubble."

"No doubt" was all Bolan said. He recalled hearing that one of the victims had been a secretary eight months pregnant.

"Hal's upset enough as it is, but that friend of his, Keating, lost part of a leg." Grimaldi had paused. "I just hope we're not barking up the wrong tree."

"That's what I intend to find out," Bolan had assured him.

After the drop, the Executioner had stashed the glide chute, adjusted his backpack and set off at a tireless dogtrot to the southwest. He had intended to reach the vicinity of the hacienda well before dawn. As it was, he barely had time to find a vantage point before the blazing sun cleared the horizon.

The Intel was to blame. The DEA had known that drug lord Luis Terrazas operated from a vast estate in the Chihuahuan wasteland, but they hadn't known that the estate was regularly patrolled by six-man teams with dogs.

Bolan had narrowly avoided each patrol. The gunners by themselves would have posed no problem. But the trained German shepherds were another story. He'd had to make sure he was downwind at all times and hadn't moved a muscle as long as the dogs were within earshot. It had slowed him considerably.

Since dawn, the soldier had seen more gunners making rounds on the hacienda grounds, some with dogs, some without.

Terrazas was known to be as arrogant as he was ruthless, but no one had said anything about his penchant for running his operation military-style. In addition to the roving guards, snipers were posted at four high points close to the main cluster of adobe buildings. The man apparently left nothing to chance.

Bolan knew it would only make his job that much harder, but then, he was used to setbacks in the field. No matter how well an operation was planned, there were always variables to deal with. The best he could hope for was that his diligent planning would cut those variables to a minimum.

He scanned the grounds yet again, ensuring he had the setup memorized.

There were four walls, but they were low and could easily be scaled. A stable, a corral and some outbuildings bordered the north one. In the center of the grounds stood the long, low house. Only two stories high, it was capped by a bell tower at the northwest corner.

Bolan knew that back at the turn of the century, hundreds of peasant farmers had worked the estate. The bell had been their signal to head out into the fields every morning and told them when to quit at the end of the day.

What interested the soldier most of all, though, were the newer buildings that covered the southern third of the estate—warehouses and other structures devoted to the drug trade.

According to the DEA, Terrazas liked to diversify. Whereas many drug lords specialized in one type of drug, Luis Terrazas was an opportunist. He dabbled in any and every illegal substance that would net him a hefty profit. Cocaine, marijuana, even heroin were all funneled through his extensive pipeline into the United States. His operation was rated as one of the largest in North America.

Small wonder the DEA had targeted him. They had tried to nail him through proper channels and been stalled at every turn by politicians, judges and police—all secretly on the drug lord's payroll. Time and again they had built a case against him, only to have it thrown out of court on the flimsiest of technicalities. Several times evidence left in the care of Mexican authorities mysteriously vanished.

So did DEA agents. Two of those assigned to bring down Terrazas disappeared. An extensive search was mounted both times, without result. On the underground grapevine, however, it was common knowledge that the drug czar had ordered them hacked into pieces with machetes, then disposed of.

If Terrazas had thought the vile murders would intimidate the DEA into leaving him alone, he had been wrong. DEA agents were a dedicated breed. Obstacles only made them try harder. And when they lost some of their own, they pulled out all the stops.

Hal Brognola believed the DEA had Terrazas worried. Why else had the drug lord brazenly marched into the DEA field office in Mexico City, along with a dozen gunners, and told the agent in charge in no uncertain terms that if the DEA continued to wage war on him, he would wage war on the DEA and hit them where it would hurt them the most?

Which made Luis Terrazas the prime suspect in the attack on DEA headquarters.

So far, Bolan had seen no sign of the man, who would stand out in any crowd. Surveillance photos had shown a tall, immensely powerful individual with a full beard and a jagged scar on his left cheek. At six feet four inches and 280 pounds, Terrazas had the build of a linebacker and carried himself like a great shaggy bear—a grizzly.

Activity near the swimming pool drew Bolan's interest. Several young women in skimpy swimsuits had emerged from a side door and were cavorting near a diving board. A brunette rolled up a towel and began flicking it at her companions, who squealed in mock terror.

The fun and games abruptly stopped when Terrazas strolled out. He had on a pair of trunks and his steely muscles rippled in the sunlight. Unlike many underworld kingpins, who grew fat and lazy once they reached the top, Terrazas had the air of a prowling tiger. He wasn't to be taken lightly.

Bolan shifted to watch the gunners. He could gauge their quality by how they behaved. Amateurs would turn to view the poolside antics. Pros would concentrate on their duties and nothing else.

Every single sniper and guard made it a point *not* to pay any attention to their boss and the bevy of beauties.

The soldier had expected as much. Penetrating the estate promised to be a challenge.

Shifting an elbow to relieve a cramp, Bolan stiffened on seeing an elderly woman in a black dress and apron appear. She carried a tray of refreshments and set the tray on a table. Terrazas spoke to her. Giving a little bow, she hurried indoors to do his bidding.

Bolan's lips tightened. He scanned the estate again and counted fourteen laborers, innocent civilians like the house servant. Some were tending stock at the corral, another worked on a tractor, still others were erecting a large shed.

Bystanders always put a crimp in the warrior's plans. His war was with the hardened criminal element that preyed on society, not with those whose only crime happened to be that they were employed by the scum of the earth.

Bolan would have to be careful. He didn't want the blood of innocents on his hands. Rather than lay waste everything in sight, it would be a search-and-destroy operation.

Lowering the M-16, Bolan folded his arms and rested his chin on them. He had a lot of time to kill before nightfall. Since he needed to be sharp to get the job done right, he decided to close his eyes and take a catnap.

For nearly a half hour the warrior slept. When he awakened, he raised the M-16 and pressed his right eye to the scope. Terrazas was gone. The three lovelies were sunning themselves. Two of them had removed their tops while the brunette had stripped down to her birthday suit to tan all over.

The soldier focused on the guards and timed them with his watch. Three pairs spaced at regular intervals made a constant circuit of the perimeter, completing a circuit on the average of once every forty-three minutes. Others roamed at will, according to no set pattern. They were the ones who would give him trouble later on.

Noon came and went, and the afternoon seemed to drag on forever. Even in the shade of the boulders, Bolan simmered.

The sun baked the earth mercilessly. Shimmering heat waves distorted objects at a distance. To the south there appeared to be a pristine lake where Bolan knew there was only more arid land.

Shortly after three the drone of an approaching plane was the signal for a flurry of activity inside the walls. Six gunners piled into a flatbed truck, which sped through the front gate and turned north. A rutted track brought it to a narrow dirt airfield a stone's throw from the hacienda.

The aircraft was a de Havilland DHC-6-2000, a vintage twin-prop airplane capable of carrying up to nineteen passengers. This one, it turned out, had been converted to haul freight. It circled the estate, then banked and came in for a perfect three-point landing. The propellers were still spinning when the door was thrown wide and two men in brown overalls hopped out.

Greetings were exchanged. One of Terrazas's lieutenants, a scarecrow in a gray suit, took charge. Orders were barked. The gunners and the flight crew began unloading crates and stacking them on the flatbed.

It had to be a drug shipment, although Bolan had no clue as to the type of narcotic. What impressed him most was the fact that the operation was being conducted in broad daylight, right out in the open. It was added proof of the drug lord's power.

Bolan figured the aircraft would depart after the crates were unloaded. But both the hardmen and the crew piled onto the truck and were whisked to a warehouse. From there the scarecrow and one of the men in overalls went into the house while the rest transferred the crates to a pallet.

The shadows were lengthening when Bolan slid a package of crackers from a slit pocket. He nibbled while checking on the guards. There had been no change in their routine.

The growl of another engine cut the hot desert air. This one belonged to a military jeep that was speeding toward the hacienda along the road that linked Terrazas's stronghold to the nearest town. Dust spewed in its wake. A tiny flag fluttered from the antenna, indicating it was a general staff vehicle.

The gunners didn't show any alarm, so evidently the newcomer was expected or came often. The jeep braked at the gate long enough for the guards to verify the identity of the occupants, then it drove on in and parked close to the front door.

Luis Terrazas himself greeted the gray-haired officer who climbed out. They shook hands warmly. Draping an arm over the officer's shoulder, Terrazas guided him indoors.

The driver, a private, lounged against the fender and lit a cigarette.

It spelled trouble for Bolan. Less than an hour remained of daylight, which might mean the army officer planned to stay the night. If that was the case, the Executioner had to put off the insertion. Even if the officer was on the take, killing him would provoke the Mexican government.

Twilight descended, and Bolan made a final check of the tools of his trade. There was a full magazine in the M-16. A 9 mm Beretta 93-R was leathered under his left arm, and on his right thigh rode a .44 Magnum Desert Eagle. A Ka-bar combat knife hugged an ankle sheath. Spare ammo and sundry devices were secreted in various pockets of his blacksuit.

Bolan didn't relish the thought of having to wait another twenty-four hours before going in. So he was all the more pleased when, shortly after dark, light spilled from the front door and the officer reappeared, escorted by the drug lord and two of the beauties. In his right hand the officer held an envelope.

The women grinned and waved as the jeep drove off. Once it was through the gate, Terrazas spoke curtly and they filed inside.

No sooner did the door close than Bolan was in motion. On cat's feet he glided from cover to cover, pausing often to look and listen. He angled toward the airstrip. No guards had been posted so he figured disabling the DHC would be a simple chore. But as he drew nearer, he saw the cargo-bay door was still open and a feeble light glowed within. Closer still, and he heard music.

The Executioner went prone to crawl the final fifty feet. On reaching the fuselage, he rose into a crouch and crept into the bay. The song on the radio ended, replaced by the chatter of an announcer. His back to the inner wall, Bolan moved forward to a doorway that separated the cargo bay from the cabin. Through it he spied a stocky man in overalls stretched out on his back on a seat that ran nearly the width of the plane, his face buried in a skin magazine.

Crouching, Bolan stalked toward the seat. He planned to knock out the hardman, then cripple the aircraft. But he wasn't quite close enough to strike when the floor under him creaked loudly.

The man, startled, sat up, upending the radio.

Bolan lunged. As quick as he was, the guy in the overalls managed to twist aside. The rifle's stock struck only a glancing blow. The man grabbed the barrel and heaved, swinging the Executioner up and over the back of the seat. Tangled together, they spilled into the cockpit, Bolan striving to retain his grip on the M-16, his adversary trying to tear it from his grasp.

The hardman, strong as a bull, flipped Bolan onto his back. A foot arced at his groin. Shifting, he took the blow on his thigh, gritting his teeth against the pain. Then, whipping both legs upward, he slammed the man into the control console.

A dial shattered. The hardman scrambled to regain his footing, but Bolan wasn't about to let him. He kicked out, his sole catching the man behind the knee. There was a crack, and his opponent fell backward.

Bolan was braced. He swung the stock into the base of the hardman's skull, then rose and stood over the prone figure. The radio still blared so he switched it off.

Using his combat knife, Bolan removed a panel from the console. At random he cut as many wires as he could reach. Others he tugged loose. When he was satisfied that it would be impossible to get the airplane off the ground, he closed the panel to disguise his handiwork.

The loose wires came in handy. Bolan bound the hardman hand and foot. In a pants pocket he found a handkerchief, which he stuffed into the man's mouth. Several loops of wire ensured the gag would stay in place. He rolled the man under the seat before leaving.

Bolan was almost to the end of the cargo bay when headlights speared the night. Instantly he melted into the darkest shadows he could find.

It was the flatbed. The brakes creaked as the vehicle coasted to a stop, and the gearshift protested being thrown into neutral. One of the two men who had left with the gunners slid from the cab. He held a small cardboard box, which he hefted while calling out in Spanish, "Hey, Pablo! Come and get your supper, eh?"

When there was no answer, the man cursed under his breath and came on board. "Pablo? It's me, Estavan. Are you hard of hearing, as well as being stupid? I went to all this trouble to bring you a hot meal. The least you can do is have the decency to answer."

Estavan headed for the cockpit. He never sensed the soldier's presence. As he drew abreast of the shadow, Bolan rammed the M-16 into the side of his skull and the good samaritan crumpled as if made of soggy paper. The box spilled, casting burritos, tostadas and refried beans at Bolan's feet.

It didn't take long to give Estavan the same treatment as Pablo. But first Bolan stripped off the newcomer's shirt and shrugged it on over the blacksuit.

Hurrying to the truck, he climbed into the cab, worked the shift and drove toward the stronghold. The panel lights were dim enough that his features were completely shrouded, but to play it safe he pulled the Desert Eagle and smashed the speedometer and the oil pressure gauge, which reduced the glare by a third. Instead of holstering the big .44, he placed it in his lap for ready use.

Bolan took it nice and slow. The gate was open and the guards were next to the right-hand wall, talking. Uzis were slung over their shoulders. He counted on their allowing the flatbed to go right on in, since it had only left a few minutes earlier.

The taller gunner looked up and moved to the middle of the road.

Tensing, Bolan rested his right hand on the Desert Eagle. If he had to, he would blast his way in and wreak havoc with the M-203 grenade launcher mounted on the M-16.

Almost at the last moment, the guard nonchalantly moved to one side and waved the truck by.

Bolan tucked his chin to his chest but gave a little wave as he entered. A glance in the rearview mirror showed the two guards moving back into the road to carry on their conversation. He headed for the warehouse where the crates had been unloaded. A spotlight bathed the gaping front door, so he veered around to the side to park. Lined up against the corrugated metal walls were empty crates and a trash bin.

Bolan replaced the Desert Eagle, grabbed the M-16, and slid out. Searching for another way into the warehouse, he sprinted to the rear of the building. In the far corner was a door. He tried the knob, half expecting it to be locked, but it opened on silent hinges. Slipping inside, he closed it softly behind him, then jogged a few yards to a pallet piled high with crates.

A minute of listening assured Bolan no one else was in the warehouse, nor had he seen anyone moving about on the grounds. Most, he reasoned, were eating supper.

Turning to the crates, the big man examined one from end to end. There were no labels, no markings of any kind to indicate the contents. It was the same with the next, and the next. The second pallet proved equally mystifying. His gut instinct was that they contained drugs, but he had to be sure.

Bolan had promised Brognola he would be on the lookout for electronic devices of the type used in the missile attack. For all he knew, they might be in the crates. Slinging the M-16 over his shoulder, he eased a crate from the top of a stack and slowly lowered it to the floor. It wasn't all that heavy. He pried off the top and found that it contained large packets of white powder. He had no need to test the contents of one to confirm it wasn't laundry detergent.

The soldier bent to replace the lid. As he lifted it, a voice rang out.

"Hold it right there. What do you think you're doing?"

CHAPTER TWO

The Executioner put a phony smile on his face and shifted, holding the lid in front of him so the portly gunner waddling down the center aisle couldn't get a good look at his clothing. "Pardon?" he asked innocently in Spanish.

"You heard me," the gunner snapped. He wore a pistol on his right hip, but he made no move to draw it. "The boss gave orders that no one is to touch the coke. Are you trying to help yourself?"

"No," Bolan said. By then the man was close enough. Bunching his shoulder muscles, the Executioner threw all his weight into a swing. The crate lid smashed into the gunner's face and blood spurted from his nose.

Stunned, the man staggered and nearly fell. Belatedly he clawed at his hardware.

The Beretta leaped clear of the shoulder rig and chugged twice in Bolan's hand. At point-blank range, the suppressor so close to the fat man's forehead that it brushed the skin, the bullet cored the gunner's brain. A glance at the wide entrance showed the inquisitive hardcase had been alone. Bolan swiftly slid the 93-R into the special holster, stooped to grip the man's ankles and dragged the body behind the nearest pallet.

About to head for the rear door, Bolan drew up short when he spied a row of gas cans against the far wall. A hasty inspection revealed six of them were full. Unscrewing the caps, he proceeded to pour the fuel over the pallets. He had to work rapidly and keep an ear tuned for footsteps.

That taken care of, he left the warehouse and moved along a row of shrubbery to the rear of the main house. Creeping to a windowsill, he saw Terrazas doing a slow dance with the brunette while the other women looked on. They would be occupied for a while yet.

The back door rattled slightly when Bolan opened it, but not loud enough to be heard above the music. The interior was cool and smelled of jasmine. A wide hall brought the soldier to a flight of stairs, which he took three at a stride. At the top he hugged the wall and counted six doors.

All the rooms were bedrooms. None contained sophisticated equipment of any kind unless one counted the whips, handcuffs and chains adorning the master bedroom.

At the far end of the corridor was another flight of stairs, which wound down into a dark den or office. Bolan removed a pen light from a slit pocket and rotated the head. The thin beam revealed bookcases on his right. There was a sofa and several chairs, but Bolan was interested only in the large maple desk and the computer that sat on top of it. It hummed with power. The monitor, though, was blank.

Lying beside the keyboard was the latest edition of a book on how to use a popular software program. The book was in Spanish, which did Bolan little good. He could wrestle with a menu and hold his own in day-to-day conversation, but technical jargon was beyond him. He had no idea how to tap into the drug lord's files.

Stymied, he rummaged through the desk. In the top left-hand drawer he found a plastic case containing dozens of labeled disks. Most of the labels bore dates, but nothing else. Were they backup files? Bolan wondered.

There was no time to lose. He raced upstairs to the master bedroom and stripped a pillowcase from a pillow. Hastening back to the office, he opened the pillowcase and dropped in every disk in the drawer and tied a knot at the open end. From a slit pocket on his leg he took a rolled up garrote and used it to fasten the pillowcase to his belt, above his right hip. By making several loops he was able to reduce the bulk and press the disk close to his body so they wouldn't restrict his movement.

Then he headed for the rear of the house. He was halfway down a hallway when voices sounded ahead and shadows played over the walls. An open door beckoned. Slipping inside, he hugged the wall. It was a dining room, complete with a grand chandelier suspended over a huge teak table that would seat twenty.

Laughter tinkled. A woman spoke in Spanish, complaining that it had been ages since she had last been to a town or city, and that she hated being stranded in the middle of nowhere. Another woman advised her to be careful. Terrazas wasn't fond of whiners.

The three beauties sashayed past. When their talk faded, Bolan slipped out and went on. He came to a junction and saw the back door off to the left. Sprinting toward it, he glanced over a shoulder, wary of having someone come up on him from behind. The coast was clear. Or so he thought until he turned around, and it was impossible to say which of them was more surprised, Terrazas or him.

The drug lord had stepped from a room a few yards away, a half-empty bottle of tequila in his hand. He gawked at Bolan a moment, stupefied to find an intruder in his inner sanctum. Then he suddenly bellowed, "Guards! Guards!" while his free hand groped under his jacket for a weapon.

Subtlety was out of the question. Bolan lashed out, planting a foot where it would do the most good. Terrazas sputtered and doubled over, in agony but still game. Livid, the drug lord yanked out a small pistol, a Walther P-5, and attempted to bring it to bear.

Bolan's right hand was closer to the Desert Eagle than to the Beretta. It would have been better to conduct a silent kill, but he had no choice. In a smooth blur he drew and fired. The blast of the big .44 was like a peel of thunder in the confines of the passageway.

The impact of the 240-grain hollowpoint at such short range was sufficient to hurl the drug lord through the air like a disjointed puppet.

Not giving Terrazas a second look, Bolan leaped over the corpse and barreled out the rear door. Cutting to the left, he headed for the end of the building. He sped around the corner and saw the bell tower atop the next one. Between it and him were two startled gunners, and a snarling guard dog on a leash.

Killers who sold their services to the highest bidder were seldom the cream of the intellectual crop. The pair confronting Bolan were cases in point. Instead of resorting to their Uzis, they unleashed the bristling dog.

Bolan had no choice. He took out the charging animal with a burst from the M-16, then elevated the barrel and took them out of the play.

There was an archway at the base of the tower, opening up to two flights of steps. Bolan took them on the fly, and from the top he could see the entire hacienda. Gunners rushed every which way, shouts and barking adding to the confusion. As yet, no one seemed to have any idea what was going on.

Stepping to the opening that overlooked the roof, Bolan hopped over the low balustrade. He sprinted to the south, aware that he had to pressure the gunners to keep them off-balance. He stopped shy of the rail.

Working quickly, the soldier took a 40 mm M-406 high-explosive round from a pocket and used the rim of the cartridge case to loosen the elevation screw on the M-203 grenade launcher. He glanced at the warehouses to gauge the range, which was well under the maximum of four hundred meters for the M-203, and adjusted the sight leaf accordingly.

It was old hat to Bolan, a routine he could practically perform in his sleep. Retightening the screw, he fed in the explosive round through the breech. It would detonate on impact, spewing three hundred fragments over a kill radius of five meters.

The warrior tucked the rifle to his shoulder, aimed and fired. Heartbeats later the grenade struck the flatbed he had parked beside the warehouse. The explosion touched off a secondary blast as the fuel tank went up in a ball of fire. Flames soared twenty feet high and licked at the warehouse wall as if hungry for something much bigger to devour.

Many of the guards hit the ground. Some headed for the front gate.

The scarecrow lieutenant materialized in the middle of the chaos, a pistol in his hand. He banged shots at the sky to draw attention, then bellowed commands, instructing the milling gunners to put out the fire before it spread to the building and destroyed the cocaine.

Bolan reached into another pocket. This time he plucked out an M-397 airburst grenade. It differed from the M-406 in that it didn't detonate on impact. Instead, a small charge kicked the grenade about five feet into the air and *then* it went off. The extra bounce seemed pointless until one realized it gave the airburst grenade twice the kill zone of the more common high-explosive round.

Bolan was dead-on accurate. The grenade hit the grass within a few feet of the scarecrow, whose scream of terror was smothered by the thunderous blast that mowed down him and all those around him.

By now the north wall of the warehouse was ablaze. A few gunners were trying in vain to stem the spread of flames.

So far none of the opposition had pinpointed the Executioner. To sow more panic, to convince them they were under attack by a large force, Bolan chose a white-star parachute round and let it fly.

The grenade detonated 180 meters above the parking area. Flaring to white-hot brilliance, it lit up the immediate area with an illumination of forty-five thousand candlepower.

Bolan crouched below the balustrade so no one would spot him. By rights, he should be getting out of there while the getting was good. The mission had been accomplished. He had what Brognola needed, and he had terminated the drug lord. There was no official reason to stay—but there was a personal one. He wanted to bring the whole operation crashing down around their ears.

A deafening whump rocked the night as the warehouse went up in earnest. The gas Bolan had spilled on the pallets had ignited in a blazing chain reaction, spewing a column of smoke from the double doors. A man stumbled from the choking cloud, his clothes afire. Screeching, he swatted at his shirt, his hair, his face. Others ran to his rescue, but they hadn't reached him when the warehouse's roof blew sky high. The concussion bowled them over like tenpins.

With no one to lead them and no way of dousing the fire, Terrazas's underlings lost their nerve. Those still able to do so flocked toward the parking area. Bolan took a bead on a burly man trying to restore order, but he held his fire when others burst from the house hollering at the top of their lungs that Luis Terrazas was dead.

That was all it took. The mass flight turned into a rout. Gunners fought with one another for seats in vehicles. Men clung to sideboards, tailgates, even bumpers. Trucks and cars streamed from the hacienda, headlights spearing the night. Those not able to catch a ride filed out on foot.

The Executioner spurred the exodus with a few strategically placed grenades. Soon all the warehouses were aflame, several sheds had been blown to bits and the tractor was a pile of charred wreckage.

Bolan watched the caravan bear to the southeast, then straightened and returned to the bell tower. According to the map, the nearest outpost of civilization was a sleepy village known as Boquillas, less than thirty miles away. Given the way the road twisted across the desert, he figured it would take the caravan the better part of an hour to get there. It would take another hour or so for them to compare notes and reorganize, which gave him a three-hour window to do what had to be done. It should be more than enough time.

Alert for stragglers, the soldier descended the tower. He moved around to the front of the house. As he was about to cross the yard to the gate, a shoe scraped behind him. Bolan dropped low and pivoted, the M-16 tucked to his side. Figures moved in the shadows. Just as he was about to spray a hail of lead, one of those figures ventured fearfully into the open.

The elderly house servant extended her hands, palms out, to show they were empty. "Do not shoot, señor!" she cried. "We mean you no harm!"

Others showed themselves. All were workers Bolan had seen earlier, and all were clearly frightened out of their wits. He was sorry they had been caught up in the firefight, but there was nothing to do now but get them out of there. "You must leave," he announced.

The matron gestured helplessly. "All the cars are gone, and I am too old to walk very far. Please, señor. Permit us to stay. We will stay out of your way."

The Executioner was tempted to give in, but it never paid to take anything for granted. Terrazas's men might reappear sooner than he anticipated, and this bunch of innocents might wind up caught in the cross fire. "Stick together and go as far as you can. Then wait until someone comes along to pick you up. It shouldn't be long."

They were too cowed to argue. Clustered like sheep, they scurried to the gate and were shortly swallowed by the darkness.

Bolan didn't waste any more time. He jogged from the estate to the boulders where he'd concealed himself during the day. He found the buried backpack, shrugged into the straps and double-timed it to the airstrip. There, he uncovered the radio, fired it up, made sure it was still set to the proper frequency and spoke a simple phrase into the microphone. "Ready when you are."

That was it. Short and sweet so no one could trace the signal. Across the border, Jack Grimaldi would be scrambling to the Phantom. Barring a glitch, the ace pilot would be over the estate in under thirty minutes.

Bolan went into the DHC to check on the bound smugglers. Both had revived and tried to get free, but all they had succeeded in doing was making their wrists bleed. They would keep.

Now came the hard part, the waiting. Bolan cradled the M-16 and took up a position at the west end of the airstrip. In his estimation it was much too short for a fighter to set down on, but Grimaldi had assured him it could be done and the man had yet to disappoint him.

A sliver of moon formed a silver crescent in the sky. A cool breeze blew from the northwest, which whispered off across the desert. In the distance a coyote yipped and was answered by another wavering wail.

The fire had engulfed all the buildings south of the house, which would go up, too, should the wind shift. Thick swirling plumes of smoke rose from the inferno, as did an acrid odor.

Minutes went by. Bolan checked his watch twice. The second time, he shifted the backpack so it hung under his left arm and took out the first flare. He had ten, all told, which should suffice if he spaced them far enough apart. Igniting it, he set it down and jogged eastward.

One by one he strung them in a line the length of the runway.

Now it was up to Grimaldi. Bolan returned to the DHC and scanned the northern horizon, then tensed on hearing the muted growl of an engine—it wasn't a jet engine and it came from the southeast.

Headlights had reappeared far out on the desert, only these were making a beeline for the estate, not driving away from it. Three, four, five vehicles in all.

Bolan took it for granted that the gunners were out for his blood until the distinctive growl of heavy trucks in tandem became apparent. He noted a uniformity to four pairs of the headlights, which could only be the case if those four vehicles were exactly the same. The one in the lead was the lone exception. It had smaller lights spaced much closer together.

The Executioner moved toward the rutted track that linked the airstrip to the hacienda. He knew the sound of a military convoy when he heard one. It reminded him of the officer who had paid a visit to the drug lord.

The man had been in Terrazas's pocket, and he'd probably do whatever it took to cover his tracks in order to keep his superiors from discovering his link to the criminal empire—that would include destroying all records of the operation. Not to mention the person who had killed Luis Terrazas.

Bolan glanced at the heavens, hoping his friend would show up before the convoy did. It wasn't in the game plan for him to kill government troops. Just because the officer was on the take didn't mean every last soldier under him was also dirty.

The convoy lumbered steadily nearer. Bolan moved to a barrel cactus and crouched. He would do what he could to keep the soldiers at bay. Failing that, he would head into the mountains.

He procured another white-star parachute grenade and loaded it into the M-203.

It took another five minutes for the military unit to reach the gate. A jeep was in the lead, undoubtedly the same jeep in which the officer had arrived. It braked a safe distance from the wall, and a man hopped out.

Orders were shouted. A squad of soldiers spilled from the first truck, spreading out in a skirmish line and advancing warily. They entered the stronghold. For a while after that nothing happened.

Bolan mentally crossed his fingers that the officer wouldn't attach any special significance to the flares. He hoped the man would assume they had been put there by the drug lord's men.

Several soldiers hurried out to the jeep to report. The officer climbed back in, a horn honked twice and the convoy entered at a crawl.

Bolan felt luck was with him. The soldiers would be occupied for a long time. The officer would want to go through the house with a fine-tooth comb, and the blaze would have to be brought under control. Long before that Grimaldi would arrive, and Bolan would be out of there.

He slipped a finger forward to the grenade launcher and flicked on the safety. Settling onto his knees, he consulted his watch once more. It had been thirty-seven minutes since he sent the message. Grimaldi should arrive at any minute.

Less smoke spiraled from the estate and the flames had dwindled a little. Dark shapes appeared on the bell tower but weren't there long.

Bolan scanned the flares. They would burn for another fifteen minutes. If they went out before the Phantom arrived, the retrieval would have to be aborted. There was no way in the world even Grimaldi could land and take off in total darkness.

The Executioner patted the ground. At least there was one factor he need not be concerned about.

Two days earlier, when the mission had first been discussed, Bolan had resigned himself to making his way to Mexico City after the hit at the hacienda, and from there catching a plane to the U.S. He hadn't rated the airstrip as long enough or sturdy enough to handle a jet. But Grimaldi, after poring over satellite photos with a magnifying glass, had been convinced that he could extract Bolan with no problem. The landing of the big DHC had proved the Stony Man pilot right.

No sooner did the thought cross Bolan's mind than the night sky reverberated to man-made thunder. As if from out of nowhere, the Phantom streaked in low over the strip from the north and barely cleared the compound walls as it roared off to the south and banked.

It was like fifty cannons going off at once. Bolan felt the ground shake and heard glass shatter beyond the wall. He also heard something else—the muffled report of a shot. Dirt erupted in a tiny geyser next to his leg. In sheer reflex he threw himself to the right and rolled. A second shot kicked earth into his face.

The two hardmen on the plane had freed themselves and were armed with pistols. Estavan, crouched beside the door, adopted a two-handed grip to steady his aim, while Pablo fired from inside the cargo bay.

Bolan had to take them down before the fighter came in for a landing. He couldn't afford the luxury of trading shots. Strident yells had already broken out in the hacienda, and it wouldn't be long before soldiers poured through the gate to the airstrip.

A short burst shredded Estavan's torso. The gunner fell and flopped about like a fish out of water.

Elevating the barrel, Bolan rained a hailstorm of lead on the cargo bay, but it was ineffective. Pablo simply ducked from sight, then popped up when the Executioner let up on the trigger. Vaguely Bolan was aware that the Phantom had looped to the west and was making its approach. Grimaldi would come in fast and hard and stop on the proverbial dime. He had to be ready.

Acting on inspiration, Bolan slid his right hand forward to the grenade launcher. The cargo door was a gaping maw impossible to miss. The white-star parachute grenade went off with a blinding flash of white light, silhouetting Pablo in its intense glare. The gunner, mewing like a stricken cat, automatically covered his eyes. It was the last act he ever performed.

A moment later the unmarked fighter rocketed onto the strip, the two afterburning turbojets screaming like banshees. In a twinkling the aircraft was halfway down the airstrip, slowing rapidly, but it still seemed certain the fighter would overshoot the last flare and plunge into the desert. At the last possible moment, Grimaldi performed one of his patented miracles.

Bolan pumped his legs to catch up. Inside the estate, truck engines turned over. He tried not to think of what would happen if the soldiers blocked off the end of the strip. Holding tight to the pillowcase, he passed flare after flare.

Grimaldi had the canopy open and had unfurled a rope ladder. "Sorry I'm late, Sarge," he called down. "I took the scenic route."

Tossing the pilot the backpack, Bolan climbed up the ladder and pulled it in behind him. Two trucks were hurtling along the road and would turn onto the air-strip at any moment. The canopy lowered much too slowly to suit him, and without another word Grimaldi punched it.

Bolan was slapped against the seat by the thrust. Twisting his neck, he saw the first troop transport brake directly in their path. At breakneck speed they bore down on it. Just when a collision appeared inevitable,

Grimaldi hauled back on the stick and the Phantom veered into the sky, clearing the truck by inches.

"See?" the pilot shouted over a shoulder. "I told you it would be a piece of cake."

CHAPTER THREE

Washington, D.C.

"You hit the jackpot big, Mack," Hal Brognola stated.

It was after regular business hours, and the men were seated in the big Fed's Spartan office in the Justice Building. Bolan had a cup of coffee resting on one knee and a copy of the preliminary report balanced on the other. He couldn't recall the last time he had seen Brognola so excited about the results of a routine mission.

"The DEA is having a field day accessing those disks you brought back. They tell me that they'll not only be able to shut down what's left of Luis Terrazas's operation, but that they now have vital intel on a score of others, as well—links to smuggling rings and gunrunners and even the Colombian cartels." A wide smile creased Brognola's rugged features.

Bolan tossed the report on the desk. "What about the army officer Terrazas had on a leash?"

"Colonel Raul Escalante. A real work of art." Brognola leaned forward. "Get this. He tried to take credit for your handiwork by claiming that he killed Terrazas and razed the stronghold. For two days he was on the front page of every newspaper in Mexico."

"And now?"

"We've discreetly passed on evidence of his double-dealing to certain well-placed individuals in the Mexican government. An official investigation is being launched. It won't be long before the good colonel finds himself on the wrong side of prison bars."

Bolan sipped some coffee, then sat back. "What about the main reason I went down there?"

Brognola tapped the report. "You'll be happy to know that we've established beyond any shadow of a doubt that Terrazas was the one responsible for the attack on the DEA headquarters. At least it was his idea and he put up the money to fund the hit. His notes indicate that he was obsessed with getting the DEA out of his hair. He figured that by showing he could strike at them anywhere, anytime, they would quit trying to bring him down."

"How is your friend doing?"

A frown passed over the big Fed's face. "Bill Keating and I graduated from the same school of hard knocks. He's learned how to roll with the punches and keep on plugging away." He paused. "To answer your question, he was pretty rattled at losing part of his leg. But they're fitting him with a prosthetic replacement, so he should be up and around in no time. His days in the field are over, though."

The Executioner made no comment. The fate that had befallen the DEA agent was one every member of Stony Man faced each and every day. Dismemberment, or worse, was the potential cost of upholding their ideals.

"Now on to the other reason I asked you in," Brognola said. "My hunch was right. There are no clear-cut references on the disk, but there are enough clues to indicate Terrazas did acquire the missile from the Wizard."

There was that name again, one Bolan had heard several times over the past year, always vaguely linked to various terrorist acts.

"We haven't learned anything we didn't already know. But we did uncover part of the guidance system from the wreckage, enough to confirm our worst fears and substantiate the rumors that keep flying around." Brognola turned to his intercom. "Would you come in, please?"

Bolan's eyebrows arched.

"I've called in a consultant," Brognola stated, "someone you know and trust. Someone who thinks our worst nightmares will come true unless we track down the Wizard, and soon." He produced a manila folder. "I've had my best people working on this one. As near as we can tell, the Wizard is implicated in seven incidents, with another three rated as possibles." Flipping the file open, he ran a finger down the first page. "There was the jumbo jet at Orly, the ferry disaster in Hong Kong, the consulate in Turkey. The attack on the Israeli parliament can also be laid at his doorstep."

All of them had resulted in great loss of life. No two had been committed by the same terrorist outfit, yet they all had one thing in common—the devices used to trigger the blasts were more sophisticated than anyone had ever seen before.

There was a rap on the office door. At Brognola's bidding, it was opened and in strolled a powerfully built man who looked as if he would be more at home on a football field than working for the government.

"Cowboy," Bolan said in greeting, using the nickname of the resident weaponsmith at Stony Man Farm.

"Good to see you, Mack," John Kissinger said amiably. Once a wide receiver with the Cleveland Browns, his pro career had been interrupted by a two-year Army stint. Later he had attended MIT, worked in the U.S. Army Department of Weapons Testing and Design and gone on to free-lance as a weapons design specialist. Now he worked for Brognola, and like all of the big Fed's people, he was one of the best in the business.

"I called in Cowboy," Brognola mentioned, "because I wanted you to have someone reliable at your beck and call." He motioned at the armorer. "Tell Mack what you've already told me."

Kissinger sank into a chair and spread his big hands on his legs. "I've spent the past eighteen hours in the lab examining what's left of the guidance system used in that missile that hit the DEA building. Now, you know me well enough to know that I'm not bragging when I say that there isn't a system in the world I'm not familiar with. But this one..."

"It's special?" Bolan prompted.

"It's more than that. It's a damned work of art." Kissinger saw the Executioner's smile and went on quickly to press his point. "Comparing run-of-the-mill guidance hardware to the device used in that missile is like comparing the crayon drawings of a first-grader to the *Mona Lisa.* Or, better yet, a paper airplane to the space shuttle." He shook his head. "There really is no comparison."

"I've heard that the Wizard is good at what he does."

"Good doesn't begin to describe him. Imagine Tesla or Edison gone bad. He's an electronics and computer genius, and it shows in every aspect of his work. Whoever this guy is, he could revolutionize the industry if he went legit. He'd be rich."

Brognola spoke up. "Maybe he sees it the other way around. Maybe he figures he can make a hell of a lot more by selling his talent under the table to those with the bucks to pay. Our sources tell us that his asking price is half a million dollars a job, plus expenses."

Bolan did some simple multiplication. "So he's made about five million in the last year alone. Probably more."

"Do you know what impresses me the most about our mystery man?" Kissinger asked. "It's the fact that every single one of his devices has worked like a charm. Half the time terrorists' bombs don't go off when they should or blow up in their faces. But not this guy's stuff. His gadgets always do the job and do it right. Do you realize what this means?"

"I'd say so," Brognola said dryly, but the weaponsmith went on anyway.

"Think of it. This Wizard is infallible. Terrorists know that they can set off bombs or missiles with one-hundred-percent reliability. No more relying on crude detonators or other faulty devices. Thanks to this Wizard, the element of human error has been eliminated. Imagine the edge it gives them now."

Bolan was thinking of something else, namely the grave security risk the Wizard posed to every government on the globe.

"The missile we're talking about is a case in point," Kissinger continued. "From what we've learned, it was launched from more than a mile away. A microchip navigation-and-targeting system guided it for blocks on end, over and around buildings, even under an overpass at one point. And all this while not moving much faster than one of those motorized toy planes people like to fly as a hobby." He whistled in admiration. "The boys who designed our Patriots could take a lesson from this guy."

"How do we find him before someone else uses one of his devices?" Bolan asked.

Kissinger frowned. "At this point, we can't. Tracing him through his suppliers won't work because he doesn't go in for specialty components. The items he uses can be found on the shelves of any computer or electronics outlet in the country. It's how he combines them that counts, and the modifications he makes."

"But we're not just giving up," Brognola added. "Bringing this Wizard to bay has become a top priority. He needs to be stopped before we have another World Trade Center fiasco on our hands."

"You've got that right," Kissinger agreed. "If those simpletons had used one of his devices, the World Trade Center would be in ruins right now."

The never-ending war raged on. No sooner was one threat eliminated than another rose to take its place. And as the years went by, those threats were becoming more and more sophisticated. It had been inevitable, Bolan supposed, that an evil mastermind of the Wizard's caliber would come along eventually.

"As it is," Brognola was saying, "we can chalk up the loss of more than five hundred lives to this bastard. Indirectly, of course, but when all is said and done, he has to shoulder the blame. And no one knows who he is or where to find him."

"Any clue as to how he contacts his clients?" Bolan asked.

"Not yet. The Red Battalion member apprehended in Turkey claimed that he knew, but he hung himself in a Turkish jail before we could interrogate him."

Kissinger frowned. "While we're waiting for the other shoe to drop, I'll do some checking around on my own. There aren't that many certifiable electronics geniuses in the world. Anyone as brilliant as he is must have drawn attention to himself somewhere along the line. Maybe in college or in industry." He shrugged. "It's a long shot, but it beats twiddling our thumbs.

"There is one bright side, if you can call it that," Brognola mentioned.

"Which is?" Bolan asked.

"As word about him has spread through the terrorist network, demand for his work has grown. It shouldn't be long before he's linked to another attack. With any luck, the next time will give us the break we need."

"Maybe," Kissinger said skeptically. "But I wouldn't give you even money that it does."

Germany

THE MAN in the green sedan couldn't sit still. He kept fidgeting and drumming the steering wheel. Time and again he glanced in the mirror to make sure he wasn't being followed. Often he licked his thin lips or plucked at his pencil mustache.

"I will make it," Otto Binder said to himself to bolster his sagging confidence. The risk he took was enormous, but he couldn't stay silent any longer. All he had to do was reach Berlin in one piece and turn over the invoices to the agent he had contacted.

Binder patted the briefcase at his side. It comforted him, knowing he had managed to get so far without being caught. Just another few hours, and his conscience would at last be clean—and he'd be safe under federal protection.

The high-pitched roar of a motorcycle snapped Binder's head around. It closed rapidly from the rear, the driver leaning into the handlebars. His female passenger clung to his back, her long blond hair whipping wildly in the wind.

Binder relaxed. They were young lovers, no doubt, who had enjoyed a ride in the country and were now on their way back into the metropolis. They bore down on him at breakneck speed, practically gluing themselves to his rear bumper. Slowing slightly, he slanted toward the shoulder, stuck his arm out the window and motioned for them to go around.

The driver's helmet bobbed as the man opened the throttle. In a blur of spinning wheels and flying hair, the cycle shot past. The blonde's white teeth flashed, and she gave a friendly wave.

Oh, to be young again, Binder reflected. If he had it to do over, he wouldn't be so serious about life the second time around. He wouldn't waste precious years trying to further a dead end career. He'd do all those wonderful things he had always denied himself. He would *live.*

A sign appeared at the edge of the highway: motorway junction. Binder remembered there being a gas station. Since his tank was less than a quarter full, he decided to stop, gas up and stretch his legs. It would be his last chance before Berlin to walk off some of his nervous energy.

Clouds had gathered to the west, a portent of predicted afternoon thunderstorms. Binder could smell moisture in the air when he rolled down his window and took several deep breaths. Soon the turnoff loomed and he braked.

The gas station wasn't very busy at that time of the day. Binder saw only one other car being serviced. He pulled close to the pumps, asked to have the tank filled and slid out. As he walked toward the building to buy a snack, he noticed the red motorcycle parked at the curb. The driver's green helmet rested on the seat. He surveyed the area but saw no sign of the blonde.

A heavyset woman accepted the money Binder handed over for a candy bar with a mechanical "*Danke.*" He unwrapped it, took a bite and stepped out to the curb. A gust of chill wind buffeted him. Ominous dark clouds were mere miles away.

Binder turned to the right, munching slowly. He was studying the design of the candy-bar wrapper or he would have noticed the woman. As it was, he nearly walked right into her. Recoiling, he blurted, "I beg your pardon, miss. I didn't see you there."

The blonde was as lovely a woman as Otto Binder had ever seen. He couldn't take his eyes off her skin-tight leather outfit. When her rosy lips curled upward and she made a self-conscious gesture at the side of the building, he went rigid, mesmerized.

"I am so sorry to bother you," she said in a silken tone, "but the door to the ladies, it's jammed. The knob turns, but the door won't open. Could you help me?"

Binder was almost too amazed to reply. "Where is your young gentleman?" he blurted, and wanted to kick himself for being so stupid.

The woman shrugged, then made a show of surveying the parking lot. "Men. They're never around when you need them."

"Well, I'm here," Binder said, salvaging the moment. He motioned for her to precede him, but she shook her head.

"After you, kind sir."

Binder moved slowly down the walk. To his right was the windowless wall of the gas station, to his left a high hedge which blocked his view of the autobahn. He was almost to the corner before he noticed there was no door to be found. "Excuse me, miss," he said, turning to face her, "but where is the—"

A strange constriction in Binder's throat cut off the rest of his question. It took a moment for him to realize what had happened because he felt no pain for a few seconds and the blonde stood there smiling at him as if nothing out of the ordinary were taking place. But it most definitely was, and the awful truth shocked him so badly that he could neither move nor speak. Someone had slipped a wire around his throat from behind.

Binder dropped the candy bar and clutched at the wire. He appealed to the woman with his eyes, but all she did was wink and keep on smiling. In a blaze of insight it dawned on him that she was standing there to keep others from witnessing his murder. She had led him into a trap.

Binder threw himself toward the wall and twisted, trying to dislodge his assailant. He glimpsed the handsome, icy face and the leather jacket of the motorcycle driver. The man's legs had to have taken root, because nothing Binder did could make him lose his balance or slacken that terrible grip.

Binder kicked, thrashed, jerked to the right and the left. His lungs seared with agony. He couldn't take a breath, couldn't scream for help. In desperation he began to whine as loud as he could to draw attention to his plight, but the smiling blonde stepped up to him and clamped her warm hand over his mouth. Those rosy lips moved again, saying words that seemed to come from a great distance.

"Aldous sends his regards, Otto. He says that he doesn't take your betrayal personally. You were a good accountant until you became greedy."

Binder barely heard. A numbing blackness had devoured his body and now gnawed at his mind. He made one last, supreme effort to tear the wire from his yielding flesh, and was swallowed by the void.

The blonde glanced at the parking lot. "No one saw," she said. "I'll fetch it, Gunther."

Gunther nodded curtly, then dragged the body behind the gas station and left it in a patch of weeds. Since he had on gloves, he left the garrote deeply imbedded in the accountant's neck.

Smoothing his leather jacket, Gunther went to the opposite end of the building. Another car had pulled into the station, but neither the driver nor the attendant was looking in his direction. He casually walked to the motorcycle, donned his helmet and forked the seat.

The blonde joined him, the brown briefcase close to her side. "It was too easy."

"You are too sure of yourself, darling Katya," Gunther warned. "One of these days it will be the death of us."

Katya laughed merrily and climbed on. She wedged the briefcase between them and pressed against it so it wouldn't be jarred loose. "You worry too much about dying, my pet," she said softly. "When a person's time comes, it comes. There is nothing we can do about it except make the most of the moments we have."

Gunther kicked over the engine, revved the throttle and slipped the motorcycle into gear. He drove onto the autobahn and took a left, away from Berlin.

It was a long ride to Chemnitz, once a bustling manufacturing center in the former East Germany. Gunther held the vehicle to the speed limit so as not to draw attention. Evening shaded the pristine hills when he rolled into the outskirts of the city and made his way along side streets to a massive industrial complex that had seen better times. Many of the buildings were vacant, thick with dust and cobwebs.

Gunther parked behind one that was still active. Leaving his helmet on the handlebars, he opened a door for Katya and followed her up a flight of stairs to another door, which was locked. She took a key from her pocket. A narrow hall brought the two of them to a lavishly furnished office, already occupied.

A man waited, seated behind a huge mahogany desk. He had the shoulders of a steelworker and a pate as bald as a cue ball. Without saying a word he took the briefcase, inspected the contents and sighed.

"Was there any trouble?"

"Is there ever?" Katya shot back. Plopping into an easy chair, she chuckled. "We delivered your message, Mr. Reutlingen. You should have seen his face."

The bald man didn't share her sense of humor. "I meant what I said. In all his years with Reutlingen Armament, Otto never gave me cause to complain." Swiveling his chair, he stared out the window and nodded at the bleak complex. "The breakup of the Soviet Union and the reunification of Germany are to blame, not poor Otto. Once, I had more business than I could handle. I supplied Moscow with more armament than any other firm in East Germany. Now look."

Gunther and Katya exchanged glances. They had heard it all before.

"Otto didn't understand that the only way I can stay afloat is to sell arms on the black market. That is why he was going to the authorities." Aldous Reutlingen faced them. "In a way, it is ironic. The black market isn't enough. If I am to avoid going under, I must be able to compete in today's market. I must have a technological edge."

"About our money," Gunther said, but was ignored.

"And I have found that edge," the arms manufacturer stated, "or at least I know of a man who can supply it for me." Reutlingen tapped a file in front of him. "I still have some influence, you know. I keep my ear to the pipeline."

"Why tell us this?" Katya asked impatiently.

Reutlingen regarded them closely. "How would the two of you like to earn two hundred thousand...in U.S. dollars?"

The blonde's grin was that of a she-wolf thirsting for blood. "Who do we kill this time?"

"This time I want the man alive," Reutlingen said sternly. "He is an electronics genius known in intelligence circles as the Wizard. He doesn't know it yet, but he is going to put his genius to work for me. My company will thrive like never before."

Gunther was all business. "Half the money up front, as usual?"

"Of course. But understand one thing." Reutlingen's features hardened. "I *need* this Wizard. He's my last hope. You will hunt him down and bring him to me, and nothing must be allowed to stand in your way. If anyone interferes, you are to dispose of them however you see fit."

"We wouldn't have it any other way."

CHAPTER FOUR

Stony Man Farm, Virginia

When Hal Brognola had remarked that he expected the Wizard to be implicated in another terrorist attack sometime soon, he had no idea it would be only two days later.

The big Fed happened to be at Stony Man Farm when word reached him. He was in a meeting with mission controller, Barbara Price, and Aaron Kurtzman. As part of an ongoing effort to increase efficiency, they met on a regular basis to review recent missions and note any areas where operational procedures needed to be improved.

This latest meeting had hardly gotten underway when the report was brought to Brognola by the chief of Stony Man communications. The big Fed had left word that he was to be notified the second anything new pertaining to the Wizard turned up.

Price and Kurtzman sat quietly while Brognola skimmed the three typewritten pages. "We'll have to wrap this up another time," he informed them. "I have to prep Striker for another field assignment." Without thinking, he added, "It looks as if he'll be walking into a real hornet's nest."

The meeting room wasn't far from the gym, where Brognola knew Bolan was working out. Rather than use the intercom, he went to deliver the news in person. As he paused in the doorway, he saw his friend scaling a thick rope suspended near one corner of the ceiling. Legs extended, muscles rippling, Bolan climbed with deceptive ease. Brognola knew how much strength that took. His shoulders cramped just thinking about it.

Bolan saw his friend enter and nodded as he descended. When close to the bottom, he let go and dropped lightly.

"It's the Wizard," Brognola said without preamble, holding up the report. "Scotland Yard suspects that he supplied a unique bomb to a splinter group of the IRA."

As Bolan bent to retrieve a towel, the big Fed filled him in.

"It happened yesterday morning. Representatives of the British government and ours were meeting at a small hotel in London. The President and the prime minister set it up to discuss covert funding of IRA activities by certain American sources. It had been in the works for months, but everyone kept a low profile. Little mention of it was made in the media."

"Security?"

"As tight as the proverbial drum. The Brits had sealed off the top floor of the hotel. Guards were posted in the stairwell and at the elevator. Absolutely no one was allowed to get by unless they showed the proper ID."

Bolan wiped his face. "What did the terrorists use? Another missile?"

"No. This time he was even more ingenious." Brognola turned to the second page. "The delegates, and there were six of them, relied on a dumbwaiter to bring drinks and snacks up from the kitchen. They had been using it for several hours without any problem when one of them rang down for tea. About three seconds after the dumbwaiter reached their floor, the bomb went off. It demolished the room and killed four of the six delegates.

"Less than half an hour later, the *Times* received a call from a faction claiming responsibility. They call themselves the Beastly Boys. The word is that they're too bloodthirsty even for the IRA. After they were kicked out, they formed their own little group. For the past month or so they kept busy robbing banks and the like. No one knew why until now."

"They were raising enough money to hire the Wizard," Bolan deduced.

"That's our guess. Anyway, two of them, posing as delivery men, slipped into the kitchen. They tied up the hotel staff, then let in two more of their buddies. One of the cooks watched them attach a device to the bottom of the dumbwaiter. They set it and ran."

Bolan headed for the showers and Brognola paced him.

"Enough of the detonator remained for Scotland Yard to recognize the Wizard's handiwork. Instead of a simple fuse or a timer, the blast was set off once the dumbwaiter had climbed a certain height."

"That's been done with aircraft before."

"True, but the detonators have always been bulky things that had to be hidden in suitcases. This one was a miniature computer, no bigger than the palm of your hand." Brognola held out the report. "Read it for yourself."

The description was verbatim. Bolan turned to the last page to discover where he fit in.

The Beastly Boys had fled England minutes after contacting the newspaper. The call, in fact, had been made from a pay phone at Heathrow.

Traveling under forged passports, the terrorists had flown to New York City and from there connected to a flight to Chicago, where they were now lying low.

"We're expecting a follow-up report any minute," Brognola said when he saw that Bolan had finished. "Everything Scotland Yard has on file." He stressed the next point not so much to remind his friend of the challenge as to offer Bolan a chance to bow out if he so desired. "We need one or two of them alive if we're to get any new leads on the Wizard."

The soldier had gone up against rabid wolves like the Beastly Boys many times before. He knew they would be hard enough to take down without having to hold back, to treat them with kid gloves, in order to leave a few breathing. He was no stranger to the risks, but he answered without hesitation. "I'll do the best I can."

"You always do."

Chicago, Illinois

CHICAGO LIVED UP to its reputation. The Windy City was in the grip of severe thunderstorms. Only an idiot would take a stroll in such weather, Bolan mused. Yet that was exactly what Michael O'Shea and Frederick Brannigan happened to be doing.

O'Shea was the leader of the Beastly Boys, a twenty-eight-year-old firebrand who had grown up on the mean streets of Belfast. At the age of fourteen he had joined the IRA. He had a passion for bombs, as a British convoy found out one balmy day on the outskirts of Belfast. Eight soldiers had been blown to bits, another ten wounded. That had been only the start of the fanatic's bloody career.

The more O'Shea killed, the more brash and uncontrollable he became. After one of his bombs harmed a number of schoolchildren, the old guard of the IRA voted to sever all ties with him. But that didn't stop O'Shea from going on to commit bigger and gorier atrocities.

Scotland Yard's psychological profile branded him as a man with no scruples, as having no conscience whatsoever and therefore no sense of guilt or remorse. In short, he was the perfect psychopath, someone who killed for the sheer thrill of killing. Blood lust, much more than patriotism, motivated him.

Brannigan was another matter. He wanted the British out of Northern Ireland at all costs. If innocents lost their lives as a result, that was unfortunate, but it couldn't always be helped. A hulking mass of muscle, he lacked the brains and the temperament to ever be more than an underling.

Ten minutes earlier the pair had emerged from the brownstone in which the Beastly Boys had been holed up since arriving in Chicago. It was owned by an uncle of O'Shea's, a man suspected of contributing large sums of money to the IRA.

Bolan had been in a room on the third floor of the apartment building across the street. His game plan called for him to wait until they went to bed and all the lights were out, then to go in fast and hard. He had counted on a few special grenades and the element of surprise to give him the edge he needed.

Then O'Shea and Brannigan had appeared.

Now, trailing them by a half block, Bolan realized there was a method to their madness. Under cover of the storm, they could go anywhere they wanted with little fear of being recognized. They were taking no chances until they were certain they had given the authorities the slip.

At the east end of the street the terrorists turned right and headed toward Lincoln Park.

Bolan had to hang back. There was little cover and several teenagers were riding bikes on the sidewalk. When he made his move there could be no witnesses.

O'Shea and Brannigan entered the park. The rain had slackened to a drizzle, but the wind was as strong as ever. It bent the tops of the maple trees and howled off across the lake like a chorus of demented banshees.

The Executioner gradually closed the gap, his hands stuck in his pockets, his head tucked low. He made it a point not to look at them except out of the corners of his eyes when he turned to view Lake Michigan or the skyline. He was only fifty feet away when they passed the conservatory. In another minute he would have been close enough to confront them. But they thwarted him by entering the zoo.

Many people had taken shelter in the various buildings and were just now venturing out again. The terrorists stopped to watch the seals cavort, then went on to the primate house.

Bolan blended into the crowd so as not to be conspicuous. He kept the pair in sight the whole time. They stared at the gorillas awhile, so he pretended to be interested in the orangutans.

Suddenly O'Shea and Brannigan came directly toward him. Bolan sank to one knee and feigned checking a shoe to see if it had a rock in it. Only after they had gone by and were almost to the door did he stand and stalk them.

The rain had stopped, though clouds still choked the sky. The terrorists left the zoo and hiked to the southeast, to the harbor. Reversing themselves, they walked northward along the water's edge.

Bolan paralleled them, using trees and brush for cover. He figured they were heading back the way they had come, but they surprised him by bearing eastward toward Lake Michigan.

The soldier was stymied again. Scant vegetation lined the lakeshore. He didn't dare get too close or they'd notice him. Drawing back into the trees, he watched the men rove along the shore. They wandered aimlessly, back and forth, O'Shea throwing rocks into the lake as the whim struck him.

Bolan was about to chalk it up as wasted effort on his part when a police car came along Lake Shore Drive and pulled into the parking lot of a pavilion close to the pair. It was a routine patrol. The officers made a U-turn and headed south, not giving the two men on the beach so much as a second look.

O'Shea, though, didn't like it one bit. He slapped Brannigan on the arm and together they hurried due north toward the bridge at the mouth of Diversey Harbor.

Breaking into a jog, Bolan reached the north end of the harbor before they did. Here there were gullies and a small area thick with undergrowth. Best of all, no one else was in the vicinity.

After checking to be certain they were headed straight toward him, the soldier dipped into a shallow gully and concealed himself in the brush. He slipped his right hand into his back pocket, slid his fingers through the loop on the handle of the blackjack he carried and balanced himself on the balls of his feet.

Bolan didn't have long to wait. The bulky outline of Brannigan's head and shoulders came into view and grew larger. Several times the terrorist glanced nervously over his shoulder.

There was no sign of O'Shea. The Executioner didn't know what to make of it, unless the appearance of the police had so spooked O'Shea that the terrorist leader had decided the two of them would be better off separating. Whatever the case, they had played right into his hands.

Brannigan tramped over the rise. The slope was slick from the rain, and he nearly lost his footing as he started down. Recovering, he turned sideways and lowered each foot with the utmost care.

The unsuspecting renegade would pass within a few yards of where Bolan crouched. Drawing the blackjack, he coiled both legs. When Brannigan drew abreast of him, he sprang, digging in his heels for purchase. But the same damp grass that had almost upended the Irishman now foiled the warrior.

Bolan's left foot shot out from under him. He regained his footing immediately, but the damage had been done. Brannigan had heard the noise and whirled, so that even as Bolan struck, the terrorist elevated a brawny arm and deflected the blackjack.

Lowering a shoulder, Bolan deliberately rammed into Brannigan's chest. They both went down in a tumble of limbs, but the Executioner was able to tuck his knees to his chest and execute a diving roll that brought him to his feet a second before the terrorist. And in hand-to-hand combat, a second was as good as eternity.

Bolan caught the Irishman behind the left ear with the blackjack. Predictably Brannigan buckled. Not so predictably, the man surged right back onto his knees and shifted. A pistol gleamed dully in the twilight, a Glock torn from a hip rig sporting a breakaway holster.

The warrior was quicker. With a flick of his wrist he whipped the blackjack into Brannigan's elbow. The terrorist bellowed like a stricken bull and the pistol went flying. As it did, Bolan brought the blackjack down on Brannigan's head—or tried to—but his adversary shifted in time and his shoulder bore the brunt of the blow.

Bolan pivoted, evading a backhand. He aimed another swing at the Irishman's temple, but Brannigan threw himself at Bolan's legs before he could connect. Tackled neatly below the knees, the Executioner crashed onto his back. He twisted and kicked loose as the Irishman punched at his groin.

A snap kick rocked the terrorist backward. Bolan gained his knees, blocked a jab and staggered his adversary with two solid hits to the jaw. The man swayed yet somehow lurched erect.

Switching the blackjack to his left hand, Bolan shot up off the ground with his right fist cocked and planted it on the point of the terrorist's chin. His entire weight was behind the blow. Brannigan's neck snapped back with a loud crack, and for a few moments Bolan thought he had broken the man's spine. He stepped aside as the terrorist pitched forward.

Brannigan groaned, raised his head and attempted to rise. His eyelids fluttered; his legs shook violently. Making a last supreme effort, the terrorist lunged. He was out like a light before he laid a hand on the warrior.

Scanning the gully, Bolan verified that no one had witnessed their clash. He pocketed the blackjack, wedged both hands under the Irishman and rolled him deep into the undergrowth. Since he had intended to take as many of the terrorists alive as he could, he came prepared.

Using duct tape, he lashed the Irishman's wrists together, then his ankles. He doubled Brannigan over and looped the arms and legs tight. He removed the throwing knife from an ankle sheath and cut a large square of fabric from the man's jacket, ample for a suitable gag.

Satisfied, Bolan straightened. Brannigan would keep for a while. Now he had to take care of the others before they missed their companion. Hurrying to the top of the gully, he scoured the park for O'Shea. In the distance, his quarry was hastening along in the direction of the brownstone.

Bolan stripped off his windbreaker and slung it over a shoulder by the crook of a finger. He threaded through the dripping trees to the south side of the street and proceeded westward. Many more people were out and about, so he had no problem losing himself in the flow of pedestrians.

O'Shea was rattled. Between the park and the brownstone he stopped a half-dozen times to look back. Each time he also checked his watch. If a police car had appeared, it was likely he would have bolted.

Soon Bolan was directly across the street from the terrorist. He acted interested in the pastries in a bakery window so the man wouldn't see his features. The reflection showed O'Shea pacing in a circle. Bolan went on. The fanatic was several blocks behind when he reached the apartment building.

In his room, Bolan dialed the number of the Justice Department's Chicago field office. When a woman answered, he gave an extension number. Hal Brognola picked up on the third ring.

The Executioner resorted to his code name out of habit. "Belasko. One package is ready. Lincoln Park." He provided directions, then added, "I'm going in now, before they can skip."

"Watch yourself, Striker."

Bolan took the back stairs down to an alley, walked a couple blocks, then turned into the alley flanking the brownstone.

A rickety fence enclosed a yard choked with weeds. Bolan tested the gate and it squeaked. Stepping to a garbage can, he climbed on top, lowered his arms as far over the fence as he could and let his duffel bag drop. The contents rattled but didn't make enough noise to be heard inside. Or so Bolan hoped. He braced a hand on the rail and vaulted over.

Crouched in the shadows, Bolan pulled the canvas bag closer and undid the zipper. He withdrew a mini-Uzi fitted with a shoulder sling and a sound suppressor, and placed it at his side. Extra clips went into his pockets, as did a pair of M-25 A-2 grenades. He already had the Desert Eagle strapped to the small of his back, under his bulky sweater. Taking out the Beretta, he fit it with its custom sound suppressor, donned his shoulder holster and shrugged back into his windbreaker.

The Executioner was about ready. The last items he took from the duffel bag were a sleek black sound detector and a small pair of earphones. Donning the headset, he adjusted the gain on the detector and pointed the tiny parabolic dish at the windows on the ground floor. The lights were on inside, but all he heard was the hum of a refrigerator.

Bolan pointed the detector at the second floor and hit the jackpot.

"—hell is keeping those morons, boyo?" a gruff voice asked. "I don't like it. Maybe we should be thinking of going to find them."

"Mike told us to stay here, Henry," another man said. "And you know how he gets when we don't listen. I, for one, am not about to buck him. He's been like a caged tiger all damn day."

Bolan suspected that the speaker was Thomas Leary, the fourth member of the Beastly Boys.

"Tell me something I don't know," Henry Cassidy responded. "I don't know which is worse, having to listen to him bellyache about being cooped up or drinking this sorry excuse for whiskey they sell here in America. Hell, if I'd known, I'd have shipped a case of the real thing over so I wouldn't have to suffer so."

Leary and Cassidy were close friends from Londonderry who had hooked up with O'Shea more than a year earlier. They were his triggermen. Thanks to them, O'Shea once escaped a cordon of British troops when the pair blasted their way out, slaying six soldiers in the bargain.

Bolan made no move to enter just yet. He wanted their leader to be there.

"Two weeks of this will about drive me up the wall," Cassidy complained. "We should have gone to ground in our own country instead of coming to this godforsaken city."

"Are you serious?" Leary asked. "After what we did, the British will leave no stone unturned in Northern Ireland to find us. Mike did the right thing. We're as safe as could be."

"Are we? You forget there were American delegates in that room, as well. For all we know, they'll sic the CIA or the FBI on us." Cassidy snorted. "That would be all we need. To really be safe, boyo, we should have gone to South America."

The warrior speculated on what was taking O'Shea so long. It made him wonder if maybe the man had gone back to Lincoln Park to find Brannigan. Then a dog barked in the alley to the east. Slipping off the headset, Bolan heard footsteps rapidly approach the fence. They halted at the gate, and the next instant the latch lifted.

CHAPTER FIVE

The Executioner streaked his free hand to the Beretta but didn't draw. He wasn't about to shoot unless he was discovered. There was little chance of that, since there was no outdoor light and he was shrouded in inky shadow at the base of the fence, well to the left of the sidewalk that bisected the yard.

The latch rasped, the hinges grated like a rusty car door and through the gate hastened a stocky man in his forties. He carried a shopping bag. After turning and looking both ways, he went up to the back door and entered without bothering to knock.

Bolan aimed the parabolic dish at the house and put on the earphones. Heavy footsteps clumped down a hall and up a flight of stairs.

"Mike, is that you, boyo?" Cassidy called out.

The newcomer didn't answer. Bolan heard more footsteps and the rustle of the paper bag, perhaps as it was hefted or switched from one arm to the next.

"Oh, it's you, Mr. O'Shea," Leary said. "With our groceries, no less. We thank you for your kindness, sir. But I'm a wee bit surprised you didn't have one of your men deliver them."

Bolan's interest perked. It had to be the uncle, Dermot O'Shea, the man the Feds suspected of funneling money to the IRA. He was a cagey one. They had yet to gather enough evidence for an arrest.

"I want to talk to that nephew of mine," the elder O'Shea declared. "Where is he?"

Several seconds of silence passed.

"I asked you a question," Dermot said in a tone that implied he wasn't accustomed to being ignored. "Where's Mike?" He paused. "And where's Freddy?"

Cassidy replied meekly, "They went for a stroll, sir. But they should be back at any time."

"They left the house?" Dermot roared. "When I gave you specific instructions not to step outside that front door? When I've gone to so much trouble on your behalf?"

"Calm down, sir," Leary said.

"Like hell I will! I've put everything on the line on your account, and this is how I'm repaid? If any of you are caught and talk, I stand to spend the last half of my life in prison. That isn't a prospect that warms the heart."

The front door opened, and it was likely that Bolan was the only one who heard it over Dermot's bellowing.

"I don't think I'm being unreasonable," the man went on. "We all have too much at stake for any of us to grow careless at this stage. You were lucky, being able to get out of England like you did. But you can't push that luck. Sooner or later the authorities will get around to questioning me in connection with the attack. They might even bug my phone and shadow my comings and goings. We have to keep our wits about us or we'll be in a world of hurt."

"We already are, Uncle."

That had to have been the leader himself. Bolan stood and made for the porch.

"Mike!" Dermot O'Shea snapped. "Where the hell have you been? Don't you know better than to go traipsing around the city whenever it strikes your fancy? Now I'll have to move all of you to another safehouse and hope—"

"Shut up, Uncle," the firebrand growled. "We have a problem. Freddy is missing."

Bolan reached the back door.

"Missing?" Dermot repeated, aghast. "What do you mean? Did he go and get himself lost, the stupid ox?"

The Executioner switched off the sound detector and placed it next to the wall. Gripping the Uzi close to his hip, he slowly turned the knob and eased the door open. Unlike the gate, it made no noise. The men upstairs were so agitated that he could now hear them without the aid of the sound detector. Mike O'Shea was explaining.

"A car drove by. I didn't like it, so I had him take a different route across the park. That way, if the coppers were on to us, we'd have a better chance of one of us giving them the slip. But he never showed up. I waited and waited but there was no sign of him."

"Oh, God!" Dermot said. "They're on to us. We have to get to my house. I have money stashed there. We can be out of the country by daylight."

Bolan crept to the base of the stairs. He could see the shadows of the men a flight above but the terrorists and their benefactor were around a corner. Pressing his back to the right-hand wall, he climbed slowly.

"Let's not be getting ahead of ourselves, Uncle," the nephew was saying. "We're not going anywhere until we find out what has happened to Freddy. Let's wait an hour. If he doesn't show up, we'll go wherever you want."

The soldier was halfway to the top. A man's shoulder was visible. Dermot's, he believed.

"Wait, hell!" Dermot said. "If they've taken him into custody, he might talk. I'm getting out of here while the getting is good."

Only six steps below the landing, Bolan had nowhere to hide when Dermot O'Shea abruptly whirled and started down. The IRA backer stopped dead in his tracks, shocked. For a few seconds they locked eyes. Bolan saw the panic that seized the other man and knew what was going to happen before it did.

"We're done for, lads!" Dermot cried, his hairy hand sweeping under his jacket. A Colt King Cobra leaped clear with the speed of its namesake.

Bolan stroked the trigger of the Uzi. Muffled rounds punched into Dermot's chest and flung the man against the wall. He never got off a shot. Leaving a smear of blood in his wake, he slid downward.

The terrorist leader stepped into view. Bolan squeezed off a short burst, aiming at the man's shoulder, but Michael O'Shea leaped around the corner a fraction of an instant ahead of the slugs. Immediately Bolan threw himself to the left. Above him a silencer chugged as an SMG spat leaden death. The section of wall where he had been standing was chewed to ribbons.

Under O'Shea's covering fire, the Beastly Boys retreated into a room and the door slammed.

Bolan bounded to the corridor. The room was to his right. He darted past it just in time, for one of the terrorists cut loose again, peppering the top panel. Standing close to the jamb, the Executioner palmed one of the spherical grenades and yanked out the pin.

More shots drilled the door. The Beastly Boys were trying to keep their adversary at bay, but in doing so they outsmarted themselves. The leaden hailstorm tore large, ragged holes out of the door. One hole was the size of a melon.

Bending, but not exposing his body, Bolan heaved the first grenade through the biggest opening. Once he released the arming sleeve, the delay element began to burn. The detonator burst seconds later, rupturing the plastic body of the grenade and spewing the CS filler. In less time than it would take a man to draw a breath, the cloud filled the room.

Bolan waited for the chemical agent to take effect. In moments it would produce coughing, vomiting and difficulty in breathing.

Sure enough, someone gasped and gurgled and broke into a violent hacking fit. A second man joined in. Someone shuffled toward the door but stopped shy of it and wildly emptied a magazine at sharp angles—high and low, right and left. The door shattered, spewing tendrils of the chemical agent that wafted low to the floor.

Bolan drew the Desert Eagle. Cassidy, wheezing and gagging, sprang into the hall and spun toward the stairs, a Sten Mark II submachine gun tucked to his side. The soldier swung the pistol, smashing it into Cassidy's skull. The terrorist toppled, firing a burst into the floor in sheer reflex.

The next moment Leary barreled out of the room, tears streaming from his eyes, mucus from his nose. He could barely stand. Disoriented, in searing agony, he saw Cassidy's body too late and stumbled over it.

Bolan slammed the Desert Eagle into Leary's head, sending him sprawling on top of Cassidy, with a gash above his ear that would require stitches to close.

Bolan backed a few strides from the doorway to avoid the gas. No sounds came from the room. O'Shea, oddly, wasn't coughing. Perhaps, Bolan mused, the man had held his breath or covered his mouth and nose. In either case, the terrorist only delayed the inevitable. The gas would sear his eyes and burn the moist areas of his body. He had to come out soon.

But as the seconds ticked by and nothing happened, Bolan became concerned. A gust of cool air suddenly blew pillowy puffs of the chemical into the hall. Guessing the cause, the soldier inhaled deeply and raced to the stairs. A few wisps passed close to his face, but they did no more than make his eyes smart. He descended to the first floor in three long leaps and at the bottom had to throw out his right arm to keep from colliding with the wall.

He ran out onto the porch. As he cleared the doorstep he glimpsed a figure darting through the gate. It was O'Shea. The man whirled, and Bolan dived flat as the terrorist fired an SMG. Then, in a blur, O'Shea was gone, fleeing westward.

Bolan got to his feet and gave chase, slapping a fresh magazine into the Uzi as he reached the alley. The brief look he'd had at the terrorist's weapon had revealed it to be a Skorpion machine pistol. The Skorpion was a favorite among terrorists worldwide because it was only ten inches long with the stock folded and lent itself well to sound suppression.

Bolan hid his own weapon under his windbreaker and ran to the street. Looking both ways, he wanted to curse.

Michael O'Shea had disappeared.

Paris, France

THE SHORT MAN'S NAME was Claude Lebel and he had lived in Paris all his life, except for two short stretches spent in prison. Neither had sufficed to make him change his ways.

Lebel was no ordinary criminal. He didn't rob or kill. He didn't embezzle or kidnap. He did, on occasion, fence stolen merchandise, and twice had paid with his freedom.

No, what Claude Lebel did better than anyone else in all of France was provide information. For a price. Never to the police, of course. He liked to live. But to anyone else willing to grease his palm, he was a veritable font of little-known facts.

Lebel's haunts were the worst dives in the city. He was on a first-name basis with the most hardened killers and thieves. He knew all the pickpockets and cat burglars. By keeping his eyes and ears open, and being a sympathetic listener when others were in their cups, he kept his fingers on the pulse of the French underworld. And since criminal elements in one country often overlapped with those in others, it was safe to say that Claude Lebel knew more about the underbelly of Europe than most men.

On this particular night Lebel had made his usual rounds and was about ready to return to his apartment. He was seated at a corner table in a seedy bar situated on the bank of the Seine, set to polish off his drink, when a stunning blonde in black leather sashayed through the door.

Every man in the place lost interest in all else.

Lebel entertained a few wild notions, then discarded them. Women like her were never, ever interested in men like him. It was an unwritten law of life. He pegged her for a tourist, but certain things didn't add up. For one, no self-respecting tourist would be roaming the banks of the Seine at four in the morning. For another, she spoke flawless French when she politely declined to join another man at a table. Downing his liquor, Lebel shut her from his mind and reached into a pocket for the money to pay his bill. He sensed rather than heard someone come up to him.

"Monsieur Lebel?"

The small man glanced up and thought he was dreaming. Beaming down at him was the vision of loveliness. "I am he."

"So the bartender told me. I am Katya."

The woman sank into the chair next to Lebel's, though she could have sat across the table. Her perfume tingled his nose and made him wish he was six feet tall and as handsome as a movie star. "Pleased to meet you, miss...?"

"Katya will do." The blonde leaned closer so that her arm brushed his. "I have been looking all over the city for you, Mr. Lebel."

Lebel's instincts kicked in and he regarded her warily. "Why would that be, might I ask?"

"I have been told by many that you are the man to see when one wants certain kinds of information."

Sitting a little straighter, Lebel smiled in false modesty. "You have heard correctly. But have you also heard that I do not give information to just anyone, and I never give it out free?"

"To be expected." Katya placed her hand on his. "If you can help me, you have but to name your price. I am trying to find a friend."

"Is that all? Perhaps you should inquire at the missing-persons bureau," Lebel quipped. "I am not in the business of finding lost sheep."

"But you might know him, or know someone who does," Katya insisted. "His name is Henri Gaston. He was a pickpocket, the last I knew, and lived in the Latin Quarter."

The name was vaguely familiar. Lebel racked his brain. "I do seem to recall a gentleman who fits that description. He was not very talented and had to leave the city quickly. I could be wrong, but I think he went to live with relatives in Germany. Berlin, I think. Perhaps you should go there and ask around for him."

Katya patted his wrist as a woman might pat a pet that had performed a trick. "It's true, then. Your memory truly is amazing. How much do I owe you?"

Lebel was amazed to realize that for the first time in his life he had given information without first receiving payment. It was a grave lapse in judgment. "Ten francs will make us even," he said.

"Is that all?" The woman handed him the money and rose. "I thank you. You have no idea what this means to me." She hurried out without a backward look.

After tending to his bill, Lebel did the same. It had been a long day and he was eager to slip under the covers. A chill hung in the night air. He pulled the brim of his blue cap low and stared at the murky waters of the river.

A few blocks from the bar, Lebel slowed and stuck a cigarette in his mouth. He was about to strike a match when a hand appeared out of nowhere and a lighter flicked to life. Scared half to death, he whirled and reached for the dagger concealed under his coat. "You!" he exclaimed.

The blond woman seemed to always smile. "I'm so sorry," she said contritely. "I didn't mean to startle you."

"You didn't," Lebel lied. He bent to the flame and puffed until the tip of the cigarette caught. "What are you doing? Following me?"

"Yes."

Lebel drew back a step. He decided that for all her beauty, he didn't like this woman. There was something about her, a quality that reminded him of the piranha in the window of the pet shop down the street from where he lived. "Why?" he demanded.

"You were so helpful about Mr. Gaston that I thought you might be equally helpful with regard to another man." Katya smiled coyly. "Although, I must be honest, I knew Gaston's whereabouts before I sought you out. In fact he was the one who told us about you. Right before he had his unfortunate accident."

"What are you talking about? What accident?" Lebel asked, more alarmed than ever. He eased his right hand toward the dagger but changed his mind when a hard object gouged the back of his neck. Ever so slowly, he turned his head and stared into the barrel of a cocked pistol held by a hawkish man in a leather jacket. "Who are you?"

It was the woman who answered. "Our identities don't matter. All that does, Claude, is that we need information." She reached under his coat and relieved him of the dagger. "How naughty of you. You're lucky I'm not one to hold a grudge."

Lebel watched helplessly as she cast the dagger into the Seine. He had no other weapon. As he had done in the past, he had to rely on his glib tongue to spare him from being harmed. "Listen, whatever you wish to know, I'll tell you. I'm an easy man to get along with. Ask anyone."

"We already have," Katya said, looping a shapely arm around his shoulders. She winked. "Make us happy, little man. Tell us all you know about the one they call the Wizard."

Chicago, Illinois

MACK BOLAN HAD a choice to make. He either returned to the house to telephone Brognola and waited around until a retrieval team arrived to pick up the terrorists, or he went after Michael O'Shea.

It wasn't really much of a choice.

The Executioner had spent a good part of his adult life waging a relentless war against evil in all its many guises. The Mob, the drug cartels, Communist regimes and Fascist dictators, terrorists of every stripe—he had fought them all. So it was no wonder he went after O'Shea. He could no more let a savage butcher escape than he could stop breathing.

Bolan hurried down the street. He wedged the mini-Uzi under his belt above his right hip so it would be handy but still concealed by his jacket. A quick check in both directions failed to turn up the Irishman. He began to turn when he noticed a man moving swiftly westward on the opposite side of the avenue—O'Shea.

The Executioner crossed against the light. Horns honked and a taxi driver insulted his lineage. He had to skirt a bus that braked at the corner, and for a few moments he lost sight of his quarry. O'Shea had apparently lost sight of him, too, and made the mistake of jumping into the air for a better look. Bolan spotted the human jackrabbit and broke into a brisk walk.

Neither of them wanted to draw attention. O'Shea moved rapidly but didn't run. He seemed more angry than scared and gave every indication of wanting to stop and open fire. The reason he didn't became clear when a police car cruised past. O'Shea spun toward a storefront until they had gone by, then resumed his flight.

Schoolchildren and delegates weren't the only ones who lost their lives due to Michael O'Shea's rabid obsession. According to the report Brognola had shown Bolan, O'Shea was in one way or another responsible for more then sixty deaths. If he wasn't stopped, in time he would make his way back to Northern Ireland to carry on his holy war. Who knew how many more casualties he would cause?

It was added incentive for Bolan to stop the man then and there. The only hitch was that for all he knew, O'Shea was the only one of the Beastly Boys who knew how to contact the Wizard. If he killed O'Shea, Brognola would lose a valuable lead.

Bolan had to decide soon. He narrowed the gap quickly and was less than a block behind when O'Shea halted and glared at him.

Over half a dozen unsuspecting pedestrians were between them. Bolan wasn't about to open fire and risk having them nailed accidentally.

The terrorist sneered, glanced at a pair of middle-aged women who were window-shopping and stepped closer to them. His hand moved under his jacket and something bulged outward. Pretending to be interested in the merchandise, he walked when they did, stopped when they did. His meaning was as clear as if he had shouted it out.

If Bolan didn't desist, O'Shea would cut loose and mow down everyone around him.

Bolan was a certified marksman. It was entirely possible he could draw the Beretta and put a slug through O'Shea's brain before the man brought the Skorpion to bear, but he was unwilling to risk the lives of so many others. He backed away, his hands held out from his body to show he wouldn't try to make a move.

O'Shea laughed. He was almost to the curb. Hurrying to the crosswalk, he fell into step behind a young mother with a baby in her arms and a toddler glued to her side. Once he had safely crossed, he paused, grinned at Bolan and gave a mocking, formal bow. Pivoting on a heel, he trailed the young woman off into the Chicago night and was soon lost to sight. And all Mack Bolan could do was stand there and watch.

CHAPTER SIX

Paris, France

Claude Lebel had broken out in a cold sweat. He had told the blonde and her icy companion all he knew. He had revealed, at their insistence, his sources for the information so they could judge the reliability for themselves. He had done all they wanted, yet he still feared for his life.

Lebel had known his share of killers. Some were driven by nothing more than a perverse drive to snuff out human lives. Others killed as part of their underworld activities, to eliminate rivals, perhaps, or to punish squealers. And then there were the professionals, killers for hire who treated their lethal trade as a business and conducted themselves with the cold detachment of robots.

Lebel liked to flatter himself that he could tell a professional at thirty paces. He was much closer to these two, so there was no doubt at all in his mind that they weren't only pros, but two of the best. When they looked at him, it was as if they were looking at a gnat or a worm or something of equal insignificance. They would no more hesitate to extinguish his life than they would that of a fly.

He was convinced they were going to. The blonde had as much as come right out and admitted that they had disposed of Henri Gaston, and it didn't take a genius to deduce why. These two were hunting a very dangerous man. They couldn't afford to have word of their search leak back to him. Anyone who might talk had to be eliminated.

But Lebel wasn't going to go quietly. They had disarmed him, yes, but he still had the wits that had kept him alive for so many years. He had another edge, too, in that he knew the area as well as he knew his own reflection. So if he could only give them the slip, all would be well.

He had been waiting for his chance even as he answered their questions. The blonde still stood in front of him, that smile of hers still creasing her lovely face. It was a deceptive smile, though, in that it didn't light up her eyes, which were as flat as those of a cold-blooded reptile.

Her companion, whom she called "Gunther," had been cast from the same unfeeling mold. Gunther let her do most of the talking and never once lowered the Bernardelli 9 mm pistol clasped in his right hand. Nor did he display the slightest trace of emotion.

Lebel's palms were sweating so he rubbed them on his pants. The pair had just glanced at each other. It wouldn't be long now before they acted.

"Well, Claude," Katya said, "you have been a great help to us. Under different circumstances, we would reward you handsomely."

The woman opened her mouth to say more. Lebel knew that once she stopped talking, the man would put a bullet into him. But she would have to move aside first. Gunther was directly behind him; the slug might pass through him and hit her. He counted on that fact as he suddenly seized her by the wrist, twisted and flung her into Gunther. Then he fled for dear life.

Lebel had hoped that the man would automatically squeeze the trigger and shoot Katya by mistake. He should have known better. Gunther's reflexes were too finely honed.

Weaving wildly, Lebel risked a glance back and saw the man drop into a crouch and take a two-handed grip on the Bernardelli. He was almost to the corner of a building when the pistol chugged once and a searing pain scored his ribs. It staggered him but didn't stop him from reaching temporary safety.

Gritting his teeth, Lebel sprinted madly northward. He reached under his coat and when his hand came out it was dark with blood. As near as he could tell, the bullet had creased his ribs but spared his vital organs.

He got to the next corner and checked on the killers, seeing Gunther take deliberate aim. But before the silencer could cough, Lebel was around the next bend and racing along a dark alley.

Lebel calmed himself and made note of where he happened to be. It was an older, run-down neighborhood. The streets were narrow and dark. By bearing to the northeast, he would reach a wide boulevard where there was bound to be people and motorists, even so late at night. Police would be on patrol. The killers wouldn't dare to follow him there.

Lebel looked back again. His pursuers were nowhere to be seen. Encouraged, he slowed a little to conserve his energy and reduce the agony in his side. He turned right at the first intersection he came to, then left at the next. Halfway down the block he entered another alley.

Here the Frenchman stopped to listen. Other than the pounding of his heart and the distant growl of traffic, the Paris night was tranquil. He had done it, he decided. He had eluded the deadly pair.

He went on at a brisk walk. Once he was at his apartment, he would bandage his ribs and give thought to how best to get his revenge. An idea occurred to him and he nodded grimly. It would be so simple. All he had to do was get word to the man known as the Wizard and let him take care of them. What could be more fitting than that?

For more than five minutes Lebel threaded through the network of streets. The Seine was far behind him. Ahead he saw streetlights and cars moving back and forth. He was safe.

Hardly had the notion crossed his mind than a shadow separated from a building to his right and came toward him. Lebel halted, horrified. It was the blonde, but she wasn't holding a gun. He looked around fearfully for sign of her companion.

"What a naughty man you are, Claude," Katya told him, her ever-present smile more chilling than ever. "Flinging me as if I were a sack of grain, and then running off the way you did. I don't mind telling you that for a while we feared you had gotten away."

"Look, I want no more trouble," Lebel said while inching to the left with the intention of dashing past her. "I know why you want me dead, but there's no need. I won't tell a soul."

"I know you won't."

Lebel went to flee, but she darted in front of him. Oddly she made no move to employ a weapon. Desperate, Lebel said, "If you've asked around about me, then you must know my reputation. I've never betrayed a trust. I know how to keep my mouth shut."

Katya slowly advanced. "Don't whine, little man. It's unbecoming of you." Stopping, she draped her hands on her slender hips and swayed gently, enticingly. "As for keeping silent, we must have a guarantee."

"I give you my word!"

"Not enough, I'm afraid." She pursed her rose red lips as if taunting him. "I can see your fear. I can sense your hatred. How ungrateful you are, little man. You should be thankful."

Lebel swallowed hard. He knew that he should try to shove past her and get away while he still could, but he couldn't resist asking, "Thankful for what?"

"For my being the last sight you will ever see. You could do worse."

Even as the woman spoke, a whisper of air fanned Lebel's face and he felt a garrote tighten around his neck. He clutched at the wire and tried to lunge forward, but it was as if he were attached to a brick wall.

He couldn't go anywhere. Lebel shifted and lashed out with both elbows in an effort to knock Gunther off-balance.

The blonde quickly stepped in close and took hold of his wrists. Lebel strained to break free, to no avail. She was much stronger than she looked, stronger even than him. His breath choked off and his lungs lanced with more torment than he had ever endured. Just as she had said would be the case, the last sight he saw was that awful smiling face of hers, and if he could, he would have bitten into her flesh and torn that mocking face to shreds.

Chicago, Illinois

MACK BOLAN WAS a man of decisive action. No sooner did Michael O'Shea melt into the flow of pedestrians than he whirled and flagged a cab that was slowly cruising toward him.

Bolan stepped from the curb and waved his left arm. Hardly had the taxi swerved to a stop than he was inside and had slammed the door.

"Where to?" the grizzled driver asked with no real interest.

"To the next main avenue that connects with Diversey."

"Huh?" The cabbie twisted to regard him with curiosity. "That would be Cicero. It's only about eight or nine blocks. Hell, you could walk there in ten minutes if you hurried."

"Take me."

The man frowned. "Listen, pal. The fare wouldn't amount to a hill of beans. I need to earn a living, not peanuts. Do us both a favor and get some exercise."

Reaching into a pants pocket, Bolan took out a small wad of bills, peeled off a twenty and handed it over. "Take me, and if you set a new speed record, you can keep the change."

It was amazing what a little incentive could do. The cabbie threw the taxi into gear and squealed out, roaring down the street.

"Stop about a hundred feet shy of Diversey," Bolan instructed.

The man shot him a puzzled look but didn't ask any questions. When he braked, the cab slewed to one side and the driver had to spin the wheel to compensate. Beaming as if he had just won the Indy 500, he asked, "How did I do?"

"Just fine." Bolan slid out and hurried to the corner. There was no sign of O'Shea yet. He figured that it would be a minute, maybe two, before the terrorist showed up, unless O'Shea had already turned onto a side street.

Bolan spotted several pay phones under an overhang and stepped to the nearest. Turning so his back was to the street, he hunched low to disguise his build, then inserted a coin and punched up the Justice Building. Brognola answered on the first ring this time. "This is your lucky night. Two more and a body are at the brownstone."

"Then that does it," the big Fed said. "Three out of four isn't bad. Which one was killed?"

"The uncle, Dermot. I'm after the leader."

"Where are you?"

Bolan was about to give his location when he pivoted to scan the pedestrians. Without warning Michael O'Shea appeared, less than forty feet away. The terrorist, strolling along as if he didn't have a care in the world, started to skirt a knot of elderly women out on a shopping spree. Bolan bent to the telephone and leaned his shoulder against it to reduce his height by another five or six inches.

"Striker?" Brognola said.

"The corner of Diversey and Cicero. No more time to talk. I'll try to take him alive for questioning, but I can't make any promises." Bolan replaced the receiver. He could clearly see the Irishman's reflection in the window of the store in front of him.

O'Shea no longer had his right hand under his jacket. A slight bulge showed where the Skorpion nestled on his right hip. He paused once to scour the sidewalk, smirked and walked on jauntily.

Bolan gauged that O'Shea would pass within three yards of him. One blow was all it would take but he had to be certain it rendered the man unconscious. If O'Shea got hold of the SMG, there would be hell to pay.

Suddenly, at the very instant the terrorist drew abreast of the warrior, a pair of teenage girls walked up and stopped smack between them. The thinner of the duo piped up with, "Say, mister, are you planning to hog that phone all night? I've got to call my mom or she'll throw a fit."

It all happened so fast.

O'Shea glanced up, saw Bolan and stiffened. The Executioner grabbed for the Uzi with one hand while trying to shove the thin girl with the other so he would have a clear line of fire. But the teen screeched in terror and swatted at his arm, thwarting him, delaying him just long enough for O'Shea to seize her friend.

Holding the petrified youngster as a shield, O'Shea swooped a hand to the Skorpion. He froze when he saw Bolan's hand on the Uzi.

For all of five tense seconds the two men stared at each other. Bolan knew that if he acted, one or both of the girls would die. Just as he knew that the fanatic had hesitated because if they were both to draw at the same time, both of them would go down. At that range neither could miss.

"Bastard! You're a damn Yank, aren't you?" O'Shea rasped. "You don't know when to leave well enough alone." He began to back down the street. "No funny moves now or the lass will die, plus as many others as I can take with me. I promise you."

Bolan wasn't about to take the threat lightly. People had stopped to gawk in horror, making perfect targets of themselves. The girl next to him cried hysterically while her friend whimpered and quaked in the terrorist's iron grip.

O'Shea was almost to the corner. "This is how it will go, Yank. I'm going around this building here and I don't want you to follow me. Do so, and this fine little girl will have her brains splattered all over the sidewalk. Do I make myself clear?"

A curt nod was Bolan's response.

"Good. There's hope for you yet." O'Shea looked up and down the street. "You can't be alone. Where are the others?"

Bolan said nothing. He was focused on the moment, his every nerve primed to explode into action.

O'Shea reached the corner. "No matter. Just make certain they know what's at stake if they press me." He snickered in contempt. "You Yanks! If Scotland Yard couldn't catch me, did you really think a bunch of stinking provincials would have a prayer?"

Bolan stayed silent, waiting. The man was flapping his gums to hear himself talk. O'Shea was strung as tight as barbed wire, and it wouldn't take much to make him snap.

"Remember what I've told you," the terrorist gritted. Backpedaling, he retreated from sight, hauling the teenager along with him.

The people nearby came to life. Some demanded to know what was going on. One man shouted for the police. A few foolishly moved to the corner to stare after the fleeing fanatic.

Bolan was also in motion but in the opposite direction. It would be only a matter of minutes before Chicago's finest arrived on the scene, and if they overtook O'Shea before he did, there would be a bloodbath.

Service revolvers were no match for an SMG and whatever else O'Shea might have on his person.

At the next junction Bolan turned south, planning to pull the same trick twice. At each cross street he slowed to glance toward Cicero. At the third intersection he abruptly halted and crouched.

O'Shea had turned onto the same street, holding the teen by the arm and propelling her along so rapidly she was barely able to stay on her feet. Several times she stumbled and was roughly jerked upright.

Bolan backed up before he was spotted. Moving behind a large garbage container, he drew the Beretta. All he needed was one clear shot. Footfalls pattered, and then O'Shea and the girl burst into sight. The soldier saw the barrel of the Skorpion jammed against her temple, and he held his fire.

The pair sped eastward. Bolan sprinted to the corner and watched until they had traveled about a block and a half and were almost invisible in the darkness. Plying the shadows, he stalked along in their wake.

A sign welcomed Bolan to Kelvin Park. Slanting to the north, he sank to one knee next to a tree trunk. Plenty of people roamed the vicinity, among them joggers and a couple of young lovers linked arm in arm. He didn't see O'Shea, and he dreaded the girl's fate.

In another few moments the lovers halted. The man looked back and Bolan realized it was the terrorist. The poor teenager appeared on the verge of collapse. A man jogging past slowed to look at them and was curtly waved on by O'Shea. The girl moaned a few words—

whether a plea or something else, Bolan couldn't tell. The next he knew, O'Shea whipped out the SMG and raked the jogger from crotch to chin. Several females screamed, including the girl. Incensed, O'Shea smashed her across the face with the Skorpion, kicked her as she fell and raced off.

At last Bolan could go flat out. He streaked after the Irishman, who was running like a man possessed. When O'Shea suddenly stopped and spun, Bolan hurtled to the right. Rounds from the Skorpion churned up the grass and he replied twice with the Beretta. He thought that he saw O'Shea recoil as if hit, but then the terrorist was off and running again.

Rising, Bolan exchanged the pistol for the Uzi. The ground sloped toward a low hill. To the north, sirens rent the night. It wouldn't be long before the whole area swarmed with police.

The IRA renegade was almost to the top of the hill. O'Shea dropped to his hands and knees so his silhouette wouldn't make him an easy target and scrambled like mad the final few feet to the crest. Shifting around, he extended the SMG.

A thin pine tree was the only cover Bolan had handy. He flattened as the Skorpion spat lead. Shredded limbs and blasted pine needles rained to the ground. Elevating the Uzi, he stroked a short burst that sprayed dirt into O'Shea's face. The terrorist ducked below the rim.

The Executioner veered to the left, bent over, tempted to end their duel if O'Shea popped up again. But the man was too crafty to be so obvious. He spied the Irishman below the hill, still heading eastward.

Bolan ran a parallel course and was pleased to see that O'Shea hadn't spotted him. The man repeatedly glanced at the top of the rise, evidently expecting him to appear there.

Going faster, Bolan gradually pulled ahead. When he had a thirty-yard lead, he angled on an intercept course, which brought him up behind another garbage container, an open green bin situated next to the jogging trail O'Shea was on. Only then did he realize the terrorist was limping.

Bolan had the man dead to rights. All he had to do was point the Uzi when the terrorist came a little closer, and O'Shea would never know what hit him. It was exactly what vermin like O'Shea deserved.

There was, however, the Wizard to keep in mind, and the many future victims who would suffer if the wave of technoterror wasn't stopped. For all of O'Shea's lust for bloodshed, the Irishman posed nowhere near the menace to society that the anonymous Wizard did. They were leagues apart.

Any good soldier learned to keep his priorities straight. Bolan had been tested in the unrelenting crucible of combat and could make split-second decisions when other men might agonize over the right course of action. As much as he would have liked to put a permanent end to Michael O'Shea's reign of terror, he had to settle for taking the man alive.

At least he had to try.

Bolan ducked and marked the terrorist's approach by O'Shea's labored breathing. He slid the Uzi's sling out of the way, cupped his hands together, and when O'Shea huffed and puffed past the end of the garbage bin, Bolan swung his arms as if wielding a baseball bat.

O'Shea was knocked down, and the Skorpion skidded off across the grass. He crashed onto his side and promptly doubled over as if in torment.

Stepping around the large bin, Bolan moved in to finish the man off. A chop to the back of the neck would suffice. But as he raised his arm for the blow, the terrorist uncoiled and speared a knife at his stomach. Bolan leaped back and felt the tip of the blade tear the windbreaker.

The renegade came up off the ground in a rush. He snarled like a wild beast and swung again and again, driving Bolan toward the garbage bin.

Bolan's back thumped against it. He ducked under a blow that would have severed his jugular, grabbed O'Shea's wrist, twisted and heaved. In a smooth shoulder throw he flipped the terrorist up and over the rim of the container. Purely by chance, O'Shea landed inside.

Instantly Bolan stepped to the right, gripped the lid and slammed it down just as O'Shea tried to stand. The man fell, cursing a blue streak. In seconds he would be on his feet again. If Bolan let him.

The soldier's hand dropped to his waist. Instead of the Uzi, he pulled the other CS grenade, tore out the pin, lifted the lid and tossed the bomb in. O'Shea yelled, but his cry was muffled by the whump of the grenade going off. Tear gas poured from the cracks around the edges.

Taking a deep breath and holding it, Bolan threw himself on top of the bin. O'Shea, in a panic, tired to force it open but couldn't. Coughing and sputtering, the terrorist pounded on the lid in a frenzy. It sounded as if he were suffocating. Bit by bit the blows weakened. Soon they stopped, and there was a dull thud.

The Executioner wasted no more time. Whipping the lid open, he stood back while the breeze dispersed most of the chemical cloud. When it was safe to do so, he moved around behind the bin and upended it. Michael O'Shea came rolling limply out like a bag of garbage. It took but a moment to drape the unconscious form over his shoulder, then the Executioner turned and headed off into the darkness.

CHAPTER SEVEN

Miami, Florida

Milo Fernstein considered himself a lucky man. In his opinion, he had the cushiest job in the U.S.A. He worked only an hour or two a day, yet he made five thousand dollars a week. Who could beat that?

On this particular day, Fernstein began the morning as he normally did. After a shave and a shower, he took a steaming mug of black coffee into his den, plunked his two hundred and sixty-five pounds into the easy chair in front of his workstation and fired up his computer.

He liked to listen to the rising hum of the hard drive as it came on-line and to see the monitor flash with the logo he had designed of a comely barbarian wench wielding a bloody sword and announcing the words, Good Morning, Handsome!

It wasn't true, of course. With his body long since gone to fat and his face pockmarked from acne, the only one in the world who would sanely call Fernstein handsome was his mother. And she happened to be notoriously farsighted.

Fernstein patted his shirt pocket, but his pen was missing. Taking a spare from a desk drawer, he set it on a small notepad next to the keyboard. As usual, he resorted to his cheat sheet, which was taped to the bottom of the monitor. Although he had worked with computers for years, he could never remember all the commands. And he dared not screw up. His employer had made that quite clear.

His employer. The words echoed in Fernstein's mind and made him smirk. How many people worked for someone whose identity they didn't know, whose whereabouts were completely unknown and who paid them in cash mailed anonymously? Still, he couldn't complain. Ever since he had responded to a message on one of the bulletin boards, he had been making more money than he ever dreamed of earning.

And the job was so easy. After being hired, Fernstein had been directed to subscribe to four different online services. Then, at specified times each day, he was to check all four services for messages sent to his computer addresses. If there were any, he had to copy the information and then telephone a number in Jamaica. That was it. It was that simple. The rest of the day could be spent as he wished.

Pausing to take a sip of coffee, Fernstein gazed out over the Miami skyline. He was no dummy. The odds were that whatever activity his employer was engaged in was illegal. Why else all the secrecy? The subterfuge? He suspected that it involved organized crime and drugs in some way or another. But he wasn't worried. If the authorities ever showed up at his door, he could honestly plead ignorance. He was simply doing the job he had been hired to do, and there was nothing illegal about relaying messages. Since he had no criminal record, it was highly doubtful he would be prosecuted, let alone do time.

He shook his head to dispel his train of thought and set down the mug. He logged on to the first service and checked his mail. There was nothing for him, so he went to the next address.

A message was waiting. As was typical, it consisted of a name and a telephone number and that was all. Fernstein jotted down both. The name had a ring to it that he was sure he would remember if he'd seen it before: Mike Belasko. Not that the same name appeared more than once very often.

None of the other addresses proved productive.

He swiveled his chair and checked the time. At the top of the hour he was to make the first call of the day. His employer had been quite specific about when he was to pass on the information. If he was late, he risked losing his job.

There was time for him to finish his coffee and read a few articles in a computer magazine. At nine o'clock he turned to the telephone. Every day the same person answered, a man with a heavy accent who took the information and promptly hung up. Fernstein had no idea who the man was or what he did for a living.

And he didn't really *want* to know.

Jamaica

EDWARD BUSTAMANTE had been a Jamaican customs official for more than a decade. His superiors regarded him as a dedicated professional who had risen through the ranks to head the office in Savanna la Mar.

There was another side to Bustamante that only a few close associates knew about. Bustamante made more money under the table than he did in his paycheck. For the right price, he was all too happy to look the other way when illegal activities were being conducted.

Smugglers knew Bustamante as a man who could be trusted. Gunrunners and drug lords relied on his lavishly greased palms to insure the orderly flow of their wares.

Bustamante had always been greedy. As a skinny child reared in a poverty-stricken section of Kingston, he had looked on men of power and influence with their fine clothes and pretty women and polished limos, and vowed that one day he would be just like them.

Earning lots and lots of money had become a lifelong obsession. One day he planned to retire to an estate he had secretly purchased near Montego Bay and live in the lap of luxury for the rest of his life.

Of the thousands of dollars Bustamante pocketed every month, fully a third of it came from one man, a man whose name he didn't know but who had seemed to know all about Bustamante on the one and only occasion they had talked, over the telephone.

The man had made Bustamante a proposition he couldn't refuse. Simply for relaying information, he would receive a large sum of cash each and every month.

For almost a year the man had been as good as his word. Several times Bustamante had toyed with the idea of tracking the man down, just to satisfy his curiosity. But he didn't. The man had made it plain that if he tried, he would pay dearly.

So on this sunny morning, when one of the usual calls came through from a man whose squeaky voice he recognized, Bustamante wrote down the name "Mike Belasko" and the telephone number he was given.

The caller with the squeaky voice was just one of several men who called regularly. Bustamante never asked who they were. He suspected that Squeaky, as he had dubbed this caller, was an American. Another regular caller sounded French. And there was a third whose accent he couldn't place.

The Frenchman had already called that very morning. So after Squeaky hung up, Bustamante did as was expected of him. He dialed a local number and relayed the information to someone with a raspy voice who always had him spell out the names twice. He did so now, both with Belasko and the name the Frenchman had given him—Katya Steiner.

That was all Bustamante had to do. He set down the telephone and grinned. Thanks to his unknown benefactor, his Swiss bank account was growing by leaps and bounds. Another year of this, and he might give serious thought to retiring early.

IN A SMALL SHACK on the docks of Savanna la Mar, a fisherman who went only by the name of Tego hung up the telephone, neatly folded a slip of paper containing the two names and telephone numbers and slipped it into the pocket of his grungy pants.

As Tego had done every day for almost a year, he left his shack and went down the pier to the berth he rented for his boat. Or rather, to the boat that had been purchased for him by the man who had hired him to take messages. It was a late-model fishing craft, the kind Tego had always dreamed of owning but had never been able to afford. Turning over the engine, he cast off and headed out to sea.

Sometimes Tego couldn't believe his good fortune. Until his benefactor came along, he had been just one of many old fishermen who lived hand to mouth with little hope for the future.

There were two things, though, that had set Tego apart from his peers. Foremost among them was the fact that he knew the West Indies perhaps better than any man alive. In his younger days he had traveled widely, from Nassau in the north to Port of Spain in the south, from Cuba in the west to Antigua in the east.

The other difference was that Tego hadn't always relied solely on fishing for his livelihood. At various times he had smuggled contraband and engaged in other activities frowned on by the law.

He believed that both things had a lot to do with his being hired by the man who lived on the island. From friends, he had learned that the man had been asking around about him long before he was approached. The man was a cautious one. There was no doubt of that.

It had been Tego who showed the man several islands that might suit his purpose. And it had been Tego who transported most of the equipment the man had flown in from the United States and elsewhere. He had known the man for many months now, yet, when he thought about it, he realized that he knew next to nothing about his benefactor.

The man was an American, the man was very smart and the man liked his privacy. That was all.

And one other thing.

Tego had seen many of the labels on the packages and equipment. While he couldn't read or write very well, he knew a name when he saw it. And the strange thing was that few of the packages and supplies were ever addressed to the same person. It was as if fifty people lived on the island.

There was only Tego's benefactor, though, and the three men who worked for him, men whose eyes were as hard as diamonds and who spent many hours shooting at targets with various weapons. Tego didn't like them very much. But as long as he was paid so well, he would keep on delivering messages and whatever else the smart man wanted.

Miami, Florida

MACK BOLAN SAT in his motel room waiting for the telephone to ring. He was a man of action and would much rather be out in the field doing what he did best. But sometimes sacrifices had to be made. In this instance, if he wanted to nail the Wizard, he had to stick to the strategy he had worked out with Brognola.

It was a sound strategy, in Bolan's opinion. By posing as someone interested in hiring the Wizard, he stood a good chance of learning where the Wizard had his base of operations.

It had, ironically, been the deceased Dermot O'Shea and not his flamboyant nephew who supplied the information they needed to put the plan into effect. Dermot had been more than an IRA money man; he had also set up a network that funneled weapons and explosives to the terrorists. And it had been Dermot who came up with the bright idea of contacting the Wizard to obtain a fail-safe device that could be used in the London bombing.

Of course, Dermot had an ulterior motive. The London meet had been set up to discuss covert American backers of the IRA, of whom he happened to be one. By blowing the delegates to kingdom come, he had derailed the investigation for many months.

To Dermot's credit, he had kept meticulous records of all his dealings, including a diary that had been seized during the Justice Department raid on his residence.

From it, Brognola had learned exactly how Dermot contacted the Wizard. The big Fed had swung into action. Within hours he had learned that the computer address to which Dermot had sent a message belonged to one Milo Fernstein.

Fernstein proved to be a puzzle. He couldn't be the Wizard, as his background was all wrong.

On his last income-tax form, Fernstein had listed his occupation as that of a "free-lance consultant." Prior to that he had worked as a programmer for a small Miami firm. The man had no links at all to the international terrorist community, so the Feds were completely at a loss to explain his connection to the criminal genius.

Bolan had flown to Miami and rented a room on the off chance that the Wizard was based in the same city as Fernstein. It was a long shot. There was no way of telling where the Wizard had his home base. It might be in another country, for all they knew.

Meanwhile, Brognola had seen to it that an appropriate message was received by Fernstein. The Feds had also put a tap on his telephone and were ready to trace incoming calls at a moment's notice.

All that had taken place more than six hours ago.

Bolan turned on the television and watched part of a ball game. Both he and Brognola agreed that tracking down the man wouldn't be easy. Anyone as intelligent as the Wizard had to have gone to great lengths to protect his identity. It was entirely possible that the Wizard conducted all of his business through underlings, which would complicate matters.

A commercial came on, so Bolan went to the sink and filled a glass with water. As he sat back down, the telephone finally jangled. He let it ring three times, then picked up the receiver. "Hello?"

"Mr. Belasko?"

"Yes."

"There is a warehouse at 1642 North River Drive, south of the civic center. Be there in one hour. Come alone."

"Who is this?" Bolan demanded, but the hum of the dial tone was his only answer. He immediately dialed the number Brognola had given him, and his friend came on the line. "Any chance of a trace?"

"Afraid not. He wasn't on long enough. We're running the address through the computer and should know everything there is to know about the place in about a half hour."

"Give me a call."

In under twenty minutes the telephone rang again. "The warehouse was built by a transport company that has since gone out of business. A magazine distributor bought it for a song, but apparently it was too big for his needs so he's been trying to rent it out for the past six months. So far he's not had any takers."

"It's empty, then?" Bolan asked.

"Supposed to be. He doesn't get down there very often. I talked to him myself and told him to stay away from the place until I give him the green light." Brognola paused. "It would make me feel a whole lot better if we had a team posted in a van a few blocks away when you go to meet this guy."

"And run the risk of the van being made?" Bolan countered. "I don't think so. If we blow this, the Wizard will be twice as cautious from here on out. I'll play this the way I always do."

"It's just a preliminary meet, anyway," Brognola said. "Odds are it'll be a subordinate, someone sent to sound you out and determine whether the Wizard should get involved."

"I have my lines down pat," Bolan promised.

"Just watch your back, Striker. A man like the Wizard is liable to throw us the kind of curve we don't run up against every day."

Bolan spent the next half hour preparing. He double-checked all the hardware in his duffel bag, made sure the Beretta and Desert Eagle were fully loaded, strapped a throwing knife to his right ankle and stuck a small flashlight in the pocket of his windbreaker.

His contact in Miami had provided him with a two-door gray sedan. The tank was full and maps of Florida and greater Miami rested on the dashboard. Headlights speared the street as Bolan left the parking lot to make the rendezvous.

Before pulling out, the soldier had studied the map and memorized the shortest route. Five minutes early, he pulled up in front of the warehouse gate. The place was supposed to be deserted, but the gate hung open and a black car was parked near an open side door.

Bolan drove in and braked alongside the other vehicle. Confident he was being watched, he made no attempt to use stealth but simply climbed out and closed the door just enough to turn off the overhead light. He left it ajar in case he needed to make a hasty getaway.

The interior of the building was pitch-black. Bolan switched on the flashlight as he strode inside and was immediately hailed by a gruff voice.

"Belasko?"

"That's me."

"Turn that damn thing off and stand perfectly still."

Bolan complied. A pair of shapes materialized out of the gloom. They had hired help written all over them. The bigger of the two moved around behind him, and hands the size of hams patted him down. In front of Bolan stood a swarthy man who favored expensive clothes and a black fedora.

The muscleman chuckled when he found the Beretta, which he placed at Bolan's feet. He whistled in appreciation as he lifted the Desert Eagle and set it down. The knife elicited no sound whatsoever.

"Planning to start a war?" Fedora quipped.

Shrugging, Bolan said, "Tools of the trade."

"And what is your trade, Mr. Belasko?"

"Let's just say I represent a certain organized crime interest that is at odds with another organized crime interest." The cover story had been solely Bolan's idea. Thanks to his long war against the Mob, he was an expert on their inner workings.

"The Mafia?" Fedora said. "I thought you guys liked to take care of your own problems."

Again Bolan shrugged, playing his part. "This is a special case."

"And you're going to tell me all about it, friend. Leave nothing out."

Bolan pretended to be annoyed. "My boss wouldn't like it very much if I aired his dirty linen. He told me not to be specific."

Fedora took out a gold cigarette case and fired a cigarette. "No offense, friend, but I have my orders, too. And my employer has made it clear that unless you tell me all there is to know about why you want to use my employer's services, you can turn right around and head back to your boss and tell him to find someone else."

Several seconds went by while Bolan acted as if he were mulling it over. "I guess I have no choice," he said. "My boss says that your boss is his best bet."

"Do tell. Go on."

"I work for Gino Gamboa of the Gamboa Family in New York City. A while ago his father died. Since then, Gino and his older brother Sam have been at odds over who gets to take over the action." Which was all true. Bolan made a point of keeping up with Mafia activities, and this tidbit was the latest out of the Big Apple.

"They're on the brink of all-out war. My boss wants to keep it from happening by taking care of Sam."

"He's going to snuff his own brother?" Fedora snorted. "Now there's true family devotion for you."

He cocked his head and studied Bolan. "I take it that you're one of his wiseguys?"

The Executioner nodded.

"How did your boss find out about mine?"

"He didn't say."

"Does he know how much he'll have to pay?"

"Half a million dollars."

"And he's willing to fork over that kind of money?" Fedora was skeptical.

Bolan smiled. "Are you kidding? Once he's head of the Family, he'll pull that much down each and every week. He wanted me to let your boss know that he'll pay whatever it takes to get the job done. A million. Name your price."

"Does Gamboa have any idea how he wants to go about it? My employer has to have all the details in advance. He's a stickler for getting things done just right."

Thankfully Bolan had already worked out the scenario. "Sam is holed up at the family compound and hasn't stepped a foot outside in weeks. Gino thinks he won't, either, until Gino is dead. So my boss needs to hit Sam there. But trying to sneak in a bomb is out of the question. No one gets close to Sam without first going through a small army of soldiers and his lieutenants."

Fedora blew a puff of smoke in the air. "Quite the challenge. All right. I'll talk to my boss. If he's interested, you'll hear from us within the next day or two. If not, you'll never see or hear from us again."

The prospect of twiddling his thumbs while waiting for the telephone to ring didn't appeal to Bolan. "That long?'' he said. ''Gino was hoping I'd have word for him tomorrow.''

The man in the hat stepped to the doorway, trailed by the hulking bruiser. ''Sorry, friend, but these things take time. We have to be careful about whose money we take. I think you can understand.''

''Sure.''

''Your story has to be checked out,'' Fedora said as he walked through the doorway. Stopping just beyond, he looked back and grinned wickedly. ''For your sake, friend, I hope it does.''

CHAPTER EIGHT

Xaymaca. James Trask liked to say the name of the island aloud, to roll it on the tip of his tongue. Xaymaca was his idea of paradise on earth and he keenly regretted that one day he would have to leave his cherished sanctuary. But it had to be. In the past year he had become one of the most sought-after men on the face of the planet. In time the authorities were bound to track him down.

By then Trask would be long gone, living in the lap of luxury where they would never, ever find him. He had always stayed several steps ahead of the law, and he would continue to do so. It wasn't really much of a contest. The police forces arrayed against him had the edge in numbers and technology, but he had his brain. And superior intellect would win out over inferior minds every time.

Trask had always known he was smarter than most. As a child he had been able to outwit his parents and other adults with astounding ease. In grade school he had applied himself just hard enough to earn passing grades while devoting most of his energy to swindling his peers of their lunch money and whatever else he could fleece them of.

Not until high school had Trask found something legitimate that piqued his interest. Electronics, and later computers, became his passion. They stimulated him as nothing else ever had.

It helped that Trask had a flair for both, a knack so rare that by the time he entered college he knew more than most of his college professors. Small wonder, as it turned out. Standard tests he was given revealed his IQ to be close to 180.

About the same time, Trask had begun to look ahead and ponder how he intended to spend the rest of his life. As much as he liked electronics, in particular microchip processing, he couldn't see himself holding down a desk job for twenty or thirty years and then retiring with a modest pension. Design engineering, programming, technical work—none of that appealed to him. A leading supplier of military hardware had approached him about taking a job, but he had declined.

No, Trask had decided that he would rather earn a lot of money quickly and then sit back and enjoy his remaining years. The problem was that for the longest while he'd had no idea how to go about it.

Then prison had given Trask the answer.

He'd gone to work for a computer manufacturer after college just to make ends meet until he came up with a better idea. Naturally they hadn't paid him what he felt he was worth, so he had helped himself to company funds and arranged the accounts so cleverly that management would never find out.

There had been a woman, though, a pretty young thing from the office pool. They had been close, or so he'd thought, and one day he had foolishly bragged about the embezzlement. And she, bless her pointy little head, had gone straight to the police.

It being his first offence, Trask had been sentenced to a year at a minimum-security facility. While there he met a drug dealer with a grudge against an informant. They had gotten to talking, and one thing led to another. On being released, Trask made a bomb for which he was paid the hefty sum of fifty thousand dollars.

That had been the beginning. Word spread among the criminal element. Trask had more work than one man could handle. He went underground, set up his own network and expanded the scope of his operation. Before he knew it, he was dealing with the big boys, international terrorists and cartel contacts and whoever else could meet his ever-bigger fees.

Now Trask was going for the gold. A year earlier he had invested everything he had into this new operation. Computers, drop boxes and selected contacts brought him plenty of business from all over the globe. As a safeguard, none of his clients ever dealt directly with him. They had to go through layers of underlings first.

Trask screened every job and took only those with which he felt comfortable. At the rate he was going, in another year he would have more than fifteen million squirreled away.

Now, seated on the veranda of his bungalow, a glass of Scotch whisky on the table in front of him, Trask gazed out over the shimmering Caribbean Sea and watched Tego's boat approach for the second time that day.

A shadow fell across the table, and Trask looked up to find Loomis standing there. Of all the people working for him, Loomis was the only one Trask had any faith in. "What did you find out?"

The thin man who liked to dress all in black frowned. Before coming to work for Trask, Loomis had been part of a Los Angeles drug operation, working mainly as an enforcer. They had met a year and a half ago when Loomis's former boss hired Trask. One day Trask had commented that he was looking for a few good men to work for him, and Loomis had leaped at the chance.

"The Gamboa Family is on the verge of war, just like this guy in Miami claims. Sam Gamboa has taken control and his brother Gino is trying to force him out."

"But?" Trask prompted. His lieutenant's tone made it plain that something wasn't quite right.

"My sources tell me that Gino is too strapped to come up with half a million in cash."

Trask sighed. "So either Gino Gamboa is trying to pull a fast one on me, or the wiseguy isn't really a wiseguy at all." He took a swallow. "What would you recommend?"

"Play it safe. Waste the guy."

The thin man's bloodthirsty outlook made Trask smile. Having Loomis to handle minor annoyances freed him to concentrate on important matters. "Give the word to Grendel. But tell him that I want this gentleman questioned first. Have Lupo break a few bones or gouge out his eyes. Whatever it takes for them to find out who he really works for."

"Will do." Loomis didn't walk off. "What about the European contact? They claim it's urgent."

"This Katya Steiner will have to wait," Trask said. "The Mexican contract is our top priority. They're offering three times my going rate, and we know they have the money."

"It's awful risky, though. I mean, hitting the DEA was one thing. But this!"

"Trust me. I'll have all the angles covered. I always do."

Miami, Florida

THE CALL CAME THROUGH almost twenty-four hours after the first one. Bolan had ordered a pizza to be delivered to his room and had just taken his first bite when the telephone rang. He recognized Fedora's voice right away.

"You're in luck, friend. Meet me in ninety minutes on the Alligator Highway, at Weston. Look for the same car you saw last night."

The line went dead. Bolan consulted a map. The Alligator Highway, it turned out, was another name for the Everglades Parkway. When the telephone rang again he knew who it would be before he lifted the receiver to his ear. "I know what you're going to say."

"I don't like it," Brognola declared. "Why meet way out there? After Weston there are no other towns for almost sixty miles."

"I have to go."

The big Fed persisted. "The Everglades are a favorite dumping ground, you know. Gangs from Miami do it all the time. Usually the bodies are half-eaten when they're found. I'm thinking of calling in a chopper. It can keep you under surveillance without being spotted."

"You think," Bolan said. "No, I'd rather you didn't. If there's an outside chance the Wizard has taken the bait, we have to play along. By their rules."

It was quite a drive from downtown Miami to Weston, so Bolan got an early start. Fedora hadn't been very specific, but Bolan reasoned that the meeting was to take place at a gas station on the outskirts of the small town. Pulling over, he parked, got out and leaned against the fender. The humidity made his shirt cling to his body. He would have liked to take off the windbreaker, but it wouldn't do to advertise his arsenal.

Ninety minutes came and went. Bolan scanned the sparse flow of traffic coming from the east, seeking the black sedan. Fifteen more minutes went by, and he began to wonder if they were going to show.

A horn honked.

Bolan spotted their vehicle. It took the exit and came slowly toward him, braking so close to his feet that the tires nearly crunched his toes. The windows were tinted, so he had no inkling of how many men were inside until the driver rolled his down.

The hulking gunner sat behind the wheel. Fedora lounged beside him. In the back seat was a third man whose features were shrouded in shadow.

Bolan didn't like the setup. Still playing his part, he remarked, "You had me worried. I thought that maybe your boss had changed his mind."

"No chance of that," Fedora said. "Hop in. We have a lot to talk about."

"Am I finally going to get to meet the big man in person?"

"Not quite. He likes to stay on the sidelines, if you get my drift. I'm the one you'll have to deal with." Fedora nodded at the rear seat. "Now climb on in, friend. We don't have all night."

"What about my car?" Bolan hedged, stalling. His gut instinct was that Brognola had been right, and he should take all three hardmen down before they did the same to him. But he couldn't, not when there was an outside chance of learning where to find the Wizard.

"No one's going to steal it," Fedora said testily. "If you're worried, lock it up. But you'll be back in no time."

Simply to buy more time, Bolan did just that. He scoured the area and saw no evidence of other gunners. As he came around the trunk, he noticed the back door of the black sedan was wide open.

"We're waiting," Fedora stressed.

Bolan slid in and closed the door. The driver pulled out, merged onto the Alligator Highway and headed due west into the heart of the Everglades. Fedora twisted around and smiled like a used-car salesman about to make a pitch.

"Yes, sir. My employer was real impressed by the information I passed on to him. His orders are that I'm to give you the royal treatment, Belasko."

"Where are we headed?"

"A special place where we can talk in private." Fedora adjusted his hat. "My name is Grendel, by the way. This big ape next to me is Lupo. And the guy beside you is Wyman. Think of us as your friends from now on."

The soldier stared out at the Everglades, which shimmered like a sea of tall grass in the pale moonlight. It occurred to him that this would be an ideal base for a man like the Wizard. Remote, yet close enough to a major metropolitan area that the man could maintain a far-flung network with no problem. The Miami airport was close, and there was no end of computer and electronics suppliers.

"As friends," Grendel went on, "we should always be up front with one another. We can hardly work together if one side doesn't trust the other, now can we?"

Bolan looked at him.

"For instance, you told me last night that Gino Gamboa was willing to pay through the nose to have his brother offed. Remember? Yet we've heard that's not quite true. Gino has been bled dry by the infighting. The word on the streets of New York is that he couldn't afford to pay a parking ticket, let alone half a million."

The Beretta was only six inches from Bolan's hand. He tensed, about to make the grab.

Suddenly the silenced snout of a pistol poked above Grendel's seat. "I wouldn't do that, Belasko, if I were you. Wyman, make sure our new friend isn't tempted to do something he'll regret."

A pistol materialized in Wyman's fist as the gunner quickly relieved Bolan of the Beretta and the Desert Eagle, which were handed to Grendel. Wyman checked both of Bolan's ankles and located the throwing knife. It went into the hardman's pocket.

"Well, now," Grendel said, visibly relaxing. "If you behave yourself, friend, you'll get to live a little longer."

"What is this?" Bolan bluffed. "My boss sent me down here in good faith and this is how I'm treated? I don't know where you got your information, but it's all wrong. Gino has plenty of money stashed away. More than enough to cover the cost of hiring your boss."

"Maybe he does, maybe he doesn't. That's what we're going to find out." Grendel winked. "But between you and me, I think you're lying through your teeth. If I'm wrong, my boss will send an apology to yours."

Lupo laughed.

"Your boss is going to regret this," Bolan warned.

"I doubt it. Mr. Trask never makes mistakes. Never. The man is so brainy, it's scary."

The same couldn't be said of those Trask hired, Bolan mused. At long last he had a name, although it might be an alias.

"Oh, look!" Grendel said, pointing to the north. "I always get a kick out of seeing those things. Ever watched one of them tear into a person, Belasko?"

Several logs floated on a stretch of water bordering the highway. At least they appeared to be logs until one of them opened a gaping maw rimmed with teeth and flicked a tail powerful enough to snap a human spine with a single swipe.

"You'll think this is crazy, Belasko, but they're poetry in motion when they go after something. For their size, they're as fast as snakes," Grendel continued. "They like to come up on their victims from below and behind. And after they get a grip with those jaws of theirs, they roll over and over until their prey stops moving. A death roll, it's called. Ever heard of it?"

Bolan didn't bother to respond.

"If it was up to me, I'd feed you to the gators. They'd finish you off quickly, with no fuss. But my employer wants answers. And since you strike me as being a tough mother, I guess we'll have to do this the hard way and make you suffer some. Nothing personal, you understand."

The car purred westward at the speed limit. Traffic was light. The farther they went, the more alligators they saw. Some of the great beasts crawled onto land and stood close to the shoulder of the road. Their eyes seemed to dance with fire in the glare of headlights.

Wyman never lowered his pistol, a .380 Colt Mustang. He did glance out the window from time to time, and once he gave a little shudder and commented, "You might like those ugly suckers, Grendel, but they give me the creeps. I keep thinking of what it would be like to have those teeth tear into me."

Grendel chuckled. "You should come to my place sometime and see me feed my piranha. Those little beauties are ten times as mean as gators."

For the longest while no one spoke. Then Grendel leaned forward and stabbed a finger to the right. "Keep your eyes peeled, Lupo. The turnoff is hard to spot. If we miss it, we'll have to go another twenty miles before there's another spot we can use."

The driver slowed. In another few minutes a gravel rest area appeared and he veered off the highway. It was a desolate spot seldom used by travelers, especially after the sun set. Grendel knew right where to go and directed Lupo to drive to the northwest, where a gradual slope led down to the very edge of the Everglades. Lupo stopped close to the rim and switched off the ignition.

A virtual chorus could be heard in the abrupt silence. Bullfrogs croaked, crickets chirped, insects buzzed. And above it all rose the throaty bellow of alligators, dozens and dozens of them.

Grendel covered the soldier with the Beretta. "Out you go, friend. And please don't insult us by trying anything stupid. Mr. Trask only hires the best."

The air was sultry, the night uncommonly warm. Bolan left his door open and stood with his hands raised to shoulder height. He wanted to give the impression that he wasn't about to make any trouble. They'd learn the truth soon enough.

Forty yards away, cars and trucks rumbled past on the Alligator Highway. None of the headlight beams came anywhere near the parked sedan.

Lupo slid out and towered over Bolan. The huge bruiser hadn't bothered to draw a gun. Lupo was the sort who relied on his brawn instead of firepower. His bulging biceps had undoubtedly seen him through many a scrape.

Grendel stepped to the front of the vehicle and beckoned. "Bring him over here. We don't want any pain-in-the-butt busybodies to notice anything. Our employer would be very upset."

Bolan was given a shove by Lupo that nearly drove him to his knees. He regained his balance, stared at the hulking hardman a moment, then moved around the rear of the car. The whole time he was covered by Wyman. As Bolan walked past the gunner, he saw that the hilt of his throwing knife jutted from the man's pocket.

Grendel inhaled. "Don't you just love the smells out here? It makes me wish I'd been raised in the country instead of in the city." He indicated a spot near the slope. "Stand here, Belasko."

Bolan found himself partially ringed by the trio. Lupo stood to the left, his massive arms folded. Wyman was to the right, his Colt as steady as ever. The talkative Grendel stood in the middle and wagged the Beretta.

"Now then. Let's get this over with. My employer wants to know who you really are and why you tried to dupe us. And please, spare yourself a lot of pain and tell me the truth."

Bolan girded himself. The blow, when it came, was a short, swift punch to the gut. He doubled over, shamming, and sank onto his left knee. The pain wasn't nearly as bad as he let on, but he wanted Grendel to think it was.

"Don't be stubborn, Belasko. We'll wring the information out of you one way or another. Why not make it easy on yourself and on us?"

Keeping his arms pressed to his waist, Bolan made no attempt to rise. He was at the very brink of the incline. Twenty feet below him lay the murky water. Out of the corner of an eye he surveyed the area. There were no alligators that he could see, which meant little. The brutes liked to lie in wait for prey, with just their eyes and snouts above the surface.

"Who do you really work for?" Grendel probed.

"The government."

Grendel smiled and looked at his companions. "See? Nine times out of ten they'll take the easy way if you give them the choice."

"Let's just get it over with," Wyman said. "I hate this place. I hate everything about this stinking swamp." The Colt drooped a couple of inches.

Just then another car pulled onto the turnoff. Its beams played over the black car and silhouetted the three hardmen. Grendel hissed and hid the Beretta under his jacket. "Wyman! Don't let them see your piece."

"Who cares if they do?" the gunner snapped, but he obeyed.

The car stopped close to the road and an elderly woman climbed out the passenger side. In her arms she held a white poodle, which she set down and patted on the back. "Be a dear and piddle for us, Muffy. That's it. Go on." The dog moved about, sniffing loudly.

Wyman cursed under his breath. "I don't believe this. We should have just thrown this clown onto a boat and taken him a mile out on the Atlantic Ocean. We'd have plenty of privacy there."

"You're not paid to second-guess those who give the orders around here," Grendel snapped.

Bolan was ready to make his move, but he waited for the other car to leave. The poodle didn't seem to be in any great hurry to heed nature's call, and the woman was growing impatient. So was Wyman, who held the Colt down close to his leg. The hilt of the throwing knife jutted farther than before.

"Look!" Lupo breathed.

The poodle was walking toward them, head bent low, tail wagging crazily. It stopped when the woman stamped her foot and called out, "Muffy! You get back here this second!"

Wyman glowered. "Stupid mutt! For two cents I'd toss it to the damn gators."

"Just stay calm," Grendel cautioned. "The boss wouldn't like it if we botch this. We have to keep a real low profile. Lower than ever, after what Loomis told me this afternoon."

"Is it a secret?"

Grendel hesitated. "What the hell. You'd find out in a few days, anyway. The boss has a new job to do, the biggest damn job ever." He grinned. "Do you remember that greaser who was hot under the collar about the DEA?"

Poised on the balls of his feet, Bolan listened intently. The gunner had to be referring to Luis Terrazas, but the drug lord was dead.

Wyman had forgotten about the poodle for the moment. "What about him?"

"Well, he got himself whacked. His people are furious. They think our government is to blame. So they're paying Trask to come up with a foolproof way to hit another target. You wouldn't guess who it is in a million years."

"The CIA? The FBI?"

"Not quite." Grendel snickered. "They want to blow away the President."

CHAPTER NINE

Marseilles, France

The call had come through an hour ago, but Bouvier had been in no great rush to relay the news. The truth was that the German pair worried him. The smiling blonde whose eyes were never touched by her mirth and the cold, quiet man who had the air of a hungry tiger made Bouvier feel uneasy inside.

The Frenchman had met more than his share of those who made their living on the wrong side of the law. In his capacity as an arms broker for terrorists of every stripe, he had come into contact with killers of every nationality.

None had ever provoked the same feeling as these two Germans.

Bouvier tried to shrug off the feeling as a case of bad nerves. He was getting on in years, he told himself, and was prone to flights of fancy. It was important to keep in mind that he was a man of influence in the criminal underworld of Europe and the Mediterranean. No one would dare lay a finger on him.

Besides, Bouvier had his bodyguard with him at all times. Rodin was built like a tank and had never been bested in hand-to-hand combat. He could produce his pistol in the blink of an eye, and he was a crack shot.

Why, then, did Bouvier fret as their car pulled into the parking lot of the hotel where the Germans were staying? Rodin opened the door for him and he eased out, his arthritic joints protesting. The hotel was perched on a hill, and below was sprawled the brightly lit city of Marseilles. Beyond lay the sparkling waters of the Gulf of Lyons.

Rodin also opened the door to the hotel. They crossed the lobby to the elevator and took it to the third floor. The bodyguard kept glancing at Bouvier as if he sensed his boss's worry, and when they reached the room Rodin slipped a hand under his light jacket and loosened the Walther P-5 in its leather holster.

Bouvier knocked once, and moments later the blonde answered the door. She took one look at him, and the corners of her eyes crinkled as if in annoyance. But it was so fleeting that Bouvier wasn't quite sure he had read her expression correctly.

"Mr. Bouvier," Katya Steiner said in her near-flawless French. "I can tell that you bear us bad news." Her beaming smile returned, and she clasped his arm in a friendly manner. "But come in, come in. Tell us about it while I pour you a drink."

Against his better judgment Bouvier let himself be drawn into the room. Rodin was right behind him. They were led past the closed door of the bathroom to a counter that fronted the pink canopy bed. Bouvier had stayed at the same hotel a number of times with his mistress and knew the layout of the rooms well.

"I must pass on the drink," Bouvier said politely. "It's extremely late and I must be getting home." He looked around the spacious room. "But where is your husband? I should think he would like to hear the news."

"Gunther stepped out for just a moment," Katya said, curling onto the edge of the bed. Her long legs were like magnets, drawing Bouvier's gaze despite himself. "Now then, let me hear what you have to say."

Bouvier drew himself up. "I'm sorry to have to tell you that the Wizard has declined. For the moment, at any rate. He is all too willing to help you, but he has a pressing job, which, I understand, must take precedence. In another month, perhaps, contact me again and I will see what I can do."

"Another month?" Katya said, and sadly shook her head. "We cannot wait that long, I'm afraid. You leave us with no other option."

"Pardon?" Bouvier said, puzzled. It was then that he heard a grunt and a thud behind him and something smacked against the back of his left leg. Shifting, Bouvier was horrified to see Rodin doubled over on the floor, his face livid, his thick fingers tearing at his own throat. Behind the bodyguard, legs planted wide, stood Gunther. Bouvier went to go to Rodin's aid when the hard barrel of a pistol was shoved into the side of his neck and the silky voice of the blonde whispered playfully in his ear.

"I wouldn't do that, not if you want to go on living."

Bouvier was helpless. He had to stand there and watch in mute terror as his trusted friend of many years was garroted. It all happened so quickly that he couldn't quite credit his senses. Rodin hardly had time to put up a fight.

Gunther unwrapped the garrote and wiped it clean on the dead man's jacket. "Now then," he said softly as he straightened, "you are going to tell us how we might find the Wizard."

Bouvier could feel the blood drain from his face. "But I thought I made that clear," he protested. "I don't know where he is. My only contact with him and his people has been over the telephone. You must believe me!"

The blonde stepped in front of him and idly nudged Rodin's body with her dainty toe. "You insult us, sir."

"What do you mean?" The full impact of what was taking place hit him, and his knees quaked. He feared that he would begin to cry like a child. He didn't want to die.

"After we were given your name by someone in Paris, we went to great lengths to learn all we could about you," Katya responded. "You're a very cautious man, it's said. Not the sort to have regular dealings with anyone you didn't know well, or had learned a lot about."

Bouvier wanted to crawl under the bed and hide.

"It's said that you have many contacts around the world," the blonde continued. "You would have used those contacts to learn what you could about the Wizard. And now you're going to share all that you have learned."

"It was very little," Bouvier said hastily. He realized his mistake when he saw her grin of triumph.

"A little is better than nothing, and nothing is all we have to go on at the moment. So start talking. And don't think to leave anything out." Katya sidled closer and lightly ran the cool steel of her pistol along the contour of his pointed jaw. "Keep in mind that we know where you live. We also know that your eldest daughter has been staying with you and your wife since the breakup of her marriage. It would be a shame if we had to come back to Marseilles to pay them a visit because you misled us. Would it not?"

Bouvier talked. He told them all they wanted to learn. And as he did, he knew they were the last words he would ever say.

The Everglades, Florida

THE VERY THOUGHT of the Wizard's evil genius being brought to bear on the President of the United States made Mack Bolan's blood run cold. To date, the man had never failed. Whatever the Wizard came up with for the Mexican drug ring was bound to work. In effect, as the old saw went, the President was as good as dead.

A squeal from the woman with the poodle made the three gunners look around. "Finally! Good girl, Muffy! Now come to mama so we can get going!"

"Idiot," Wyman muttered.

The Executioner was braced. He saw the woman climb back into the car, and the instant it pulled out, he exploded into action. Lupo had already faced him, but the other two were just turning so only he had time to react. The bruiser wasn't holding a gun, though. All he could do was roar a warning that came much too late.

In one swift step, Bolan was next to Wyman and spinning the gunner even as he yanked the throwing knife from the jacket pocket. Grendel fired. The slug narrowly missed Bolan's ear as he gave Wyman a hard shove that sent the gunner stumbling into Grendel and threw them both off-balance. Lupo bellowed and charged while trying to tug a snagged pistol from under his shirt.

Spinning, Bolan raced down the slope. He was almost to the bottom when his own Beretta coughed twice. The rounds would have nailed him in the back had he not launched into a dive that carried him the final few feet. A different gun blasted as he neatly cleaved the water and stroked toward the bottom. Whoever fired, missed.

The water was blacker than the night itself. Bolan couldn't even see his own arms. Suddenly he scraped the bottom and slanted upward to keep from being entangled in tendrils of vegetation that clung to his wrists. He swam farther out into the pool, staying well below the surface, and tried not to think of the consequences should he blunder into a hunting alligator.

At least Bolan had the throwing knife. It wouldn't do much good against a gator, but it was better than nothing.

A muted voice reached him from the shore. Grendel was barking orders. Bolan expected them to spread out and try to catch him in a cross fire when he came up for air.

What they didn't know was that Bolan had taken a deep breath before he went under, and he intended to stay under until he came to a wall of reeds. The only problem was that the reeds were sixty to seventy feet from the bank. His lungs might not be up to the task.

Bolan kicked for all he was worth. By twisting he could vaguely make out the surface, no more than a lighter shade of black against the backdrop of sky. He thought that he glimpsed a long, dark object floating at the top, off to his left. Fortunately it made no move toward him. His chest began to ache. Swimming smoothly, he sought some sign of the reeds. Just when he was about to go up for air, he reached them.

Bolan rose and clung to the stalks as he quietly gulped breaths. He had to have made some noise rising, and sure enough, Grendel called out.

"Over there! Those reeds rustled!"

A small flashlight lanced the darkness. Bolan ducked just before the beam played over where he had stood. The light shone back and forth for a half minute, then swept off to one side. Warily he rose until his head was out of the water.

"I don't see him!" It was Lupo who had the flashlight.

"Keep looking, damn it. We can't let him give us the slip."

Bolan parted the reeds and paddled to the east. His plan was to circle around to the highway and catch a ride back to Weston. As much as he wanted to take the three gunners down, it was more important that he get word to Brognola of the threat to the commander in chief. If something should happen to Bolan, the Feds would never find out.

The reeds were thicker than Bolan had counted on. They made a lot of noise, too, if he pressed against them too hard, which forced him to pick his way with care. The whole time, he stayed alert for alligators and snakes. Cottonmouths inhabited the Everglades in droves, as did coral snakes.

It was eerie, gliding through the swamp late at night with the chorus of wildlife in full swing. Most of the creatures had fallen silent when the shot rang out, but they didn't stay quiet very long.

Bolan had covered no more than thirty feet when an enormous shape to his right caught his attention. Freezing, he studied the pool and made out the telltale bulge of a large alligator's snout and eyes. It was looking right at him.

The soldier stood stockstill. Movement was known to attract the brutes, just as it did sharks and other predators. He saw it swim slowly toward him and gripped the knife more firmly.

Lupo inadvertently came to Bolan's aid. The gunner had been sweeping the flashlight back and forth across the pool. The beam passed over the alligator, then flicked back again. Apparently the gator didn't like it, because a few moments later it sank straight down with hardly a ripple.

Bolan didn't twitch a muscle. For all he knew, the thing was still coming toward him and he wasn't about to incite it to attack.

"Where the hell is he?" Wyman fumed on the shore.

Grendel answered. "How should I know? Keep looking."

"I just saw a gator," Lupo told them.

Wyman snorted. "Who cares?"

"Shut up, both of you!" Grendel snapped.

Thanks to their petty bickering, Bolan had their locations pegged. They were spaced about fifty feet apart. Wyman was the nearest. He could see the vague figure of the gunner moving slowly eastward, a pistol held in a two-handed grip.

Bolan eased eastward, too, moving parallel to the highway, which was elevated above the level of the swamp. The rumble of passing cars and trucks wasn't quite loud enough to drown out the sounds made by the creatures around him. That proved just as well for Bolan, since a faint swirl of water was the only warning he had when an alligator did bear down on him.

Hearing the sound, the soldier turned and set eyes on a sinuous shape as it arrowed out of the darkness. It was no more than twelve feet away, closing the gap swiftly.

Bolan raised the knife to strike. But as he did, the gator unexpectedly went under. Its streamlined form veered past on his left, so close that his legs were buffeted by the wash and its tail scraped his shin. Why it hadn't carried through with the attack, he had no idea. But he wasn't staying there to wait for it to try again.

Pushing through the reeds, Bolan came to another, smaller pool. He struck off toward the shore and was halfway across when the metallic click of a hammer being cocked alerted him to a new peril.

The Executioner dived. He never heard the shots, since Wyman's pistol was fitted with a silencer, but he did see the bubbles churned by the two slugs that ripped through the water near his head.

Instead of going back the way he had come and retreating into the swamp, Bolan angled toward the shore, certain he knew where Wyman was standing. His chest nearly brushed the bottom as he stroked strongly. Suddenly he was in water so shallow he could stand, and almost directly above him reared the distorted figure of the gunman.

Wyman had the pistol fully extended and was sweeping it from side to side. His gaze was fixed on the reeds bordering the pool.

Just as Bolan had anticipated.

The soldier surged up out of the water like a human missile. His left arm looped around Wyman's head even as he drove the six-inch blade of his knife into the man's chest. The gunner let out a strangled cry and threw himself backward.

Bolan went with the motion, stabbing twice more before they hit the ground. Wyman, in a panic, tried to club his adversary with the pistol instead of firing it into his side. Rolling to the left, Bolan pulled the gunner along with him, stabbing as he did.

Wyman tried to push Bolan off but the gunner was rapidly growing weak. The Executioner saw the pistol swing toward him and swatted the silencer aside with an elbow. Twice more he buried the throwing knife. On the last thrust, Wyman went rigid, gurgled deep in his throat, clawed feebly at Bolan's face with his free hand and died.

The soldier rose into a crouch and listened for the gunner's companions. Seventy feet away the flashlight swept the swamp, but it didn't go anywhere near him. Apparently neither had noticed.

Bolan picked up the fallen pistol. It was a rarity for a pro, a Taurus PT-91, a .41 Action Express sporting a 10-shot magazine. The sound suppressor was a custom job, short and stubby but quite effective. He rummaged in the man's pockets and came up with two spare clips, which he shoved into his own pants pocket.

After yanking the knife out, he wiped the blade clean on Wyman's shirt, then slid it into his ankle sheath and fastened the Velcro strap.

Now all Bolan had to do was reach the highway without being seen. But at the spot where he had come ashore the bank was much steeper than it had been at the rest stop, and it was coated with loose gravel. He'd need wings to reach the guardrail above without making noise.

Another way was for Bolan to go back into the water and head east until he found a culvert or a notch in the bank for rain runoff, which he could scale. But the thought of venturing among the gators again wasn't appealing. He had lucked out the first time; he might not the second time around.

It was Lupo who decided the issue by shouting, "I don't see hide nor hair of him, fellas. How about you?"

"No," Grendel said softly. "He's either laying low or a gator got him." He paused. "Wyman, any sign at your end?"

Bolan darted to the bank and pressed his body flush so it would blend into the terrain.

"Wyman? Did you hear me?"

When there was no reply, Lupo bellowed, "Yo, Wyman! Do your ears still work or what? Answer us, damn it!"

Raising the Taurus, Bolan took a hasty bead on Lupo. He couldn't see the man clearly, but he had a fair idea where to put the slugs thanks to the flashlight. Before he could squeeze off a shot, though, Grendel guessed the truth.

"Turn out the light, you fool! Now."

Lupo did, just as Bolan stroked the trigger. Whether he scored or not was impossible to say. There was no outcry, no return volley.

Flattening, Bolan crawled to a knob of earth ten feet past the body. They had a fair idea of where he was and would be coming for him. Let them. Propping his right arm on the knob, he probed the night.

Without warning, the dirt close to his arm erupted in a fine spray. Bolan replied in kind, rolled to the right and fired two more times. He saw a form drop but couldn't determine whether it did so on its own or whether his shots brought it down.

In a firefight it didn't pay to stay in one place very long. Bolan scrambled to the right, closer to the water. A frog sprang out of his path and landed in the swamp with a loud splash. Immediately a silencer coughed over near the slope and tiny geysers dotted the surface of the water.

One of the shots winged the frog. The amphibian flipped wildly about, raising a racket. It drew a round from Lupo, the only one whose gun didn't have a silencer. The pistol boomed twice and thunder echoed off across the Everglades. He shot way too high.

Now Bolan knew where the muscle man had gone to ground. Sighting on a black blob, he fired and was rewarded with a fiery oath. The blob scooted to the left and somehow vanished.

Then, for the longest time, none of them made a move.

Bolan had time on his side. The gunners could hardly afford to lie out there until daylight. They would lose the advantage their numbers gave them. And there was the very real likelihood that some of the shots had been heard by passing motorists who would notify the police. Gator poachers were a problem in the swamp, and the public was encouraged to turn them in.

All Bolan had to do was wait the pair out.

The frog had stopped flopping around. The shots had silenced all the creatures close at hand but not those in the distance. Somewhere a gator had to have caught hold of something because a tremendous splashing broke out, ending in a high-pitched squeal.

A large shape abruptly appeared in the middle of the pool. Before Bolan could identify it, the animal went under. From its size it had to have been an alligator. He focused on the slope leading to the rest stop and thought no more about it for the time being.

Sooner or later the gunners were bound to go up that slope. It was the only way to their car unless they were foolish enough to try to scale the steeper banks on either side.

Bolan studied the incline. By now his eyes were so well adjusted to the dark that he could detect any movement within twenty yards.

More minutes went by. A horn honked on the highway, and Bolan automatically glanced around. When he looked at the slope again, a figure was a third of the way up. He promptly fired and the figure cried out and toppled. But the man was only wounded and squeezed off five shots of his own while flat on his back.

Some of the lead came much too close to Bolan. He flipped a few feet to the right, raised his pistol to shoot again and discovered the figure was gone, lost in brush that grew close to the bank.

Bolan could afford to be patient. He replaced the partially spent magazine with a fresh one. While he liked the feel of the Taurus, he missed the Beretta and the Desert Eagle. He knew full well that when a man had used a gun long enough, firing it became second nature. It sounded corny, but the weapon and the user became one. A shooter was always much more accurate with a weapon he fired often than with one he hardly ever used.

The brush parted, and a silencer coughed.

Bolan shifted, aimed, fired three times at a patch of clothing. Or he hoped it was a patch, anyway. The gunner sank from sight.

Based on the size of the figure, Bolan suspected it was Grendel. There had been no sign of Lupo for some time, and he wondered if perhaps he had reduced the odds without knowing it.

Again the brush moved and a pistol spat lead. None of the shots came near him. Bolan was about to squeeze the trigger when it occurred to him that Grendel was being strangely careless. It was almost as if the man in the Fedora were shooting just for the sake of shooting, as if he were trying to draw the warrior's attention and keep it on him. But that would mean—

Bolan didn't get to finish the train of thought. The next second a pair of arms like dripping wet pythons clamped on him from behind, and he was bodily lifted into the air and shaken as if he were a rag doll.

"You're mine now, mister!" Lupo snarled. "All mine!"

CHAPTER TEN

Mack Bolan was no stranger to unarmed combat. When he had to, he could kill with his hands as readily as with an M-16, pistol or knife.

Experience had taught the soldier that it wasn't always the strongest or even the quickest who survived a hand-to-hand clash. All the strength in the world did a man no good if he didn't know how to use that strength the right way.

So as those constricting bands of steel closed around him, Bolan didn't lose his head. Others might have thrashed and struggled in vain. The Executioner let himself go limp. Lupo felt his grip loosen and shifted to get a better one. In that instant Bolan struck. He whipped his head back into the bruiser's face while at the same time he rammed the heel of his left shoe on top of Lupo's instep.

Both blows were delivered with jarring force. Bolan felt the cartilage in Lupo's nose yield with a distinct crunch and heard a bone in the huge man's foot crack.

Lupo cried out and staggered but didn't let go. Enraged, he shook the soldier as a bear might shake a cougar. Bolan tried to angle the Taurus high enough to plant a slug in Lupo's torso, but his arms were pinned just above the wrist. He could barely move either hand.

"You'll pay for that," Lupo grated in his ear. "I know how to inflict pain like you wouldn't believe!"

So did the Executioner. Bolan whipped his head back a second time, aiming at the bigger man's mouth. There was a louder crunch, and moist, warm drops of blood splattered Bolan's nape.

Lupo roared in fury. The muscle man suddenly flung Bolan hard to the ground, but he didn't let go entirely. He had the presence of mind to clamp a hand onto Bolan's right wrist to prevent the soldier from using the pistol. With a savage wrench, he twisted the arm, trying to make him drop the Taurus.

Bolan held on as long as he could. He wasn't about to sacrifice his elbow when there was no need, so he released the gun just when it seemed the limb would be snapped in two like a dry twig. Lupo relaxed his hold a little, just enough for Bolan to be able to spin in a half circle and drive his foot into the gunner's belly. It was like kicking solid iron.

"Surprised, little man?" Lupo said in contempt. "I'm going to bust every bone in your body and then stomp you to death. And do you know what? There isn't a damn thing you can do about it."

The threat didn't worry Bolan. Grendel did. He expected the gunner to show up at any moment. Distracted as he was by Lupo, it would be easy for Grendel to drop him. He risked a side glance to see if the gunner was approaching.

Suddenly Bolan was wrenched upright. His shoulder flared with agony. Before he could set himself, an iron fist rammed into his stomach, doubling him over. His head swam. The grip on his wrist eased, and he clutched at himself with both hands.

"That's just for starters," Lupo said. "Once I get warmed up, you'll wish that you'd never been born."

The man was either an idiot or a rank amateur. One of the rules of unarmed combat was to always keep your mouth shut. Talking gave a foe time to think, to strike or to turn tail and flee.

Bolan wasn't about to run off. He girded himself, one eye on the muscle man, and when Lupo's huge arms swooped toward him, he slipped in between them, straightened and arced his right fist upward. His knuckles connected with the point of Lupo's chin.

The bruiser rocked on his heels but didn't go down. Growling like a rabid dog, he swung both fists.

Bolan evaded the clumsy blows, slipped to the right and delivered a pair of short punches to Lupo's ribs. The hardman countered with an uppercut, which did no more than fan the soldier's cheek. Ducking under the swing, Bolan executed a sweep kick that caught Lupo low down, behind his legs, and knocked him to the ground.

A huge foot streaked at Bolan's face. He bent, dived to one side and slipped around behind the muscle man as Lupo began to sit up. Before Lupo could guess his intent and try to thwart him, Bolan applied a headlock with his left arm. In the same motion he clamped his right hand on his adversary's jaw.

The bruiser grunted and struggled to rise.

Shoulder muscles rippling, Bolan gave a quick twist to one side even as he jerked straight up and back. The snap of the spine was like the report of a small-caliber revolver. Immediately Lupo melted into a disjointed heap.

Bolan crouched and spun, seeking the other killer. Grendel should have been almost upon him, but there was no trace of the man. Puzzled, Bolan flattened and waited for the gunner to give his presence away. After a couple of minutes passed and nothing happened, he rose partway and searched for the Taurus. He thought that he knew exactly where it should be, but it wasn't there. Figuring that during the struggle it had been sent flying, he made a circuit of the body, without result.

Grendel still hadn't appeared. Bolan wasn't about to waste more time, so he carefully moved toward the bank. He scooped dirt into his left hand to fling into Grendel's eyes if the gunner jumped out at him, but for some reason the man in the fedora never appeared.

Bolan went up the bank like a crab, scuttling on his hands and knees to keep from outlining himself against the rim. One peek over the top showed him why Grendel hadn't attacked.

The car was gone.

Standing, Bolan tossed the dirt aside. He brushed off his pants and jacket and tucked in his shirt to make himself presentable as he made for the Alligator Highway. There might not be many motorists willing to pick up a lone man traveling on foot in the middle of the Everglades late at night, but he had to try. If no one stopped, he'd walk clear to Weston. Then it would be on to Miami and a meeting with Brognola.

They had a crucial decision to make.

The Caribbean

JAMES TRASK WAS in his personal lab on Xaymaca when the call came through.

The original owner of the bungalow had built an addition, which was nearly as big as the bungalow itself, and it was here that Trask had set up his tables and arranged the standard tools of the high-tech trade. Some of the equipment, such as a multichannel analyzer and a signal generator, had cost him a small fortune. Other things, such as an oscilloscope and a voltmeter, he rarely used. But they were all essential to his work, as were the various explosives kept in a safe in a corner of the room.

At the moment, Trask was bent over a drawing board, T square in front of him, pencil behind his ear, pondering the logistics of the scheme he had come up with to dispose of the President of the United States. It was a challenge, and Trask loved challenges.

He had been surprised to learn that Luis Terrazas was dead. But then, few drug lords lasted very long. If the law didn't get them, those hoping to move up in the ranks often did.

Adolpho Garcia, the man who had stepped into Terrazas's shoes, had been one of the drug lord's lieutenants. He was a vicious man, as Trask recollected, prone to random acts of raw violence. Which was of no consequence so long as Garcia didn't try to renege on their contract.

It had been a bigger surprise to learn the identity of the man Garcia wanted hit. Trask's first impulse had been to send word back for Garcia to take a flying leap off the nearest cliff. Killing the President was bound to draw more heat than all the other contracts Trask had taken, combined.

Then Trask had thought about the idea some more, and the longer he did, the more it grew on him. A million and a half dollars was nothing to sneeze at. The bonanza would enable him to retire that much sooner.

And so what if it was the President? Trask told himself. Presidents had been assassinated before. Sure, the Secret Service was a factor, but they were human. They had their flaws, just like ordinary law-enforcement types.

The more Trask had thought about it, the less formidable the job became. In a way, a sitting President was an easier target than most because the President had a weakness, an Achilles' heel a smart person could exploit.

Every President lived at the White House. No matter how often or far he might travel around the country, he always came back to the same place. To put it in hunting terms, the White House was the President's den, his lair. And every savvy hunter knew that the surest way to bring down game was to track it to its lair.

Once Trask had picked where to strike, he had to pick how to go about it. The idea of a missile similar to the one used in the DEA attack appealed to him, but he dismissed it.

Ever since a small private plane had crashed on the White House lawn, security had been stepped up. A new radar system had been installed, he'd learned, while agents armed with surface-to-air missiles were now posted on the roof. An incoming missile, even one cruising at treetop level, would likely be blown out of the sky before it could detonate.

No, what Trask needed was something that could fly even lower yet still go fast, a craft that could fly at ground level one moment and high enough to get over the White House fence the next, a craft that could carry enough explosive to level the Oval Office. And most of all, it had to be a craft that was highly maneuverable.

Trask had mulled the problem for more than an hour before the obvious answer hit him between the eyes like a ton of bricks. He had whooped for joy. It was so simple, yet so effective, that it had to work. He would use a modified remote-control helicopter, the kind flown by hobby enthusiasts every weekend in the park across the street.

It was as Trask sat working on the fuel-to-weight ratio that there came a knock on the door. "It's open," he announced.

Loomis came in. He wasn't a man who showed much emotion, but he was clearly annoyed at the moment. "I've just heard from Grendel."

"And?"

"He didn't learn a damn thing. This Belasko character killed Lupo and Wyman and got away."

Trask sat up. "Did he say how it happened?"

"He claims that Belasko took them by surprise."

"All three of them? No, that couldn't have been the case unless they were stupidly careless. I gave Grendel specific orders. If he had carried them out to the letter, there wouldn't have been any problem."

"What do you want done?"

Through the east window Trask could see the rising sun. He had been up all night. Tiredly rubbing his eyes, he said, "Grendel has become a liability. See that he is disposed of. Attend to it personally. Then recruit someone to replace him."

"Do I try to find this Belasko?"

"Don't waste your time. In all likelihood the man is an undercover government operative. Probably one of their very best. You could no more find him than you could a needle in a haystack. No, don't worry about him. Unless Grendel was foolish enough to—" A thought gave him pause.

"Sir?"

"I may have been remiss, Loomis. Grendel came highly recommended, so I took it for granted he would be trustworthy. Perhaps I was wrong. Before you terminate his services, question him most carefully. Find out everything he told Belasko."

"And if the jackass has put the operation in jeopardy?"

"Then make Mr. Grendel suffer before he dies. Make him suffer as no human being has suffered in centuries. And when you are done, take his body to the Everglades and feed it to the alligators." Trask smirked. "I understand he's always had a fondness for them."

It was shortly after eight o'clock that morning when Edward Bustamante, the Jamaican customs official, received a strange phone call. He was reviewing a ship's manifest when the intercom buzzed and his secretary came on the line.

"I'm so sorry to bother you, sir, but there's a lady on line two who insists on talking to you."

"Who is she?"

"She won't give her name or state her business, but she claims it is a very important matter. I wouldn't have troubled you had she not said she would keep calling back until she was put through."

Bustamante frowned. "I'll take the call. Thank you." It sounded to him as if the caller was one of his many criminal contacts, yet he had told them all in no uncertain terms never to do anything that might imperil his position by arousing suspicion. "This is Edward Bustamante."

A silken female voice responded. She purred her words, speaking slowly and clearly with just a hint of an accent. Dutch, perhaps. "Thank you for taking my call."

"Do I know you?" Bustamante demanded.

"You haven't had the pleasure yet," the woman said, "but you will soon enough."

"Explain yourself."

"Do you truly want me to? Can you guarantee that your line is secure?"

Alarm bells went off in Bustamante's mind. Of course he couldn't.

"I thought so," the woman continued suavely. "Suffice it to say that my partner and I are in a certain line of work in which you might be of great help. Naturally there will be compensation for your work on our behalf. A very large compensation, I might add, much more than you are normally used to getting."

A new customer. Bustamante was interested but cautious. "If you don't mind my asking, how did you hear of me?"

"Through a mutual friend whose name I shouldn't mention until we meet in person. I hope you don't mind."

Bustamante did, but he wasn't about to press the issue and possibly ruin a new deal.

"In fact," the woman went on, "one of the reasons I'm calling is to set up a meeting. My partner and I expect to take the next flight to Kingston. We should be in Savanna la Mar by tomorrow evening. Where could we get together?"

"The Fairmouth Club at eight would be ideal."

"We can talk in private there?"

"Most assuredly. The owner is a close friend. He has a booth at the back that I use whenever I need to."

"Excellent. The Fairmouth Club it is."

Sensing she was about to hang up, Bustamante said, "Wait. How will I know you and your partner? Can't you at least tell me your name?" It occurred to him that he should run a background check before the meeting, just to be safe.

The woman made an odd comment. "A rose by any other name would still be a rose, would it not?" She laughed merrily, as if at a great joke. "My name, Edward, is Katya Steiner. I look forward to meeting you."

"The same here, my dear."

Miami, Florida

MILO FERNSTEIN LOOKED forward to an easy day. There had been no messages when he checked in the middle of the morning, and something told him there would be none later that afternoon. He had half a mind to call it quits early and head into downtown Miami, where he could treat himself to lunch at his favorite restaurant. Then he would spend four or five hours making the rounds of computer stores, looking for new software.

But Fernstein knew he didn't dare go. His anonymous employer had made it clear that if he ever failed to check his mail three times each day as required, he'd pay dearly.

He had to settle for fixing his own lunch. Since he was trying to lose weight, he opened a can of chicken soup and went to pour it into a pan. He stopped when the doorbell rang. "Who is it?" he called.

"Package, sir. Special delivery."

Fernstein ordered a lot of items through the mail, but he couldn't think of one due to arrive in that manner. Placing the can on the counter, he headed for the door. "Are you sure you have the right address?"

"If your name is Milo Fernstein, I do," the man answered, sounding as bored as could be. "Just sign for it, will you, mister, so I can finish my route."

Amused by the man's impatience, Fernstein threw the bolt and turned the knob. He started to pull the door inward when it exploded into motion of its own accord, slamming against him and knocking him back over an easy chair.

"Federal agents! Do not move!"

Astounded and stunned, Fernstein lay there trying to collect his wits. He saw men in suits barge into his modest living room, saw one dressed in a deliveryman's uniform straddle him and point a pistol the size of a cannon at his forehead while flashing a shiny badge.

"Milo Fernstein?"

"Yes, sir?" Fernstein's brain kicked into gear, and he knew without asking why they were there and what was going to happen next. He even predicted the next words out of the federal agent's mouth.

"You are under arrest."

The rest was all a blur. He was dimly aware of someone reading him his rights while someone else rolled him over and another person slapped handcuffs on his wrists. He realized that it all had to be connected to his wonderful, cushy job, and he wanted to beat his head against the wall for being lamebrained enough to take it.

How long before he learned?

When something seemed too good to be true, it usually was.

HAL BROGNOLA had an unlit cigar clamped in the corner of his mouth and his brawny hands clasped behind his back. He stared out over downtown Miami without noticing the impressive skyline, which was lit up like a Christmas tree. He had too much on his mind.

Mack Bolan entered the room. Without being asked he took a seat in a chair next to the desk.

"Anything yet?" he asked when his friend simply stood there.

Brognola turned and gestured. "Not a damn thing, Striker. We've run Milo Fernstein through the wringer and come up dry. Apparently the fool just answered an ad and never met his boss face-to-face. It's just the sort of slick setup I would expect from a man like the Wizard."

"So it's a dead end?"

"I wouldn't go that far. We're running a check on all the phone calls he's made since he took the job, but it's going to take a while."

"If only we knew how much time we had."

Brognola nodded and wearily sank into his chair. "The way I see it, we have two avenues we can pursue. One is to go after the drug ring and put them out of operation before they can get their hands on whatever hardware the Wizard makes for them."

"Do we know who has taken Terrazas's place?"

The big Fed shook his head. "Our Mexican contacts are working on it. Whoever it is, you can bet he'll be on his toes after what happened to his boss. Which will make him that much harder to locate and deal with."

Bolan listened to a police siren shriek in the distance.

"Our second avenue is to step up our hunt for the Wizard and stop him before he can hand over the bomb or missile or whatever the hell he comes up with to kill the President," Brognola said. "At least we have a name to go on now. Trask." He said the word as he might the name of some disease. "It's probably an alias, but we're running it down anyway. The same with Grendel. I've got my fingers crossed that we'll nab him and he'll be able to tell us where to find his boss."

"It's a long shot."

"What isn't in this business?" Brognola picked up a pen and tapped it on the desk. "I've relayed word to the President, of course. The Secret Service has been put on alert, but that's all he's willing to do. He won't change his schedule. He won't cancel any of his speaking engagements."

"Did you really think he would?"

"No." Brognola sighed. "I suppose it was bound to come to this sooner or later. The drug cartels have murdered hundreds of judges and politicians in South America and Mexico. It was only a matter of time before they went after our own leaders. It was only a matter of time before they brought the drug war to American soil in a big way.'' He took out the cigar, scowled and placed it in an ashtray. ''If Trask and the new drug lord prevail, we'll have passed over that invisible line that separates civilized society from near anarchy. We can't let that happen.''

When Mack Bolan answered, his tone was as sharp as tempered steel. ''Don't worry. I'm not about to.''

CHAPTER ELEVEN

It was more than twenty hours later that the Feds got the break they needed. The check of Milo Fernstein's phone records bore out what he told them about having to call a certain number at certain times every day. The man cooperated fully once he realized how much trouble he was in.

After being told that his employer was a prime suspect in the DEA missile attack that had made all the headlines, making him an accessory to murder and a slew of federal charges, Fernstein fainted dead away. On being revived, he was so eager to tell all he knew that the agents interrogating him could hardly get a word in edgewise. But he knew little that was of any use.

They had better luck with the man in the fedora.

There were four people named Grendel listed in the Miami telephone directory. Two were women, another a retiree, the third an accountant. A check of voter registration turned up no others. Tax records were consulted, and it was there that they hit pay dirt.

A man by the name of Arthur Grendel had won a thousand dollars in the lottery two months earlier. As required by law, he had signed a standard form before he received the money.

A check of criminal records turned up that an Arthur Grendel had done time for manslaughter. A model prisoner, he had been paroled early and promptly disappeared. If not for his slip when he won the lottery money, the Feds would never have found him.

This information wound up on Hal Brognola's desk, and Bolan volunteered to go after him.

The address Art Grendel listed on the lottery-winnings form turned out to be in a seedy neighborhood near the waterfront. Bolan slowly cruised down the street, reading the numbers on the buildings. When he saw the one he was looking for, he frowned. It was a bakery.

He proceeded to the next intersection and made a U-turn. About a hundred feet from the bakery he pulled to the curb. Unfolding a newspaper, he pretended to read while studying the building. The bakery was still open but would close in fifteen minutes, at six. There were apartments in the upper story, accessed by a flight of stairs that ran up the side of the building. As Bolan looked on, an elderly woman stood on the landing, made sure the door was locked behind her and carefully descended.

Bolan idly watched her amble off down the sidewalk, then noticed a gray sedan driving up the street. Three men were inside, and as the vehicle neared the bakery it slowed. The men craned their necks to study the second floor. A dozen yards past the building, the vehicle braked. The man in the back seat hopped out and moved into the recessed doorway of a pawn shop.

He stood there as if inspecting the items in the window, though he was actually keeping an eye on the stairway.

The three had the latent cruelty in their features so typical of hardmen. Bolan had tangled with far too many not to recognize killers when he saw them. He slouched in the seat in order to be inconspicuous and glanced at the side mirror.

The gray sedan continued on a hundred feet or so and parked. The driver and a lean man in black turned to watch the building.

This was an unexpected development. Bolan decided to stay where he was for the time being and see what happened next. He had no doubt that the hardmen were linked to Grendel. In what way, he would very much like to find out.

In a short while the bakery owner put a Closed sign in the window. Bolan felt there was a good chance the man also owned the apartments, but he wasn't about to go over and question him with the three hardmen looking on.

Gradually twilight fell. Most of the businesses, including the pawn shop, closed. Kids playing in yards the size of sandboxes were called inside for supper. The number of pedestrians thinned out.

Bolan saw the elderly woman return, bearing a bag of groceries. She started up the stairs, fumbling in her purse for her keys. The tall guy in front of the pawn shop, who wore a shiny gold watch, motioned to the others, then dashed to the foot of the stairs. He waited until the unsuspecting woman had inserted her key and pushed on the door, then he went up taking three steps at a stride and was right behind her as she stepped inside. The woman finally noticed him. She recoiled as if scared. The man had to have said something that reassured her because she smiled and closed the door.

Bolan had a fair idea why the guy had gone inside. He was proved right ten minutes later when a familiar figure in a fedora appeared at the corner and strolled toward the building with a newspaper under one arm and a box containing a pizza in the other hand.

It was Grendel. He sniffed the box a few times and smiled as if he couldn't wait to take a bite. He was so preoccupied that he never noticed the gray sedan or Bolan.

Grendel went up the steps, opened the door and went in. He reappeared in less than a minute, wearing a worried expression, his arms held out from his sides. Behind him, one hand in the bulging pocket of his brown jacket, trailed the tall gunner. They headed straight for the gray sedan. Grendel and the man in black exchanged words before Grendel was forced into the back by the tall gunner and the vehicle pulled out.

Bolan twisted the ignition as the gray sedan wheeled from the curb. He made a tight turn and shadowed them, staying as far back as he dared without running the risk of losing them. When they stopped at a light, he was four cars behind. From where he sat, he could see Grendel and the man in black arguing heatedly. The other two were listening. None was paying attention to the traffic around them.

The killers made for Biscayne Boulevard and headed north along the palm-lined avenue, eventually turning off Biscayne and heading toward the docks. They stopped in a parking lot next to a quiet marina. Grendel was hemmed in by two of them and ushered down the pier to a large cruiser. He had the look of a man being led off to face a firing squad. All four men went below.

Bolan parked. He loosened the new Beretta in its shoulder rig and slid out of the vehicle. Pulling up the collar of his windbreaker, he shoved both hands in his pockets and headed for the cruiser. Many other boats crowded the marina, everything from runabouts to yachts. No one paid much attention to him.

When he was directly across from the cruiser, Bolan slowed. Voices wafted up from below, too muffled for him to tell what was being said. None of the gunners was topside, nor were there any lights. He quickly walked to the vessel, slipped over the gunwale and padded to the ladder that would take him to the cockpit. Climbing, he poked his head above the upper deck to confirm that he was alone. Then he scaled the final rungs and crept forward.

A window on the starboard side of the cabin was open. By leaning over the flying bridge, Bolan could hear the men clearly. Someone with a gravelly voice was speaking.

"—tell me what I need to know before we're done. I guarantee it."

Grendel spoke, and he was unable to mask his fear. "But I've already told you everything I can remember, Loomis! It went down exactly the way I told you."

"Yeah. Right." Loomis snorted. "Do you think I was born yesterday? How could this guy get away if the three of you had the drop on him, like you claimed?"

"I told you. There was this woman with a mutt. She distracted us for just a few seconds but it was all Belasko needed. He tore into us before we could get off a shot. The man is a pro, I tell you. Greased lightning. You had to be there to see him in action. Then you'd know."

"If I had been there," Loomis said stiffly, "Belasko would be dead." He paused. "Willy, bring me the black bag over there on the table, would you?"

There was brief silence, then Grendel blurted, "Oh, my God! What the hell is that thing for? You're not thinking of using it on *me,* are you?"

"As a matter of fact, I am." Loomis sounded as if he were enjoying himself. "I used one of these once before, a couple of years back. There was this tough guy who wouldn't tell me what I wanted to know." Loomis laughed. "But by the time I was done, he couldn't shut up."

"You can't!" Grendel whined. "Please, Loomis. I'm begging you. Just ask your questions and I'll answer the best I can. There's no need for this. I've always been loyal to the organization. You know I have."

"I know," Loomis conceded. "But it's not your loyalty that's in question. It's your competence. Mr. Trask is afraid that you may have gone and jeopardized the whole operation. He sent me to find out if you have."

Grendel was scared to death. "I haven't! I swear! I did just as I was told. Belasko doesn't know a thing." He gulped. "What do you take me for, anyway? Do you think I'd be dumb enough to give anything away? Come on. Be reasonable."

A peculiar whirring sound wafted from below. It took Bolan a few moments to recognize it for what it was—an electric drill. He could barely hear Grendel over the noise.

"Loomis! No! You can't do this! Please!"

The frantic plea had no effect. As Bolan had long ago learned, there was no honor among thieves and even less among killers. When they had a job to do, they did it, and it didn't matter to them if their own mother was the one they had to dispose of. He heard a loud scraping, as of a chair being moved across a floor. Then Loomis barked an order.

"Tom, get behind him and hold the chair steady. Willy, you turn on the radio and crank up the volume. Then go close that window. We don't want anyone to hear his screams."

Bolan had heard enough. It was time to interrupt their little party. Straightening, he went to turn but stopped when a metallic click warned him that he was no longer alone.

"Not a twitch, pally, unless you want to look like a sieve. You get me?"

The soldier shifted his gaze to the left. A gunner was on the ladder, only his head and shoulders visible. He had an autopistol trained squarely on Bolan's back.

"Hold your arms straight out and step to the console."

Bolan was tempted to take a flying dive over the side, but the man had him cold. Reluctantly he complied. The rustle of clothing told him the gunner had climbed up onto the deck.

"Don't move."

There were a half-dozen loud thumps. Bolan knew the man was stomping on the deck to get the attention of the men below. It worked. The music, which had just begun to blare, was cut off.

"Leon? Is that you? Loomis wants to know what the hell is going on up there?"

The gunner behind Bolan shifted. "Get up here, Willy. Pronto. I caught some joker snooping around."

In no time the pair had stripped Bolan of his weapons and were guiding him below. He was alert for any opening that might present itself, but none did. One of the gunners shoved him through a doorway into the main cabin.

Grendel was strapped to a chair, his face as pale as a sheet. The man in black, who had to be Loomis, stood next to a counter, holding the drill.

"Well, well, well," Loomis said. "What do we have here?"

Grendel beamed like an idiot. "That's him! That's Belasko! The SOB who pulled the fast one on us last night."

Loomis's brow creased. He beckoned. Willy and Leon shoved Bolan and prodded him at gunpoint to stand in front of the man in black. Loomis studied the big man closely. "Your first name is Mike, as I recall, isn't it?"

Bolan didn't reply.

Loomis was unfazed. "Well, Mike, we were just talking about you. Grendel there claims that you're the toughest thing on two legs. I think that maybe you're a lousy Fed. Could it be that we're both right?"

Again Bolan kept quiet. He hoped to incite the man in black into making a blunder, but Loomis was too smart for that.

"Suit yourself, Mike. But trust me. You'll answer my questions eventually." Loomis looked at the gunner named Leon. "Where there's one Fed, there are always more. Fire up the engine and take us out to sea, where we can continue this without having to worry about more uninvited guests dropping in."

The gunner nodded and hastened out.

"Hey!" Grendel said. "What about me? Now that you have Belasko, you can cut me loose, right? I mean, why question me when you can question him?"

Loomis spun. "I want to be sure I have this straight first, Art. You did say that you never told this guy anything? That you kept your mouth shut last night and attended strictly to business? Is that true?"

Grendel nodded vigorously, as if his very life depended on it. "Yeah. That's the gospel. Now do me a favor and cut me loose."

Stepping to the chair, Loomis leaned down so his face nearly brushed Grendel's. "If so, then maybe you can explain to me what Belasko is doing here? How did he know where to find us? And don't try to tell me it's just a coincidence."

Licking his lips, Grendel glanced at Bolan, then at the thin man in black. "I don't know how he found us. Honest to God, I don't."

The next moment the cruiser rumbled to life. The running lights came on. No one said a word until the craft was under way. Engine puttering, it cruised from its berth and headed due east, making for the open sea.

"Now then," Loomis said with a sneer, "let's get down to cases. I need information, and one of you is going to give it to me whether you think that you will or not. Since Art is already in the hot seat, I might as well start with him."

"No! This isn't fair! I never did anything wrong! I swear to God!"

The plea fell on deaf ears. Loomis revved the drill, gripped the gunner's wrist and speared the quarter-inch bit into the man's forearm. Blood and flesh splattered every which way. Grendel started to scream, but the gunner named Tom clamped a hand over his mouth.

Loomis, grinning, reversed the drill and slid out the spinning bit. Red drops glistened on his cheeks and chin as he winked at Bolan and said, "Be patient, Mr. Belasko. Your turn is coming right up."

Jamaica

EDWARD BUSTAMANTE didn't know what sort of woman would show up at the Fairmouth Club at the appointed hour, but he certainly didn't expect a ravishing blonde in a revealing black dress. The woman and her companion were escorted to his booth by Orlando, the owner, under orders from Bustamante.

Orlando was just one of many nightclub owners who paid the customs man to look the other way when liquor shipments came in that were much larger than the manifest claimed. The profits to be made from goods not subject to customs duties and taxes were enormous.

Bustamante smiled widely and accepted the woman's slender hand. "It is my great pleasure," he assured her.

"And mine," Katya Steiner said with just the right hint in her eyes and tone. She introduced her partner, Gunther, saying, "He and I have a strictly business relationship."

"How nice," Bustamante said. On shaking the man's hand, he was surprised at the tensile-steel strength in her partner's fingers but he thought little more of it.

For a half hour they made small talk. Drinks were brought. Appetizers followed. Steiner told about their flight and how excited she was to be in Jamaica for the first time in her life.

Bustamante held his curiosity in check for as long as he could, then he asked bluntly, "Perhaps now, dear lady, you will be so kind as to explain more about the nature of the business in which you are involved."

Katya scanned the noisy crowd. "I don't know. Are you sure it's safe?" She indicated the walls of the booth and the overhead light. "One never knows when other ears are listening. I have a policy of never discussing my business in public. I do hope you'll understand."

The customs inspector thought she was being much too cautious, but he didn't criticize. Many of those he dealt with were paranoid about being found out by the authorities. For that matter, so was he. "What do you propose, then?"

The blonde edged closer and draped her warm hand on top of his. "I have a room at the Imperial. Perhaps we could talk there after our meal."

Bustamante couldn't get over the contrast between her pale skin and his own dark skin. The thought of being alone with her made his mouth go dry. He looked at her partner, but Gunther appeared not to have noticed.

"Would that be all right?"

"Most certainly," Bustamante said, annoyed that he had a frog in his throat. He tried to keep from ogling her cleavage but couldn't. It would be hard for any man to think straight around such a woman, he mused.

Katya chatted on during the meal and afterward accepted an offer to dance. Bustamante was amazed at how light she was on her feet, at her graceful movements and poise. She had the body of a professional athlete.

The Imperial was only four blocks from the Fairmouth Club. Rather than take a cab, Katya suggested they walk so they could enjoy the cool night air.

Gunther coughed lightly. "If you will excuse me, I have some other business to attend to. I will join the both of you in, say, two hours."

"Whatever you wish," Bustamante replied, inwardly giddy at the idea of being alone with the blonde. He gave a little wave as her partner walked in the other direction and hailed a cab at the corner.

Katya tugged on his elbow. "Let's go. You can tell me about yourself as we stroll."

"There isn't much to tell," Bustamante said with false humility.

"Oh, come now. My contacts tell me that you have your fingers into every pie in Savanna la Mar. You must know everything that goes on in this city."

"I do try to keep on top of things."

The blonde laughed. "I bet that you do." Holding his arm, she hustled him toward the hotel while rattling on about the wonderful climate and the beautiful island. She asked dozens of trivial questions.

Bustamante politely answered each one. She was so amusing that it never occurred to him that all her chatter might be intended to keep him from thinking straight until it was too late. Like a lovestruck teenager, he strolled along at her side until they were close to the Imperial.

"Maybe we should go up the back way," Katya suggested slyly. "Being seen together at the club is one thing. But if we are seen together here, the police might become suspicious."

Bustamante was going to ask why the police would even care. But before he could, she pulled on his arm and hurried him down an alley. The rear door to the hotel, which automatically locked when closed, had been propped open with a brick. He didn't attach any special meaning to it as he slipped inside and trailed the vivacious blonde to the second floor.

Katya unlocked the door and ushered him in. She flicked on the lights, saying, "Make yourself right at home while I slip into something more comfortable."

The suites at the hotel were first-rate. The customs inspector chuckled to himself as he eased onto the plush sofa and loosened his tie. This night, he told himself, would be a night to remember.

In due course Katya Steiner returned from the bedroom. But instead of the nightie Bustamante expected her to have on, she was clad in leather from neck to toe. He blinked, then smiled. "Oh. I see. You're one of those."

"Not hardly, moron."

Bustamante didn't know what to say. Her silken tone had become rock hard, and she was staring at him as if he were some kind of insect to be crushed underfoot. He was about to point out that she was being quite rude when something flashed past his eyes and an odd constriction suddenly shut off his air. At the same instant, Katya Steiner drew a small pistol fitted with a sound suppressor, leaned down and rammed the barrel into his groin.

"Now, Mr. Customs Inspector, you and I are going to have a long talk. If you don't answer, or if you try to call for help, my partner, Gunther, will throttle the life from you. Bit by bit by bit. Understood?"

Bustamante nodded. He didn't know what he had gotten himself into. At that moment he felt more afraid than he ever had in his life. And something told him that the worst was yet to come.

CHAPTER TWELVE

Loomis enjoyed his work. Time and again he drove the drill bit into Grendel, shearing flesh, piercing bone. He wore a sadistic grin that widened when Grendel tried to tear himself loose from the chair.

Already six holes dotted Grendel's right arm from wrist to shoulder. Blood oozed down over the chair arm to form a growing puddle on the floor.

The Executioner stood with his hands half-raised, covered by the gunner called Willy. His Beretta and Desert Eagle were a few yards away, lying on the counter, well out of reach.

As Loomis bent to use the drill again, Bolan made a squeamish face and shifted as if to avert his gaze. He had an ulterior motive. He needed to see exactly where Willy stood before he committed himself to a course of action. The young gunner was five feet behind him and slightly to one side, holding a Springfield Armory M-911 A-1 pistol.

The whirring drill slowed once again and Loomis stepped back to admire his handiwork. He nodded at Tom, who pulled his hand away from Grendel's mouth.

"How are you holding up, Art?"

"Go to hell!" Grendel sputtered. Sweat caked his face and his eyelids fluttered.

Loomis laughed. "Come now. You brought this on yourself. You know as well as I do that our employer is a stickler for doing things right. He doesn't tolerate mistakes. He doesn't make them and he won't have people working for him who do."

Grendel shuddered and bit his lower lip. He was in tremendous agony and it showed.

The man in black hefted the gory drill and looked at Bolan. "Changed your mind yet? Are you ready to tell me who you work for?"

Bolan shook his head.

"Well, then, let's see if I can make you see the light," Loomis cracked. Revving the drill, he nodded at Tom, who covered Grendel's mouth.

Grendel screamed as the drill bit slowly neared his temple. He went into a frenzy, vainly tugging at the rope that restrained his wrists and ankles.

"Watch this, boys," Loomis said to his men. "You'll learn something here."

Willy glanced toward the chair, which was the cue for Bolan to whirl and seize hold of the hardman's wrist. The soldier jerked the arm just as Willy pumped the trigger twice. The .45 boomed and bucked. Bolan had swung the arm so that the pistol was pointed in the direction of the chair. He'd hoped to nail Loomis, but the first slug cored Grendel's forehead and the second hit Tom square in the sternum, driving him back against the wall.

Loomis spun, bellowed in rage and sprang, thrusting the drill at the Executioner. But just as he was about to drive the bit into Bolan's back, he ran out of cord. The plug shot from the socket, and the drill promptly died. He drew up short, then cast the drill aside in disgust.

Bolan was struggling with Willy. He rammed the man's wrist against his knee in an effort to make him drop the pistol, but the hardman clung to the gun and tried to knee his adversary in the groin. Pivoting, Bolan avoided the blow and at the same time slammed his elbow into Willy's nose. The gunner cried out and staggered but still wouldn't let go of the pistol.

To Bolan's left, Loomis was reaching under his jacket. The soldier kicked out with his left leg, striking the man in black in the knee. It shattered with an audible crack. Loomis, cursing, sank to the floor but drew a pistol as he did. Bolan kicked him again, in the mouth, and Loomis toppled.

There was no time to lose. The Executioner delivered an uppercut to Willy that lifted the young gunner off the floor and sent him flying into a chair. Wheeling, Bolan darted to the doorway and bounded through just as Loomis fired. The bullets bit into the jamb. And then Bolan was racing along the corridor to the companionway that would take him to the deck.

"Leon!" Loomis roared. "Belasko is heading for the deck! Stop him!"

It was doubtful the gunner at the wheel heard the yell above the rumble of the engine, but Bolan was taking no chances. He hurtled into the door at a full run, smashing into the top panel with his left shoulder. It exploded outward as if blown apart by a grenade.

Without slowing, he dashed across the cockpit, inhaled deeply and dived over the side.

A pistol blasted on the upper deck, but the rounds tore into the gunwale instead of the Executioner.

Bolan cleaved the surface smoothly and was enveloped by cold salt water. He arced down and to the right. The huge shadow of the cruiser moved off but didn't go far. In moments the roar of the engine dwindled as the throttle was shoved back and the wheelman started to swing the craft around.

The soldier stopped stroking and held stationary ten feet down. He marked the position of the boat, then swam to intercept it. As it came toward him, he dived even deeper, the dull throb of the twin propellers like the rumble of thunder in his ears. He had to be deep enough when the cruiser passed over him to keep from being ground to bits by the props.

The sleek prow knifed through the ocean toward him, the water hissing like a nest of angry snakes. Bolan could tell it would be close. He dived even deeper, not daring to look as he pumped his limbs for all he was worth. The sea was dismally dark and grew even more so as the cruiser eclipsed what little light penetrated to his depth.

The throb of the engine seemed to fill the sea. He knew the vessel was mere yards above his head. Then prop wash rolled over him.

The cruiser slowed to a crawl, then the engine stopped.

Bolan was running out of air. He swam around to the port side of the boat and slowly rose until he was inches from the hull. Covering his mouth with a hand to muffle the sound, he sucked in air and listened.

Loomis was spewing every oath known to man. "Willy, help me up these damn steps!" he ordered. "I can't hardly move my leg."

Up on the control deck, Leon called out, "I don't see any sign of him yet!"

"Keep looking!"

A searchlight swept the area behind the cruiser and on the starboard side. Bolan caught glimpses of it as it swung back and forth. Hidden in the shadows, he scoured the hull for a ladder or some other way of getting back on board.

"Nobody could stay under this long," Leon said. "Maybe he took a slug or drowned!"

Loomis had reached the lower deck. "I said to keep looking!" he snapped. "We're not leaving until we find the body. I want to be sure."

Bolan quietly moved toward the bow. If he could reach the rail, he'd be able to pull himself up and possibly take them by surprise.

Another searchlight abruptly pierced the darkness on the port side. Bolan flattened against the boat, partially screened by the curve of the hull. The light would have to strike him directly for them to spot him.

"I hope the guy is still alive!" Willy said. "I owe the scumbag. He cost me three teeth."

"Quit yapping and find him!" Loomis roared. "If he isn't dead, don't worry. You'll get to take your turn."

Bolan edged nearer to the prow. The rail was a good six feet above him, much too far for him to grab. But the loop of a tie rope hung over the edge, dangling three feet overhead.

Coiling, Bolan surged upward as high as he could. His fingertips brushed the rope, but it was too slick to grab hold. He fell back into the sea and immediately pressed against the hull.

"Did you hear that?" Willy asked. "I thought I heard a splash." The light passed a few feet above Bolan's head and then out over the ocean.

"It was probably just a fish," Leon grumbled. "I don't see why we don't just get out of here. We're too far out for this guy to reach shore. He'll drown before he can reach land, or else the sharks will get him."

"Not this guy," Loomis said. "That idiot Grendel was right all along. This bastard is trouble with a capital *T*. You'll go on searching until I say differently."

Bolan watched the searchlight. It swept in a steady pattern from right to left and back again. He figured it would be safe to try for the rope when suddenly Willy cried out, "Look there!"

A large fish broke the surface and looped back down in a glistening spray.

"You idiot!" Loomis complained. "Does Belasko have fins? Pay attention to what you're doing!"

The light swept farther out from the craft. Bolan arched upward again, extending his arms to their limits, his fingers clawing to snag the rope. This time he succeeded, but his weight made the rope uncoil and he slipped back into the water. He saw the searchlight coming toward him and quickly ducked under the surface. The light passed over the spot he had occupied, lingered a few seconds, then roved to the right. There was no outcry.

Bolan broke the surface gently. Getting a firm grip on the rope, he climbed swiftly, careful not to let his wet palms slip. When he was just below the rail, he lunged upward and snagged it. With a firmer purchase, he was able to slip up and over and lie flat on the foredeck facing the cabin.

From his new vantage point Bolan could see the beams playing over the Atlantic on both sides of the cruiser. He couldn't see the killers, nor could they see him. Crouching, he moved to the cabin and straightened. There were only two ways to reach the stern. He either swung around to one side and followed the rail to the cockpit or he climbed onto the flying bridge. There was no ladder, but he decided to try climbing. It was the one move Loomis and company wouldn't expect.

Bolan reached up and took hold of the thin edge at the top of the cabin window. The window was tinted, yet he could still see Grendel slumped in the chair and the legs of the other dead gunner.

The soldier slowly pulled himself upward. When his head drew level with the bottom of the flying bridge, he reached up with his right hand, seeking a new grip. For all of five seconds he hung there, unable to find the handhold he needed. Then he found a groove in the windshield barely wide enough for his fingers. He wedged them fast, pressed his right knee against the lip of the window and gingerly raised his other arm.

Suddenly Bolan's right hand began to slip. Straining, he clamped his fingers into the groove and managed to do the same with his left hand.

By bracing the sole of his foot against the window ridge, Bolan gained enough leverage to go higher, to reach the very top of the windshield. He raised his eyes to the rim and peered over.

Leon stood aft, near the end of the upper deck, swinging a handheld spotlight. There was no sign of Loomis, but Willy was visible on the lower deck. He was doing the same as Leon.

"I'm telling you that we're wasting our time, fellas," Leon declared. "Belasko is shark bait by now. What say we head on in, Ed?"

The man in black was as cranky as a wounded bear. "We'll head in when I say so and not one minute sooner. Fire up the engine and make a circuit of the area. He's got to be out there somewhere."

Bolan knew that Leon would spot him the minute the gunner turned. He hauled himself over the windshield, slid down over the control console and dropped to the deck.

Leon was backing toward the wheel while continuing to sweep the light. On hearing the warrior's shoes slap on the polished wood, he spun, a gleaming pistol in his right hand.

The Executioner was faster. In a flash he was on the gunner, his left forearm deflecting the gun while at the same time he landed a bruising right on Leon's jaw. The blow drove the gunner to the rear. The searchlight clattered at Leon's feet as Bolan closed in to finish him off.

Gravity took over, though, and the gunner, yelping in alarm, fell from the deck. He still held the pistol. Arms flung outward, Leon crashed onto a deck chair. The hardwood top of the chair caught him across the upper spine. He screeched, rolled onto the lower deck and was still.

Willy hadn't moved from his position. Loomis was propped against a cockpit freezer in the corner. Both gawked a moment, then Willy elevated his pistol and banged away like a madman.

Bolan hit the deck. He still had no weapon, no means of fighting back. The .45's magazine cycled dry and Willy swore a blue streak. Bolan heard a new clip slapped home and was about to climb up on the console and lower himself to the foredeck when the man in black spoiled his plan.

"Go on up there and finish Belasko off!"

"What?" Willy countered. "Are you crazy? If I go poking my head above the ladder, he's liable to blow it off."

"If he had a gun he would have used it by now," Loomis declared. "Do as I say! Climb the ladder and kill him. Now! Unless you'd rather answer to Trask."

Bolan scanned the flying bridge for something he could use as a weapon. But it was a lost cause. The helm seat and bench seat were bolted to the floor, and it would be impossible to remove the throttle lever to use it as a club.

A foot scraped on a low ladder rung.

The warrior's gaze fixed on the portable searchlight Leon had dropped. Its brilliant glow bathed the control console. Crawling over, he grasped the handle, then slowly slid toward the top of the ladder. He made certain not to jiggle the light or to turn it in any manner so that Willy wouldn't know that he had gotten his hands on it.

The gunner had all the stealth of a drunk orangutan. His feet clunked on every rung, and he was breathing loud enough to be heard back at the marina.

A few inches shy of the edge, Bolan halted and flattened. He locked his eyes on the top rung, watching and waiting. All was quiet for several seconds, then a hand groped the rung, grabbed hold and tensed. He heard the gunner take a breath and knew Willy was about to pop up.

It took another ten seconds for the hardman to get up the nerve. Extending the .45, Willy rose and looked to the right and the left when he should have been looking straight ahead.

With a flick of the wrist, Bolan reversed the searchlight, shining the bright beam right into Willy's face. The gunner, briefly blinded, tried to bring the Springfield Armory to bear.

Bolan smashed his fist into Willy's face and grabbed at the pistol, but both the .45 and its owner went flying from the ladder and hit the lower deck with a sickening thud. Bolan glanced down and saw that the man was out cold.

Loomis, however, wasn't. The man in black had a 9 mm pistol, which he raised and fired three times so swiftly that the shots sounded like one.

Slugs tore into the wood along the rim as Bolan flipped out of harm's way. He moved back from the edge and rose to his knees. As he saw it, it was a stalemate. Loomis couldn't scale the ladder with a busted knee, and Bolan couldn't very well take on the killer with nothing but a spotlight.

Then the beam fell on the control console, and Bolan smiled.

The engine still idled in neutral. It responded superbly when the soldier threw the starboard and port throttles wide open. Roaring like a jet, the cruiser shot forward, churning the water in its wake. It started so abruptly that there was a loud crash from the lower deck and Loomis squawked in pain.

Bolan spun the wheel to the right, his hands flying. The craft sheared the ocean at a steep angle. Even as it made the turn, he spun the wheel in the other direction. The cruiser tilted wildly. Again he cut the wheel sharply. Belowdecks, glasses, pans and other items were smashing to the floor. Glass shattered. A great rending noise added to the din.

"Damn you!"

The bray of sheer rage came from the lower deck cockpit. In his mind's eye Bolan pictured Loomis being buffeted from rail to rail, frantically trying to catch hold of something for support. He twisted the wheel again and again. Then, just as quickly as he had started, he let go and ran to the ladder.

Loomis was nowhere to be seen.

Bolan gripped the side rails and bent down to look into the passageway below. No one moved. No shadows flickered. He wondered if perhaps Loomis had been pitched overboard and rose to survey the ocean.

Suddenly an SMG thundered below. A deluge of heavy-caliber slugs punched through the floorboard of the upper deck almost directly under the wheel. Some ripped into the console itself.

Swinging over the side, Bolan slid down the ladder and stepped close to the passageway. A hasty peek showed the man in black at the other end, firing into the ceiling. The SMG ran empty, and Loomis smoothly inserted a fresh magazine.

"How do like those apples, bastard! Hold on. There's more where that came from." Loomis took an awkward step and pressed the trigger of the subgun, stitching the ceiling in an X pattern. Stopping, he tilted his head back.

"No answer, Belasko? Come on. Don't be a wuss. Show me your stuff. Come down here and take this from me."

Bolan would very much like to. Like a hawk, he watched as the killer advanced a few more short, hobbling paces and slanted the barrel. Loomis fired again, chewing the wood above to bits, heedless of the slivers that rained on his head and shoulders.

Once more Loomis exchanged magazines. He had two more jutting from a back pocket. Working the bolt, he sent a short burst into the ceiling. In the narrow confines of the passageway, the racket was enough to shatter eardrums. When he stopped, he cocked his head to listen.

Bolan eased into a crouch and propped his left hand on the floor, like a linebacker about to rush an opposing line. Loomis, staring intently at the ruptured ceiling, seemed puzzled. The killer frowned, then faced toward the steps. Bolan drew back so he wouldn't be seen. He was in shadow close to the opening. If Loomis came out without bothering to look both ways, it would all be over in seconds.

But the killer didn't appear.

Bolan strained his ears to hear above the roar of the racing engine. A hopeless task. Edging to the jamb, he looked and was mildly surprised to discover the passageway to be empty.

In addition to the door into the main cabin, there were two others closer to the steps. Loomis might have ducked into any one of them.

The soldier decided not to wait out there for the killer to come to him. Like a greyhound charging from a chute, he sped to the nearest doorway. The room contained two beds, a dresser and an open closet. He hastily checked the drawers and the bottom of the closet in the hope of finding a weapon but came up empty-handed.

On to the next room. Bolan found himself in a small galley. A loaf of bread sat on the counter, a dirty pot was in the sink. He slid out a narrow drawer filled with silverware and cooking implements. Among them was a large butcher knife. Bolan pulled it out, tested the edge on his finger and crept to the hall. It wasn't much but it would have to do.

The cruiser continued to race landward. Bolan tried not to dwell on what would happen if it collided with another vessel or a buoy. He had to see this through. He couldn't go topside until the killer had been dealt with.

The soldier moved to the passageway. There was no doubt Loomis had retreated into the main cabin. Unfortunately there was only one way in, and Bolan had a hunch the man in black was just waiting for him to show himself, with the SMG covering the doorway.

Hanging from a rack above the sink were four dish towels. Bolan grabbed all of them and stalked forward. A few steps short of the doorway, he slung two over his shoulder. Taking the remaining two, he moved as close to the jamb as was prudent and hurled them through the opening.

The subgun thundered. There was no way of counting the number of rounds fired, but Bolan estimated half the magazine was expended before Loomis realized his mistake. And the second the SMG stopping firing, Bolan gave a yell, pounded his feet as if he were charging into the cabin and heaved the other two towels inside.

Loomis was caught flat-footed by the same ruse twice. He squeezed the trigger without thinking, his back braced against the far wall so he could stay on his feet. When he saw the towels, he tried to let up but the damage had been done. The magazine had gone dry.

The Executioner threw himself into the room and saw the man in black claw at another magazine. He was halfway across the cabin when Loomis yanked out the spent magazine, three-fourths of the way across when Loomis slammed the new magazine home. And just as the killer snapped up the SMG to fire, the Executioner plunged the butcher knife into Loomis's throat with so much force that the man's neck was pinned to the wall.

Bolan wrenched the subgun from his adversary's grasp and stepped back. The killer glared at him, defiant to the last. Loomis tried to speak but could only wheeze. He'd die a slow, lingering death unless Bolan delivered a merry round. The subgun chattered, punching leaden rivets into the twitching form.

In the silence that followed, Bolan turned and headed for the upper deck. He had a boat to bring under control. Then he had to give Brognola the bad news that they were no closer to catching the Wizard.

CHAPTER THIRTEEN

The night didn't turn out to be a total waste.

Brognola had his people go over the cruiser with a fine-tooth comb. The effort yielded results when one of the federal agents thought to check the contents of a small wastebasket in the main cabin.

A handful of crumpled receipts turned up. All were from different electronics and computer outlets in Miami, and dated nine months to a year earlier. Several fuel receipts were also found, two of them showing the *Hephaestos,* as the craft was named, had been serviced in Jamaica within the past year.

The well-oiled machinery of the Justice Department swung into full gear. Calls were made. Businesses visited. Within twelve hours of the time Bolan docked the boat at the marina, he walked into Brognola's office and saw the big Fed grinning for the first time in many days.

"We think we're on to something, Striker. We're about ninety percent sure that the Wizard has his base of operations somewhere in Jamaica. The authorities there are being very helpful. They have feelers out, trying to learn more for us. Quietly, of course."

"But do we have anything concrete?" Bolan got to the heart of the matter.

"Yes and no. There are few electronics outlets in Jamaica that carry the type of high-tech equipment and components the Wizard would use. The police are checking them out for leads." Brognola leaned back and locked his fingers behind his head. "The Kingston chief of police told me that it's more likely the Wizard has whatever he needs smuggled into the country, so they're working on that angle."

"How soon before you expect to hear something?"

"We've already had a few interesting developments. For one thing, the police had been keeping their eye on a customs official in Savanna la Mar. They suspected him of being strongly involved in a number of smuggling operations. And they know for a fact that within the past year he allowed sophisticated electronics gear to slip into Jamaica unnoticed."

"Then all they have to do is bring him in for questioning."

"Would that they could. The gentleman's name is Edward Bustamante, and earlier today he was found dead in an alley. Someone used a garrote on him and damn near severed his head off his neck. The police are going through his records and his home to see what they can come up with."

"Do you think the Wizard had him killed to cover his tracks?"

"Impossible to say at this point. But it's a given that the Wizard knows something happened to Loomis. What worries me is that he might fly the coop before we can close in."

"How about the name we came up with, Trask. Anything there?"

"Not yet. I wouldn't be surprised if it's an alias. Whoever this guy is, he covers his tracks better than most. He must have a slew of false identities he can fall back on if need be."

Bolan went to the window. They weren't making progress fast enough to suit him, not when the clock was ticking on the plot to assassinate the President. "Anything new on the Mexican drug ring?"

"We've learned that a guy by the name of Adolpho Garcia has stepped into Luis Terrazas's shoes. Garcia has to be the one who put the contract out on the Man. So far, though, we've had no luck tracing his whereabouts. Once we do, you'll get a green light."

The soldier pondered the factors involved. He wasn't about to sit around and wait for something to break. The adage about the best defense being a good offense came to mind. "If Jamaica is where the Wizard is, then that's where I should be. I'll take the next flight. Can you arrange for a liaison?"

Brognola didn't seem the least bit surprised. "Consider it done." He took a black address book from an inner pocket and consulted it. "And if anything develops on Garcia, I'll pass on the word. Hopefully, by going at this from both angles, we can stop Trask or whoever he really is before he chalks up the President as his next victim." Brognola put a hand on the telephone. "Just think of what that would do for his reputation. Every terrorist and drug outfit in the world would seek him out. He could name his own price from here on out."

Bolan had already had the same thought, which made it imperative that he stop the Wizard. No matter what it took.

Jamaica

KATYA STEINER and Gunther Merzig weren't surprised when a policeman showed up to question them about the death of Edward Bustamante.

Katya answered the knock at the door and feigned shock on seeing the tall black officer in his crisp uniform and cap. "What may I do for you, sir?" she asked ever so politely.

"I am Lieutenant Sangster," the policeman introduced himself. "I apologize for disturbing you, Miss Steiner. But I am here as part of a murder investigation."

"Oh, my," Katya said, looking flustered. "Certainly. Come in, won't you?"

Sangster was led to a sofa, but he declined to sit. Pulling out a small notebook and pen, he began by saying, "It is my understanding that you spent some time last night with Customs Chief Bustamante at the Fairmouth Club. Is this correct?"

"Yes, we did," Katya said as Gunther came from the bedroom. "A most charming man." She scooped her purse from an end table and produced a business card that identified her as a purchasing agent for Hamburg

Importers in Germany. "We are in the import business. We specialize in raw fruits, bananas and such."

Steiner had her cover story rehearsed. She knew that if the police were to phone the number on the card, an old woman she had hired to sit by a telephone in a small apartment in Hamburg would answer and pretend to be a secretary. The woman would confirm her false identity. "My firm is thinking of importing various goods from your country."

"So that is why you met with Bustamante? In your business capacity?"

"Yes," Katya said. "We were told that he knew a great deal about the importing and exporting business in Jamaica, so we met to seek his advice." She smiled. "He is a most engaging man. He kept me laughing for hours."

"I am afraid he will never do so again. He was killed last night. Strangled with a wire, we believe."

Katya recoiled in horror. "How awful!"

"When was the last time you saw him?"

"He walked me to the hotel. We arranged to meet again tonight at the same time. Oh, my! How could this have happened? Who would do such a thing?"

"We will find out soon enough," Sangster vowed. He asked more questions, sounding the pair out to his satisfaction. The woman's sincerity impressed him. In his opinion, they weren't likely suspects since they lacked a motive and would hardly be stupid enough to remain in the country after brutally killing a man. When he was done, Sangster thanked them for their help and departed.

Gunther walked to the door and listened to the officer's footsteps recede. "Did you see how he looked at you? I think you made another conquest, my dear."

"Nonsense, darling. This one was all business. But we convinced him, I think. Which buys us the time we need to do what has to be done."

Gunther waited while she went into the bedroom to change from the prim dress she had on into the black leather she preferred. "It's too bad that idiot Bustamante didn't know more," he mentioned while waiting.

"Did you think it would be easy? Our prey this time isn't a bumbling accountant. Think of it as a chess match. We must go through many pawns, rooks and knights before we get to the king himself."

"Bustamante was a pawn," Gunther said. "And the information he gave us will probably lead us to other pawns."

"Do I detect a hint of impatience?"

"For once, yes. The money Reutlingen will pay us is enough to see us through the rest of our days. We can shed these false identities and move to Switzerland as we have always dreamed of doing."

The blonde came out, her hair done up in a ponytail, a squat pistol in her left hand. She pulled her jacket aside and wedged the Walther under her belt, on her left hip. "I never thought of you as a romantic. Tell me true. You'll miss this life just a little, will you not?"

A rare grin creased the cold man's lips. "Maybe more than a little. I like this work."

"So perhaps we should keep our hand in, eh?" Katya clapped him on the back and they went out, taking the stairs to the ground floor and exiting the hotel through the rear door. She stooped, picked up the brick and tossed it into the alley. "There is no need to keep this here any longer."

"So where to first?"

"Our friend the customs inspector gave us three names. Antonio is the computer man. He will be easiest to locate so we should go talk to him now. Then, if we need to, we will hunt down the importer, Gordon."

"What about the old smuggler, Tego?"

"All Bustamante could tell us is that he hangs around the waterfront a lot. That isn't much to go on. Tego will be the hardest to find so we will save him for last."

MACK BOLAN STARED OUT the small window of the commercial jet and saw the humped green back of Jamaica spread out below. The plane came in low over the north shore and the spine of high mountains. Soon Kingston unfolded below. He heard the oohs and aahs of tourists but didn't share in their childlike delight. He had to stay focused on the deadly business awaiting him.

The immigration officer hardly gave Bolan's false passport a second glance. His small travel bag was spared the scrutiny of customs, and in minutes he was threading through the crowd to the terminal entrance.

He almost missed seeing the skinny black man in a white suit who held a large card bearing his name. Warily he went over.

"Mr. Belasko?" the man said heartily. "I am Eric Mandeville. I believe you were told I would meet you."

"At my hotel."

"Ah, yes. There has been a change in plans. Our friend has learned that a large shipment of electronics equipment was sent to Savanna la Mar from the States about a year ago. He believes we should focus our search on the west coast instead of here in the capital." Mandeville gestured. "I took the liberty of arranging to have a private plane ready to fly us there as soon as you arrived. Our friend made it clear that urgency is most important."

"Then let's go."

In fifteen minutes the soldier was back in the air, seated in a comfortable twin-prop Cessna, winging westward. Mandeville had shown credentials that identified him as being on the personal staff of the prime minister. Bolan suspected that he had been paired with Jamaican's equivalent of Hal Brognola, but Mandeville never admitted as much.

The man was a friendly chatterbox. He went on at length about the crime plaguing his country. Smuggling was epidemic. Drugs were rampant. As in America, it was all the authorities could do to slow the tide.

"Whatever I can do to help, you have only to ask. The police, the armed forces, they are all at my disposal. Although I do understand that it would be best for all parties if secrecy is maintained."

Bolan tactfully sounded the man out on how much he knew.

"I know that the man you are after has been supplying arms to terrorists. And it enrages me that he has taken refuge in my country. Jamaica, it seems, hasn't come so far from the old days when pirates haunted our shores."

The flight was short. In under forty minutes they were circling the scenic port city. Mandeville gazed down. "I was born and raised here, you know. Savanna la Mar is my home, but I haven't been here in quite a few years."

A car awaited them at the airport. Mandeville, not the driver, walked around and opened the trunk. "You can place your bag in here, Mr. Belasko," he said, smiling.

Bolan understood why when he saw a Colt Combat Commander, a Beretta Model 85-F and a Kris knife lying on a green blanket along with a box of .45 ammo for the Colt and .380 ammo for the Beretta. A pair of leather holsters lay near the fender.

"I'm sorry these aren't the exact firearms Mr. Brognola requested," the Jamaican said, "but I didn't have much of a selection to choose from. My countrymen aren't as gun crazy as you Americans. Most of them don't even own one."

"These will do just fine," Bolan assured him. He crammed the weapons and ammo into his bag before slamming the trunk lid.

The streets of Savanna la Mar were crowded. Traffic congestion was worse. It took them a half hour to reach the Falstaff, a hotel built back during the days when Jamaica was part and parcel of the British Empire.

"This is one of the finest in the city," Mandeville said. "Only the Imperial is better, but it was booked up."

The accommodations were more than adequate. Plush carpet covered the floors. Mahogany furniture and wall paneling gave his suite the feel of a ritzy home. He went into the bedroom, removed his jacket and slipped on the shoulder holster for the Beretta and the hip holster for the Colt. The Kris blade went up his left sleeve. When he came out, his contact was on the telephone.

"A police officer is on his way up," Mandeville reported. "He's one of the best on the local force. I personally had him assigned to the Bustamante case."

In short order Bolan was being introduced to Lieutenant Thomas Sangster, a strapping black man whose backbone was as stiff as his uniform.

"I have learned nothing new about the customs inspector's murder since last we spoke, sir. Those who work at the club and many of the patrons who were there have been questioned. So far we have no solid leads."

Mandeville wasn't very happy. "What about the other matter?"

"There is no record of an American named Trask being anywhere in the city in the past year," Sangster said. "As you instructed, I have also been discreetly asking around about computer and electronics shipments. Again I regret to report no real progress." He hesitated as if unsure whether to say more.

"What is it, Lieutenant?"

"Well, sir, I don't know if this has a bearing or not." Sangster eased a notebook from his shirt pocket. "About three hours ago a computer dealer named Antonio was found dead in the back room of his store. It appears that he was killed with a garrote, just like Edward Bustamante."

Bolan remembered his last talk with Brognola. Had he been right? Was the Wizard trying to cover his tracks?

"That isn't all, sir. Not quite an hour ago the body of an importer named Charles Gordon was discovered in his home—"

"Let me guess, Lieutenant," Mandeville interrupted. "He had been garroted to death."

"Yes, sir. Quite frankly, I don't know what to make of it. There's no direct link that I can uncover between Bustamante, Antonio and Gordon. All three are suspected of shady dealings, but not with one another."

"Do you have people following up that angle?"

"Even as we speak. I have told them to leave no stone unturned. And I gave orders to be notified if anything of interest came up." Sangster closed the notebook and squared his wide shoulders. "So how do you want me to proceed, sir?"

"Take us to the scenes of the crimes."

Bolan felt it would be a waste of time but he held his tongue. Until another lead materialized, he had nothing else to do.

A policeman stood guard outside the closed computer store. The stockroom was a mess. All the drawers in a desk had been torn out and the contents scattered over the floor. Papers were everywhere—invoices, receipts, order forms. It was plain that the killer or killers had been hunting for specific information. Sangster explained that someone would be by later to gather up all the papers and sort through them.

Charles Gordon's study was in the same shape. The desk and a pair of file cabinets had been ransacked. Two bookcases had been toppled and a painting ripped from the wall.

"We speculate that the suspect was looking for a safe," Sangster remarked.

"Any fingerprints?" Mandeville asked.

"Not one. Whoever committed these murders is a professional." The officer stared at the outline of a body etched in the middle of the hardwood floor. "Which makes the use of a garrote all the more puzzling, sir. A gun or even a knife would be better."

"Not if the person knows how to use one properly," Bolan offered. "And this one evidently does."

Sangster shook his head. "Strangulation is too sloppy, sir. A bullet or blade to the heart is instantly fatal. But a victim being choked can struggle, can call out for help. There is too great a chance of something going wrong."

"The Mafia would disagree," Bolan said. "In Italy it's one of their favorite ways to dispose of traitors in their organization. A skilled garroter can kill another person in under ten seconds and the victim never gets to draw a breath, let alone shout or scream."

"I couldn't believe that unless I saw it with my own eyes, sir."

"The issue is moot," Mandeville said. "Whoever is committing all these murders isn't a member of the Mafia. Their influence in Jamaica is very limited."

Bolan noticed a stack of yellow sheets close to the desk. They were all inventory lists of merchandise imported within the past twelve months. It was as if someone had been searching for a specific shipment, or a *type* of shipment, which made no sense and spoiled his theory about the Wizard trying to cover his paper trail. If Trask was to blame, the mastermind would have destroyed all the records, not merely rifled through them.

As they were about to leave, the driver entered and informed Bolan's liaison that he had a call on the car phone. Mandeville excused himself.

Bolan sifted through more of the papers, trying to discern a pattern. He could feel the police officer's eyes on him the whole time, so he said, "Is something bothering you, Lieutenant?"

"Curiosity is all, sir. You must be a man of great importance, judging from the way Mr. Mandeville treats you. Yet you don't have the look of a politician. If I was to hazard a guess, I would say that you are an American spook. Is that the correct expression?"

"I'm not a spy."

"So you claim, sir. But if you don't mind my saying so, a real spy would never admit as much, now would he?"

"Does it really matter who I am?"

"No, sir. I have my orders. And I will obey them to the best of my ability."

"You are a good cop, Lieutenant. That is another American expression."

Mandeville returned shortly. "I'm most sorry, Mr. Belasko, but that was the prime minister. My presence is needed in the capital on a crucial state matter." He put a hand on the officer's shoulder. "If you have no objections, I'll leave you in the capable hands of Lieutenant Sangster."

"I don't mind," Bolan said.

"Good." Mandeville faced his subordinate. "Understand this clearly. Mr. Belasko is to have a free reign to do as he pleases. You are to extend him total cooperation. And if anyone gives you any trouble, you are to refer them to me. I won't be gone more than twelve hours. Any questions?"

"No, sir."

Mandeville again apologized to Bolan before heading for the airport. The lieutenant telephoned for a patrol car, which picked them up in ten minutes. Sangster took the wheel, drove the patrolman back to the station house, then turned to Bolan.

"Right. Now we can do whatever you want, sir. Would you care to return to the Falstaff?"

"I'd rather carry on with your investigation. What were you planning to do next?"

"Question contacts along the waterfront. If someone has been smuggling electronic materials, someone else is bound to have heard of it."

Sangster parked on a street that overlooked the harbor and entered a bar as seedy as any Bolan had ever seen. The customers were sailors, fishermen and wharf rats of every stripe. Sangster made the rounds but turned up no leads.

During the next hour the Executioner and the cop visited three more dens of iniquity. At the last, Sangster cornered a bartender and grilled him. Bolan thought the man was putting them on when he screwed up his ferret face and scratched his thin patch of hair.

"Electronics? It seems to me that I did hear someone say something about that."

"Think, Beakman," Sangster prodded. "Remember, your licence is up for renewal in a few weeks."

Beakman scowled. "There's no need to threaten me, Tommy. I've always been straight with you. As for the electronic nonsense, I seem to recall old Tego telling me a week or so ago that he had been delivering a lot of that stuff to an island a ways out. He was in his cups at the time, but I don't think he was making it up."

"Do tell," Sangster said.

"Do you know him?" Bolan asked.

"Yes. And I know where he calls home." Sangster slipped Beakman a bill, and they walked out into the brilliant sunlight.

"Is this man dangerous?"

"Old Tego? No, sir. He's a harmless fisherman who does odd jobs from time to time." Sangster chuckled. "Don't you concern yourself, Mr. Belasko. The worst that can happen is Tego will bore us to death."

CHAPTER FOURTEEN

A run-down shack stood at the north end of the harbor. Weeds and rusted tin cans choked the small strip of ground in front. Nearby was the last pier, while to the north a long, rolling beach wound into the distance.

The Jamaican police officer marched up and knocked once on the rickety closed door. "Tego. This is Lieutenant Sangster. Open up."

When there was no reply, the officer lifted the wooden latch and pushed. The door creaked open on hinges as rusty as the tin cans. "Well, what do we have here?"

Bolan followed Sangster. Judging by the shape the shanty was in and all the trash, he thought the inside would turn out to be a dump. Appearances were deceiving.

A new rug covered the floor. In one corner stood a folding table and two chairs, both looking as if they had just been taken from a carton. A small dresser stood against one wall, and other than a light layer of dust, it showed no sign of wear or tear. On top rested a large portable radio. A new lantern hung from the ceiling. In the far corner was a folding cot with hardly a speck of dirt on it, and a telephone was mounted on the left-hand wall.

Sangster stepped to the cot and fingered a new blanket sloppily folded on top. "So. Beakman was telling the truth. Tego has come into a windfall." He gestured. "The last time I was here, about a year ago, the old man owned a couple of ratty blankets and a three-legged stool."

"Could he have made enough from fishing to buy all this?" Bolan asked.

The officer snickered. "Not unless he has gone into the whaling business. Most fishermen barely earn enough to make ends meet. They live hand to mouth, as so many of our people do." He stepped to the dresser and examined the radio. "No, our friend Tego is up to his old tricks again, I suspect. Many years ago he was one of the best smugglers in the Caribbean."

"Where should we start looking for him?" Bolan prompted.

"Let us check his boat first," Sangster said.

The afternoon sun blazed down as they walked along the pier past fishing boats and a few pleasure craft. At a berth halfway out, the officer halted and stared at a sleek Streamliner tied to the dock. "This is Tego's berth, but the last I knew he owned an old boat barely able to stay afloat." Cupping a hand to his mouth, he hailed the Streamliner. "Tego! Come up on deck! This is the police."

A dry cackle was the only response, and it came from the next craft, a square-hulled boat built decades earlier. Seated cross-legged on the bow was a bearded fishermen mending a net. "You're wastin' your time, guv. Old Tego ain't to home."

Sangster clasped his hands behind his back and walked over. "Your face is familiar, sir, but I can't recall your name."

The fisherman cackled again. "My face better damn well be familiar. You hauled me in two years ago for makin' a public spectacle of myself."

The officer nodded. "Arquette. You were drunk at the time, and prancing down the middle of the street with no clothes on. I had my duty to perform."

"Mercy me. Your duty," Arquette said sarcastically. "And now I reckon you're here to do your duty with Tego?"

"My business with him doesn't concern you. If you know where he is, I would be grateful if you would tell me."

"Would you now?" Arquette said, mocking the policeman. Then he looked at Bolan and something he saw in the soldier's eyes made him blink and cough. "Well, I wouldn't want it said that Bill Arquette never helps the law out when they need a helping hand."

"I'm listening," Sangster said.

Arquette shifted and jerked a thumb northward. "Most afternoons when he's not out on his new boat, you can find Tego feedin' the gulls. He takes bread to that rocky point about a kilometer from here. Do you know it?"

"Yes. Thank you."

Bolan and the policeman turned to go but were stopped by the fisherman's next remark.

"I swear. That Tego is gettin' right popular."

Sangster arched an eyebrow. "How do you mean?"

"Why, the two of you are the second ones today to be lookin' for him. Not ten minutes ago there was this guy and gal almighty interested in his whereabouts."

The officer's reaction interested Bolan. Sangster tensed and went rigid in the face.

"A man and a woman, you say? Can you describe them, Arquette?"

The fisherman set the net in his lap. "I'd not be likely to forget this pair. The man was big and strong, sort of like your friend here. But his eyes were even meaner. I swear, when he stared at me, I felt like I was being sized up for a grave plot." He paused. "Ever been nose to nose with a shark or a barracuda, Officer? It gives you goose bumps, just like this guy does."

"And the woman?" Sangster asked urgently.

Arquette smiled dreamily. "Now there was a beauty if ever I saw one. Hair like gold, she had, and a body as ripe as a melon. She was all dressed in shiny black leather. Seein' her was enough to make me wish I was forty years younger. Those lips. That face—"

"Thank you," Sangster said. Pivoting on a boot heel, he nearly ran toward the shore.

"Mind filling me in?" Bolan said, keeping pace.

"I know those two, Mr. Belasko. I questioned them in connection with Edward Bustamante's death, but I dismissed them as suspects."

The worried officer turned left and sprinted along the beach. Bolan did likewise, staying a few steps behind. It was hard to run in the loose sand wearing shoes. They came to the crest of a low dune.

Sangster shielded his eyes with a palm and scanned the shoreline ahead. "They've had too much of a head start. We'll never make it in time. If Tego dies, it'll be my fault."

Bolan made no comment. He scoured the sand as they sped onward. There weren't many prints to be seen, indicating the beach was seldom used. Savanna la Mar wasn't quite as popular with tourists as Kingston and Montego Bay.

The belt of sand thinned. More and more boulders had to be skirted.

Lieutenant Sangster was breathing heavily, his face beaded with sweat. But he made no move to unfasten the buttons of his uniform jacket or to remove his cap. He was spit and polish down to the bone.

"It isn't far now," the policeman said. "Just over the next rise."

Bolan slipped a hand to the Colt and undid the snap to free the pistol for a fast draw. He wasn't even going to try to take the man and woman alive. Whoever they were, they had already killed three people, and they'd do the same to him and Sangster without hesitation. He glanced at the lieutenant to advise the officer not to take needless chances. The next moment they reached the crest of the knoll.

Spread out below was the rocky point mentioned by Arquette, a bony finger of land that poked fifty or sixty feet into the sea. Seated on a flat boulder at the water's edge was a grizzled old man in shabby clothes. Beside him lay a loaf of bread. He had part of a slice in his right hand and held it high, waiting for one of the ten to twelve circling gulls to swoop down and snatch the morsel from his grasp.

But it wasn't the fisherman who interested Bolan the most. Slinking toward the unsuspecting Tego was a tall man with a short length of wire clasped at his waist. The man moved with the smooth stealth of a jaguar, his whole attention riveted on his quarry.

On the shore next to the rocky point stood the blond woman in leather. She grinned, as if at a secret joke. But Bolan knew better. She couldn't wait to see Tego strangled. He'd met her kind before, thrill killers whose main pleasure in life was to watch others die. If it had been up to him, he wouldn't have given either of them a chance.

Sangster, however, always went by the book. On sighting the pair, he placed a hand on his service revolver and hollered, "All right, you two! Stand where you are! I'm going to place you under arrest!"

The man and woman reacted like a pair of cobras. They whirled and bared their fangs. In the woman's case it was a small pistol, a Walther that she leveled in a two-fisted stance. The man snaked a Norinco 9 mm pistol from under his jacket and took quick aim at the policeman.

Bolan leaped, catching hold of Sangster around the knees and tackling him just as the two pistols cracked. The policeman cried out and clutched at his shoulder.

Letting go, Bolan rolled to the right and whipped out the Colt Combat Commander. He was just in time to see Tego stand and dive into the ocean. The man with the garrote had taken a snap shot at him but apparently missed.

The Executioner sighted on the killer, but the blonde fired, her slugs kicking up dirt inches from Bolan's face. He rolled again to throw off her aim.

The hawkish man on the rocky point was making for shore with all the speed of a track-and-field Olympian. He zigged and zagged while the blonde provided covering fire. They were a finely honed team.

Bolan fired. The round fell short of the man's flying feet. He compensated, then squeezed off another shot. The tall man staggered, recovered and kept on running, banging off several rounds at the knoll. With lead flying at him from two directions, the Executioner had no choice but to hug the ground.

That was when Lieutenant Sangster joined in, his service revolver booming three times. Although he was right-handed, he had to use his left thanks to the neat red hole in his right shoulder. Needless to say, he missed.

The pair of killers concentrated their fire on Bolan, as if they sensed that he was the greater threat. He snapped off two shots as they fled up the beach and into the trees, but neither seemed to have an effect.

"Stay here," Bolan said, pushing erect to give chase.

"Not on your life," Sangster replied, standing unsteadily. "I must apprehend them."

Bolan didn't want to have to look out for the wounded policeman, as well as his own skin. "Mandeville said that you're to do as I say, remember? And I want you to go check on the fisherman. We need him if we're to find the Wizard." Without waiting to see if the Jamaican would obey, he plunged down the knoll and made for the forest. Precious moments had been wasted. He had to overtake the killers quickly or he'd lose them.

The foliage closed around Bolan and he darted behind a tree. No shots rang out. He'd half hoped the pair had lain in wait to ambush him, but they were too smart for that. These were professionals in every sense of the word, and a pro never took a needless chance. When a pro blew a kill, he or she got out of there as fast as possible. The unwritten rule of survival was simple—run away to live to kill another day.

Bolan palmed the Beretta in his other hand. Angling to one side, he ran an *S* pattern and drew up in the shelter of a thicket. The woods were unnaturally quiet. Not a single bird chirped. Not a lone insect buzzed.

The killers had to be close by.

Going prone, Bolan scoured the area at ground level for movement. He spotted a white cat, of all things, crouched next to a log, but he failed to spy the deadly blonde and her companion. Then he took a closer look at the cat and saw that it was peering intently at a cluster of high weeds to the east. So he did the same.

At first Bolan discerned no reason for the feline's interest. Had the weeds not rustled, he would have gone on. But when they did, he pointed both pistols at the spot. Time seemed to drag. Finally the stems parted. He had both trigger fingers tensed to shoot, but he held his fire.

Out ambled a small pig.

Rising, Bolan jogged eastward. It was doubtful he could catch the pair now. They'd had too much of a head start. He came to a gully and took the steep slope carefully. At the bottom, as plain as the nose on his face, were five bright drips of fresh blood.

Bolan scaled the other side and found more drops on the rim. The man was wounded, perhaps badly. It would slow the pair. He still had a chance if he hurried.

The dense growth hindered him. Bolan had to skirt tangles of vines and tracks of brush so heavy it would take a bulldozer to open a way through. Several times he came across more blood, and tracks. From the prints, he gathered that the blonde was supporting the man with her shoulder.

Somewhere ahead a twig snapped. Bolan drew up and squatted. They were certain to be watching their backs, and he wasn't going to blunder now that he was so close. Creeping forward another thirty feet, he detected motion among the trees.

It was them. Side by side, they hurried as best they could, the man hobbling and grimacing in pain, the woman straining to keep him on his feet.

Bolan tried to get a clear shot, but there were too many trees. Stalking them, he slowly narrowed the range until he was almost near enough to guarantee he could drop them both, trees or no trees. That was when he heard a car horn honk.

Twenty feet beyond the killers the vegetation abruptly thinned at the border of a highway. The vehicles moved at a crawl, some bumper to bumper.

The Executioner knew that he couldn't let the killers reach the thoroughfare. He lowered his gaze to the pair and saw that they had spotted him. The man was already bringing the 9 mm pistol to bear. Bolan threw himself down as leaden hornets buzzed above him. When he rose high enough to return fire, the pair was in full flight toward the highway. The woman fired this time. Again Bolan had to dive to the ground.

Their intent was transparent. By keeping him pinned down, they would be able to reach the highway.

Tucking his knees under his chest, Bolan flung himself up and raised both pistols. The killers were almost there. He stroked the Beretta's trigger, but as he did his quarry rolled onto the ground and crawled the last few yards on their hands and knees.

Bolan hurtled after them. There was a scream and a shot, then a second shot. Metal rent with a grinding roar; broken glass tinkled. The reason became apparent when the soldier reached the highway.

A man lay on his back in the middle of the road. He was in the grip of convulsions caused by a bullet hole in his side. Another man lay sprawled out of the open door of a station wagon on the other side of the highway.

A second loud crash drew Bolan's attention to the south, where a compact car zipped toward town using the crowded shoulder. It scattered pedestrians and bike riders as if they were mere bowling pins, knocking many over, sending others flying. Men, women and children were run down with no regard whatsoever.

The Executioner shoved the pistols into their holsters while running over to a man who stood beside a bicycle. The Jamaican was in shock, his mouth agape. He came to life when Bolan yanked the bicycle from his grasp and jumped on. His shouts of outrage were wasted. Bolan pumped the pedals furiously and shot off in pursuit, weaving among the injured and the dead.

Bit by bit, Bolan gained. With the twists and turns of the road and the number of pedestrians, the car could go only so fast. Bending low over the handlebars, he stroked in a steady rhythm and shifted the bicycle into a higher gear. A dazed woman, blood seeping from a gash in her forehead, stumbled in front of him. He barely swerved in time.

The soldier could see the killers clearly now, could see the man urging the woman to go faster. Seconds later the man looked back and glared at him.

The glint of metal alerted Bolan a fraction of an instant before the rear window of the vehicle exploded outward. He banked the bike to the left, nearly clipping a car. None of the shots scored. Bolan pedaled on, confident that in another minute he would overtake them.

The piercing bleat of a whistle intruded.

There was a congested intersection up ahead. At the very center stood a uniformed police officer, directing traffic. His gloved hands swirled every which way. To an outsider it might appear that he was swatting at a horde of mosquitoes, but his precise movements kept the traffic flowing, if at a snail's pace.

The officer heard the shriek of a woman mowed down by the compact. He held up his hands, bringing all oncoming traffic to a halt, then darted toward the shoulder. Planting his boots at the point where the shoulder merged with the intersection, he boldly gestured for the compact to stop.

The killers, of course, weren't about to.

Bolan lifted his head to shout a warning, but it was too late.

At the very last moment the policeman woke up to his lapse in judgment. He clawed for the revolver at his side, but he had just started to lift the flap when he met his end.

At close to fifty miles per hour the compact slammed into him. He crumpled as if he were a human accordion, jolting the car into the air as it rode right over him. When Bolan reached the spot, it looked as if every bone in the poor man's body had been broken and his skull had been crushed.

The blonde and her partner were already well across the intersection, fleeing up a hill.

Bolan had no hope of catching them now, not with the bicycle. But off to his right a young man sat on a motor scooter. Bolan leaned the bike against a telephone pole for the owner to find and ran to the scooter.

"You saw what just happened. The people in that car are murderers. I'm trying to catch them. Will you help me?" Bolan wanted to borrow the scooter and continue after the killers by himself. The man nodded, then pointed at the seat.

"Hop on. I'll take you."

Since arguing would enable the pair to get away, Bolan had two choices. He either did as the man wanted or he simply threw the Jamaican off the scooter and took it. He settled for sliding on the back of the seat.

The young man gunned the motor and took off much too fast, causing the front wheel to leap skyward. Just when a collision with a car seemed certain, he regained control and raced up the hill. "I should have asked for some identification. Are you a policeman, by any chance?" he inquired nervously over his shoulder, shouting to be heard over the roar of the scooter and the stalled traffic.

"Of sorts," Bolan admitted. "I'm working with Lieutenant Thomas Sangster of the Savanna la Mar police."

The man relaxed a little. "Ah. I know of him. He's always getting his picture in the paper for arresting criminals. A good man, they say."

By this time the compact had reached the top of the hill and was almost out of sight. Bolan wished he could will the scooter to go faster, but its owner was pushing the vehicle to its limit. Whining noisily, it was less than halfway to the crown.

Sirens yowled to the east and north.

After a seeming eternity the motor scooter sped up over the crest. Below them the road curved sharply around a bend. Trees hid whatever lay on the other side.

The young man took the slope almost as recklessly as he had taken the first turn. The rear of the scooter fishtailed, and Bolan had to grab the Jamaican's shoulders to keep from being thrown off. A ditch loomed on their right. For a few seconds Bolan was sure they were going to end up in it, but the driver regained control.

They swept around the curve. In front of them was a quarter-mile straight stretch to another intersection. The driver looked and blurted, "Where's their car?"

Bolan was wondering the same thing. They flashed past a side street, and he glimpsed the compact a couple of blocks away. "Turn around!" he shouted. "They took that last turn."

The young man braked unevenly and wheeled. He had a hard time holding the scooter steady. At the side street he stuck out his arm to signal before turning.

By all rights the red compact should have been two or three blocks farther, but it sat right where Bolan had last seen it. As they approached he noticed both front doors were wide open. He was off the scooter before it stopped rolling. Running flat out, he came to a broad avenue thronged with foot and vehicular traffic. He looked both ways, knowing it was futile.

It was just as Bolan figured.

The blonde in black leather and the man who favored garrotes were long gone.

CHAPTER FIFTEEN

The small flotilla of seven boats approached Xaymaca in the chill of early morning. Six of the craft were Jamaican police vessels. In the lead was Tego's boat.

Mack Bolan, Lieutenant Thomas Sangster, Eric Mandeville and two Jamaican policemen were on the fishing boat with Tego. The warrior now carried an M-16, courtesy of the government liaison, and had spare magazines squared away in his back pockets. He squinted against the bright glare cast by the glassy sea and studied the island.

After the firefight at the rocky point, Tego had tried to evade Sangster by swimming under water close to the shore. But the alert officer had spotted him and hugged the water's edge until he came up for air. At gunpoint the old fisherman had reluctantly waded ashore.

Tego had been taken to police headquarters in Savanna la Mar and grilled for hours. He had refused to say a word at first, until Bolan mentioned that it might be the very man Tego worked for who had tried to eliminate him. After thinking that over, Tego offered to lead them to the island in exchange for immunity from prosecution.

The police hadn't been inclined to cut a deal. About that time, however, Eric Mandeville arrived from the capital and took charge. He agreed to Tego's terms. Preparations were made. All the police craft in the area were rounded up, and Sangster personally picked thirty of the best officers on the force to go along.

They were well-armed, dedicated men, yet Bolan had reservations about the plan. He'd much rather have gone in alone, and had said so to Mandeville. But the government man refused to hear of it. The Wizard had violated Jamaican soil; he had to be brought to bay by Jamaicans.

The wind was still, the waves mere ripples. A haze shrouded the green island. Bolan fixed binoculars on it and saw a pair of lushly forested hills that flanked a dock and several buildings.

The island was supposed to be uninhabited. Mandeville had told Bolan that back in the days before the coming of the whites, Jamaica itself was called Xaymaca by the Indians. Much later a government mapmaker bestowed the name on the small island in homage.

Bolan had tried to glean information about the island's defenses from Tego. It went almost without saying that a man like the Wizard was bound to have installed a formidable security array. The fisherman was no help whatsoever, though not through any fault of his. Tego had never been allowed to set foot off the dock. He had glimpsed a bungalow nestled high up on one of the hills but could never get close enough to see much else.

Bolan could only hope they had the element of surprise in their favor, but it was a long shot. Milo Fernstein had been arrested. Loomis and Grendel and the other gunners were dead. The Wizard was bound to have guessed why he had lost contact with all of them.

So far there had been no further word from Brognola. Trask might be the Wizard's real name. It might not. Not that his identity mattered. The important thing was to close down his operation before the President of the United States and countless others became his victims.

Xaymaca now lay four hundred yards away. It was the picture of peaceful serenity, deceptively so in Bolan's opinion. No people were visible—not at the dock, near the buildings along the shore or higher up where the bungalow perched. Yet someone should have been up and around by that time.

"It appears we caught them napping," Mandeville declared. "I doubt they'll put up much of a fight."

Sangster smiled. He had switched uniforms and wore his right arm in a sling. "If they do, sir, my men can handle them."

Bolan wasn't as confident. The fishing boat cruised to within three hundred yards and still nothing happened. There was no outcry, no alarm sounded. It was almost as if the island were deserted.

A boathouse stood close to the dock. Its outer doors swung open suddenly and out came a tiny craft. Bolan had to study it a moment before he recognized it as a motorized scale model of the PT boats used in World

War II. It had a high antenna attached for remote-control guidance. And as he looked on, the motor churned to full power and it shot toward them at amazing speed.

"What the devil is that?" Mandeville asked, then laughed. "This Wizard character must be insane. He attacks us with a toy."

Bolan lowered the binoculars and swung the slung M-16 around so he could grab hold. "We have to blast that thing out of the water before it gets too close."

"Whatever for?" Mandeville queried. "A boat that size couldn't hurt us even if it rammed our vessel."

"It could if it's loaded with explosives."

As the soldier spoke, the PT boat began to weave from side to side in an ever wider pattern. The high-pitched whine of its motor was like the drone of a lawnmower.

Mandeville picked up a battery-powered bullhorn and quickly stepped to the bow. "Attention!" his voice boomed across the sea. "When that model boat is within range, you are to open fire. Do not let it reach us. I repeat. Do not let it reach us. We believe it is wired to blow up on impact."

Bolan watched the police officers check their Lee Enfield rifles, leftovers from the days when Jamaica was part of the British Empire. More modern arms were extremely hard to come by. He was the only member of the strike force armed with an M-16, which Mandeville had told him were as rare as hen's teeth.

Sangster and the officers moved forward so they would have clear shots. Almost in unison three bolts were thrown and rounds chambered. The men sank to one knee to steady their aim.

The PT boat was almost within range. Bolan tucked the M-16 to his shoulder and sighted on the tiny craft, but no sooner did he do so than it swerved to the right. He compensated, and it swerved to the left. The boat promised to be extremely hard to hit.

Mandeville raised the bullhorn. "When you are ready, men, fire at will!"

Moments later the Jamaican police complied, a ragged volley ripping from each craft. Small geysers spewed all around the PT boat, but no one hit the speeding target.

Bolan let off his first rounds. Relying on full-auto would be a waste of ammo, so he had the selector lever set to semiautomatic fire. His shots missed by a hair. Tracking the PT boat with the front sight, he bided his time, trying to detect a pattern that he could exploit. There was none. The thing moved at complete random, never repeating the same maneuver twice in a row.

The police were pouring a steady fire at the small craft. They worked their rifles with practiced precision, taking deliberate aim when they shot. On a field of battle that would have been a plus. But with the PT boat growing closer by the second, their deliberate movements worked against them, slowing them.

Bolan moved to the port side. It was apparent the PT boat had zeroed in on the police vessel closest to the fishing boat. He braced his legs against the gentle rise and fall of the deck and sighted broadside on the Wizard's toy. Making a rough guess, he estimated the PT boat could carry four or five pounds of plastic or some other kind of explosive, which would be more than enough to blow the police craft out of the water.

Suddenly, just as Bolan touched his finger to the trigger, small jets of fire spewed from the rear of the PT boat. The sight reminded Bolan of afterburners on racing cars. It rocketed toward the police craft as if shot from a cannon. He fired a short burst and thought he heard some of the rounds smack into the tiny boat's side, but they had no effect on the guidance or propulsion systems.

It never slowed. Some of the officers on the doomed police craft cried out. The man at the wheel tried to turn aside. But there was no denying the inevitable. The explosion tore the craft to pieces.

Bolan ducked and shielded his face as an enormous fireball devoured the helpless officers. As the flames and smoke rapidly dispersed, debris rained from the sky—bits and pieces of wood, plastic and flesh. Artificial thunder rolled off across the sea and echoed off the high hills.

The Jamaicans were stunned. Boats idling, they gaped at the charred, twisted debris. One man raised his arms to the heavens and wailed as if he had just lost his dearest friend.

Mandeville uttered the sentiments they were all feeling. "How can this be? What manner of man can do such a thing? It is diabolical!"

"Stay alert," Bolan cautioned. "He's bound to have more tricks up his sleeve."

As if to accent the point, an officer on another boat pointed at the shore and cried out, "Look! What is that?"

All eyes swung around to behold the door to a large shed sliding open. From out of its dark depths, moving on a narrow track similar to the kind used on rides at amusement parks, slid a square flatcar. It automatically braked at the end of the track. On top of the car stood a large metal tripod, which in turn supported a long rectangular metal housing.

"What the devil?" Lieutenant Sangster blurted as the tripod swiveled from right to left and back again.

Bolan had seen tripods like that before. The blunt snouts that poked from the housing confirmed his hunch. "It's a missile launcher!" he shouted. "Take evasive action!"

The Jamaicans tried. They veered the police craft and bore down on the beach, trying to reach shore before the launcher was activated.

Only Bolan knew they didn't stand a prayer. The setup in the shed reminded him of the Vigilant missile system used by the British. A gyro autopilot made automatic elevation and azimuth adjustments and maintained velocity control. It was a superb system, made even more so by the certainty that the Wizard had upgraded it with high-tech components. It wouldn't surprise Bolan if the missiles were heat seekers.

Tego frantically spun the wheel. His boat, faster than the rest, was nearest to the dock, on the off side from the shed.

Bolan was ready to dive overboard if a missile came toward them. There would be a split-second warning, hardly enough to move a muscle let alone leap into the water. But he wasn't about to meet his end meekly.

With a riveting hiss and growling roar the first missile streaked from the launcher. In the blink of an eye it struck one of the police vessels. The explosion this time was louder and more devastating. There was virtually nothing left of the boat or its occupants.

Hardly had the reality of the awful loss sunk in than a second missile was fired. This one arced too high. The autopilot compensated, and the missile executed a loop that lanced it into the prow of the last police craft in the line. Two of the officers attempted to jump to safety but they barely cleared the rail when the detonator went off.

Bolan braced for a third missile. No more were fired, and the ravaged flotilla neared its destination. He replaced the M-16's magazine while scanning the shoreline for hardmen. There had to be gunners somewhere, he reflected. The PT boat and the missile launcher hadn't activated themselves.

Tego slowed the fishing vessel to avoid ramming into the dock. He was bent over the wheel, staring fearfully landward, as if afraid of being sniped at.

Which was a distinct possibility, Bolan mused. Keeping low, he gripped the rail with one hand, gauged the distance and vaulted up and over when the boat was close enough. He alighted on the balls of his feet near a stack of crates and promptly ducked behind them. Propping an elbow on the top one, he trained the M-16 on the shore to provide covering fire, then yelled, "Everyone off and hit the dirt!"

Mandeville was the first to comply. The government man came armed with a matched pair of stainless-steel Smith & Wesson Model 5906 9 mm pistols. He had shunned using an Enfield, and had confided in Bolan before they left Savanna la Mar that he had no idea how to use an M-16. "I'm not much of a marksman. I like to spray the area with lead and just hope I hit something."

Bolan had advised Mandeville to hit the deck if a firefight broke out, but the man had ignored him. The Jamaican insisted on facing the same dangers as those under him.

Now, with the liaison safely shielded by crates, Bolan signaled and the rest leaped from the fishing boat. Sangster and another man tied the vessel fast. Meanwhile, the surviving police craft arrived. One berthed at the dock while the last two were purposely beached on either side of the short pier.

As had been arranged in advance, the policemen fanned out in a line along the shore. Only sixteen of the original thirty were left.

Bolan, Mandeville and Sangster were at the middle. On the trip to the island, the soldier and the liaison had talked it over and agreed that Bolan should assume tactical command once they set foot on Xaymaca. He did so now by motioning for the others to stay down while he rose and sprinted to the shed in which the missile launcher had been concealed.

A quick look showed Bolan that the shed was otherwise empty. It had been built for the specific purpose of concealing the launcher. Warily moving to the rear corner, he saw several cables that came out the back of the shed and angled into the ground. He suspected that the lines ran underground up to the bungalow, where the control console was located.

Returning to the open door, Bolan motioned. The Jamaicans rose and started to cross the strip of sand. Unexpectedly there was a tremendous crump and one of the policemen was flung into the air as if he were a rag doll. Sand and earth flew in all directions. The officer smashed onto the ground with a sickening crunch. He made no move to rise. There was no point in rushing to his aid. The man was obviously dead.

A mine. Bolan studied the shore closely. Sometimes when mines were buried, the dirt on top of them later settled, leaving telltale shallow depressions. Not so in this instance. Whoever buried them had done a top-notch job.

"Mr. Belasko!" Sangster called out. "What do we do? My men aren't equipped for this."

Bolan wracked his brain. So far the Wizard and his men hadn't shown themselves, but they were bound to at any moment. If they did, they'd be able to pick off the stranded policemen at their leisure. He had to get those men to safety. But how? Bolan scoured the beach once more and inspiration struck.

A wide path led from the edge of the forest to the bungalow. Judging by tire tracks in the dirt, he knew that some sort of vehicle used the path to transport supplies up to the Wizard's lair. That same vehicle had to be able to safely cross the beach between the dock and the edge of the forest.

Sure enough, Bolan spied a long row of smudge marks that had once been clear tracks. Someone had erased every last vestige of tire prints, but in doing so they had failed to take into account that by brushing out the tracks, they left smudge marks where the tracks had been.

"Look here!" Bolan shouted, pointing. "It's a safe path through the mine field."

Mandeville looked but shook his head. "I see nothing. What do you mean?"

The lieutenant moved gingerly forward. "Wait! I think I understand! Follow me, all of you. Step exactly where I step, and you'll be all right."

Bolan had to admire the policeman's courage. Sangster crossed swiftly, licking his lips with every stride he took. Once he gained the cover of the vegetation, the rest were quick to imitate his example. Bolan stepped to the path and scanned the slope above.

"It is probably booby-trapped," Mandeville commented.

The warrior nodded. They would be better off melting into the forest, and he said as much. But no sooner did several of the men rise and advance than one of them screeched in mortal agony and toppled back into view. He looked like a porcupine. A score of short spears bristled from his chest and legs. Dead on his feet, the man pitched onto his face.

Bolan ran over to him. The policeman had blundered across a trip wire, which triggered an ingenious device. Twenty hollow metal tubes had been attached in four rows to a man-size frame. Each tube operated on the same principle as a pellet gun in that the spears had been propelled by cartridges of compressed gas. The Vietcong had nothing on Trask.

Mandeville and Sangster joined him.

"This is horrible," the liaison said. "Half our force has been eliminated, and we haven't even had a glimpse of the fiend we're after. How many more must perish before we find him?" Sadly he shook his head. "If I had it to do over again, I would bring in a battalion of soldiers."

The lieutenant squared his shoulders. "My men can do the job, sir. Don't give up on us."

Mandeville faced Bolan. "What would you suggest? Do we take the path or work our way through the forest?"

"It doesn't seem to matter," Bolan said. "To be on the safe side, I'd like to go on up the path by myself. I've had a lot of experience along these lines."

This time Mandeville didn't debate the issue. "Very well. But we'll follow close behind in case you're ambushed or taken out of commission. After the slaughter I've witnessed today, I won't rest until this Wizard is in custody or dead."

Bolan moved to the path. The tire tracks were clearly imbedded in the soft soil, so he had no problem placing his feet on top of the tread marks on the right side. He did so because he reasoned that if there were triggering devices planted along the pathway, they'd be in the middle or along both borders.

Still, Bolan couldn't be positive. A genius like Trask wouldn't be predictable. Alert for trip wires and electronic sensors, he placed each foot carefully. He dared not rush.

At the same time, Bolan had to keep watch for hidden gunners. He surveyed the trees, the brush, the grass along the path. When he had covered fifty feet, the rasp of a rifle bolt being thrown made him glance over a shoulder. Mandeville and the policeman had started up after him. He wanted to wave them back but knew the government man wouldn't listen.

Bolan spied a wide shelf above. Parked to one side was an orange tractor, and hitched to the tractor was a trailer. Now he knew how the Wizard's equipment and supplies had been hauled from the dock. He took a few more steps, then halted when one of the policemen cried out. The warrior shifted.

Several of the Jamaicans were in the middle of the path instead of stepping in the tire tracks as Bolan had done. The first man had stopped in astonishment and was pointing at a peculiar metal rod that had popped up from under the earth directly in front of him.

It had to be a triggering device. Bolan was about to warn them to take cover when a series of metallic clicks sounded up above. The noise came from the shelf, where an M-60 machine gun mounted on a tripod had just materialized out of nowhere. He heard the link belt ratchet into firing position in the chamber and threw himself to the right.

"Get off the path! Find cover!"

The warning came a second too late. The gas-operated weapon cut loose with a vengeance. Capable of firing six hundred rounds per minute, the M-60 chewed up the path below the projecting rod, dicing the base of the hill in an *S* pattern. Policemen scrambled for cover, but several weren't quite fast enough and paid with their lives.

Bolan saw the rounds sweep toward Sangster, who rolled aside in the nick of time. Rising, the soldier sprinted toward the shelf. The heavy chatter of the M-60 brought to mind the killing fields of Vietnam, where countless had seen service. He locked his eyes on the muzzle in case it swung toward him.

Electronically guided, the machine gun swung in a tight arc, back and forth, while the belt fed through at the proper speed. It seemed to have a limitless supply of ammo.

Then Bolan reached the rim and flattened. He sighted on a large black box that had been mounted to the underside of the weapon, just behind the trigger grip. Cables ran out the bottom of that box into the soil. It had to be the control mechanism.

Bolan emptied his magazine on full-auto, generating a hailstorm of slugs that punctured the side of the black box. Sparks flew. There was a loud crackling and smoke poured from the holes like water from a sieve. As suddenly as the M-60 had begun to fire, it stopped.

Three bodies dotted the path. Sangster rallied the rest and led them onward. Mandeville stood over the slain officers a moment, his head bowed.

Bolan had seen enough good men die that day. He hurried on before they could catch up, sticking to the track marks. Soon he reached the end of the path. The bungalow loomed before him.

No hardmen appeared to challenge him. No machine guns or missile launchers rose up out of the ground to blast at him. The bungalow was as still as death.

"Wait up, Mr. Belasko!" Mandeville called.

Fully aware that the dwelling probably harbored its share of nasty surprises, Bolan ignored the liaison and slipped inside. The instant he did, the door locked itself behind him.

CHAPTER SIXTEEN

Mack Bolan never, ever committed a foolhardy act. He was too disciplined a person to act on reckless impulse. Above all else, he was a tactician. Planning and strategy were everything to him. It explained why he never went up against an enemy without first learning all he could about that enemy. It was simply not in his nature to leave anything to chance if it could possibly be avoided.

In the heat of combat, Bolan's fertile mind worked like a whirlwind. He didn't so much react to situations as he acted on them.

The Jamaicans thought the Executioner was crazy to rush up the slope alone and enter the den of the murderous Wizard by himself. Yet it was a calculated gamble on his part to spare more of them from being mowed down. They were no match for the Wizard's many lethal booby traps. Unless something was done quickly, there was a very real likelihood none of them would ever leave the island alive.

When Bolan heard the click of the door being locked, he instantly whirled and crouched. The door was made of wood, so he could still get out that way if he had to by shattering it with a burst from the M-16. And there were also two small windows through which he could escape. He was far from trapped.

The warrior strained his ears to catch other sounds. A wall clock ticked loudly. A small refrigerator hummed next to a sink. He hoped to hear the louder hum of a generator but didn't. Yet there had to be one somewhere, or maybe two or three. The Wizard's many devices required an ample power source.

Bolan warily crossed the kitchen to an open doorway. Beyond lay a hallway. There was no trip wire that he could see, so he checked both jambs for hidden sensors but found none. The doorway appeared safe, yet Bolan didn't cross the threshold. He had a gut feeling that something was wrong, and he wasn't going to go any farther until he found out what.

Then he glanced up at the lintel. A pair of opaque glass eyes peered back at him. Each was recessed into the wood about six inches from either jamb. Backing up and stepping slightly to one side, he extended the rifle barrel and passed the muzzle under one of the electronic eyes.

Bolan had no idea what would happen but he never figured on a dozen metal spikes bursting up through the floor. Anyone entering the hall would have been impaled. Crouching, he examined the razor sharp tips of the spikes. All were coated with a sticky brown substance. Poison, he realized.

Looking around, Bolan spotted a closet in the corner. He opened it and removed a broom, which he took with him to the hall. Before stepping over the spikes, the

Executioner poked and prodded the floor beyond and ran the broom handle up and down both walls and along the ceiling. Nothing happened.

Cautiously, Bolan advanced. He tested the floor with the broom every foot of the way, his eyes constantly searching for sensors. About ten feet from the kitchen he suddenly halted.

The floor didn't look right. A few feet way, in the very middle, a square section about six inches wide was elevated a fraction of an inch above the rest of the floor. It had to be another triggering device, a pressure plate that would activate when weight was placed on that particular spot.

Bolan took a long stride over the plate and kept on going. On his right was a doorway. A glance revealed an empty bedroom that he decided to search later.

As the soldier neared the next door he heard another hum. But it wasn't the purr of a generator. Rather, it was the muted whine of a computer, a state-of-the-art model with a large 234 color monitor and a laser printer that he saw a moment later. File cabinets lined one wall. Another was devoted to bas-relief maps of every corner of the globe. Tacked to a third wall were circuitry schematics and handmade sketches of electronic devices. It was a treasure trove of information. But there was no sign of the Wizard or any of his henchmen.

Bolan didn't know what to make of it. Clearly Trask had flown the coop. Yet why, then, had a man as intelligent as Trask neglected to take so many crucial papers along?

He carefully moved to the cabinets and opened the first one, which was empty. So was the second, and the third. A closer look at the schematics on the wall showed that most had been clipped from technical journals. The hand-drawn diagrams were for simple triggering devices, not sophisticated detonators or the like.

Bolan stepped to the chair in front of the computer. He pressed the seat with the broom handle. When assured it wouldn't blow up if he sat down, he did so and faced the monitor. It was blank except for the bright yellow cursor that blinked on and off like a miniature neon light.

Just to see what would come up, Bolan pressed the Enter key. Text appeared on the screen. It was a letter, and it began with To Whom It May Concern. Bolan read on.

> I must congratulate you on reaching this room unscathed. It must have been difficult to overcome my computer-controlled defense array. I hope you won't be too terribly disappointed that I'm not at home. A skilled chess player, like a good general, knows when to attack and when to cut losses and retreat. And I have always been extraordinarily good at chess.
>
> After all your effort, it must be upsetting to learn that the most you have done is set my timetable back by a few days.

Xaymaca isn't my only sanctuary. By the time you read this, I'll be well on my way to one of the hideaways I keep in reserve for this very contingency.

Oh. Before I forget. This entire bungalow is wired to blow. I installed a seventy-second delay to give you time to read my note. It was triggered when you pressed your first key on the keyboard.

There was more, a final mocking paragraph, but Bolan didn't stick around to read it. Hurling himself from the chair, he ran from the room. He reminded himself to leap over the pressure plate. A single jump also took him over the toxin-tipped stakes.

Tucking the M-16 to his side, Bolan called out, "Get away from the door!" in case any Jamaicans were on the other side. Then he stroked the trigger. The panels splintered and dissolved under the withering autofire.

Lowering a shoulder, Bolan slammed into the door like a human battering ram. It exploded under the impact, and then he was in the sunlight and racing toward the rim of the shelf. Rooted in place on the path were Mandeville, Sangster and the rest of the assault squad.

"Run!" Bolan shouted. "The place is going to blow!"

The Jamaicans fled. The Executioner was right behind them as they crossed the shelf and poured down the slope. Time was almost up.

"Hit the dirt!" Bolan warned, and heeded his own advice. He slid when he landed, scuffing his elbows and knees. They were the least of his worries as above him the bungalow went up.

He felt the earth under him shimmer and shake as his ears were assaulted by a roar like that of an erupting volcano. A gust of hot wind fanned him, followed by a choking cloud of dust. The debris was next, raining like oversize hail, pelting him and the Jamaicans. One man cried out in pain. Bolan covered his head with both arms and didn't move until the crack and crackle of falling objects died out.

Slowly he rose, swiped at lingering tendrils of dust and coughed. Off to the right lay a policeman with a five-foot length of slender wood imbedded in his lower back. The man was alive but wouldn't be for long. Others were tending him, so Bolan climbed back up to the shelf.

The bungalow was gone, a smoking crater all that remained.

The soldier stared at it a moment, then, in turn, at the doomed policeman, at the men who had been mowed down earlier by the machine gun, and at the shed that had housed the missile launcher. It dawned on him that Mandeville had been right. Of all the terrorists Bolan had ever gone up against, the Wizard had to be one of the most diabolical. If anyone could come up with a way of circumventing presidential security and assassinating the chief executive, it was Trask.

Somehow, some way, Bolan had to stop him before it was too late.

HAL BROGNOLA had a file on Adolpho Garcia waiting on his desk for Bolan to see when the Executioner returned to Miami. The big Fed listened impassively as Bolan recounted the events of the day.

"We almost had him," Bolan noted.

"At least we have the bastard on the run," Brognola said. "Despite what he claimed, we must have put a major crimp in his operation. Even if he has another network in place elsewhere, it'll take a while to get every element running as smoothly as his Miami operation. I'd say we've set the Wizard back a month or better."

"Let's hope so."

Brognola looked as if he hadn't slept in days. He ran a hand across his face and yawned. "On to other matters. I've relayed the names of that blonde and her friend to all appropriate agencies, including some overseas, such as Scotland Yard and Interpol. Maybe we'll get lucky. Their MO is unique in that not many pros prefer a garrote."

"What I'd like to know is whether they work for Trask or whether they were trying to find him themselves."

Brognola straightened. "I assumed they were covering his tracks."

"So did I, until Tego told me that he had never seen the pair before. Yet he had met Loomis and the other gunners. It made me wonder."

"Hmm. Maybe you're on to something. But they can't be government agents, not with their penchant for spilling blood. So either they're free-lance or they've been hired by a third party to track down Trask." The big Fed balled his fist and propped his chin on it. "But why? Is there a contract out on him? Or is there a lot more to their involvement than I suspected?" He gave a sheepish smile. "Thanks. I almost overlooked a crucial angle."

"What about Trask? Anything new on his real identity and background?"

"I wish. Cowboy called a while ago to tell me that he might be on to something. Said he'd know by tomorrow sometime."

"So once again we're left holding the bag."

"Not quite." Brognola pushed the file across the desk, then stood. "Take a gander at this. I'll be back in a while to see how you want to proceed."

The file was an inch thick and contained every scrap of Intel the Mexican government had on Adolpho Garcia. Age, 39. Height, five feet eight inches. Weight, 210 pounds.

Garcia had been raised in Mérida on the Yucatán Peninsula. Always causing his parents grief, the final straw had come at the age of ten when he threatened to stab his father. They had abandoned him, and Garcia had taken to the streets. After several brushes with the law, he left for Mexico City and fell in with the criminal element.

Before long Garcia earned a reputation as a triggerman. He drew the interest of Luis Terrazas, who took Garcia on as a lowly gunner but in a short time made him one of his top lieutenants.

Garcia was put in charge of enforcement and carried out his job with ruthless abandon. When a rival drug czar tried to muscle in on Terrazas's action in Mexico City, Garcia and some cronies disguised themselves as priests and gunned the man down as he came out of his favorite restaurant.

Another time Garcia was sent north of the border. One of the middlemen in the Terrazas pipeline had gone bad and was skimming drugs and money off the top. As a warning to other underlings who might get the same idea, Garcia hacked the culprit to pieces with an ax. After that, no one dared cheat Terrazas again.

Unfortunately Garcia hadn't been at the stronghold during Bolan's penetration. By all accounts, the psychopath was in Colombia at the time, cementing Terrazas's ties to a cartel. Informants had told Mexican authorities that Garcia had been incensed when he came back and learned of Terrazas's death. He had personally killed two other lieutenants for failing to protect their boss.

A short power struggle had ensued to see who would step into Terrazas's shoes. In less than six hours' time, Garcia had beheaded one pretender to the throne and had another tossed alive into a pit of rattlesnakes.

Now Adolpho Garcia was the sole head of the drug empire. His first order of business was rumored to be paying back those he held responsible for the death of Luis Terrazas, namely the United States government. He had vowed that he would take the life of the President before too long, and he was willing to pay the Wizard top dollar to insure the job was done right.

Bolan tossed the report on the desk, rose and walked to the window. He leaned on the pane and watched a fire truck wind through the streets below, its lights flashing, siren wailing.

It disturbed Bolan to think that after all he had been through, he was right back at square one. Disposing of Terrazas had no impact whatsoever on the drug empire Terrazas created. Now a man who was twice as cold-blooded ruled the roost. The situation was worse than it had been when Bolan agreed to take Terrazas down.

Added to that was the unsettling fact that the Wizard had gotten away. Trask was free to do as Garcia wanted, and there was no telling how soon the plan would be carried out.

It was a nightmare scenario.

The vast resources of the Justice Department and related agencies were hard at work trying to find the Wizard. Given his track record, Bolan wasn't confident they'd succeed before Garcia struck.

The only bright note in the bleak picture was that Mexican authorities knew where Adolpho Garcia was setting up shop. He had moved the base of operations from northern Mexico to his old stomping grounds on the Yucatán Peninsula.

But while the Mexican *federales* had a good idea where to find Garcia, bringing him in was another story. He had learned his lessons from Terrazas well. Evidently he had certain high-ranking political and military officials in his pocket. No one could get anywhere near him.

Or so Adolpho Garcia believed.

Mack Bolan was going to prove the butcher wrong.

Jamaica

LIEUTENANT SANGSTER was catching up on paperwork at his desk when someone rapped on his office door. A young policeman named Domingo stood there holding a sheet of paper. "Come in," Sangster said.

The man entered and snapped smartly to attention. His uniform was crisply clean, his shoes had been polished to a fine shine. In short, he was everything Sangster like to see in his men, and he put Domingo at ease with a friendly smile.

"What have you uncovered?"

"I have made the rounds of postal offices as you requested, sir. None of those in the city limits have any record of unusual shipments made within the past day or two."

"That's too bad. I had high hopes it would pan out."

The young policeman smiled slyly. "It did, sir."

"But you just told me differently."

"I know, sir. None in Savanna la Mar were helpful. But on a hunch I went to a few of the rural offices. And a man at the nearest one to the north recalled sending off several large packages for an American who was in a very great hurry."

Excitement coursed through Sangster, but he didn't let it show. "A tourist, maybe?"

"I thought of that, sir, and questioned him most carefully. It was his opinion that this American didn't act like a typical sightseer." Domingo paused. "I examined the customs form. This American shipped electronics equipment to an address in the States."

Sangster half rose out of his chair, then caught himself and sat back down. "What kind of equipment?" he asked excitedly.

"The American told the postal worker that one was a radio and another a cassette player. The worker inspected them, as required, and okayed their shipment."

"But?" the lieutenant prompted when his subordinate grinned.

"When I pressed him, he admitted that the equipment wasn't like any other he had ever seen. He said as much to the American and was told they were the very best components money can buy."

The reports Sangster had been working on were completely forgotten. This took precedence. He had reasoned that if the Wizard had to flee the country quickly, say on a commercial flight, the man wouldn't have been able to take much with him. Yet it seemed logical that an electronics genius would have certain pieces of equipment he wouldn't care to part with. So Sangster had sent out Domingo to make the rounds, never really expecting the officer to turn up anything.

"There is more," the younger man said. "This American paid for the shipment with cash. The worker told me that this man had the biggest wad of bills the worker had ever seen. His exact words were 'as thick as a telephone book.'"

"You obtained the address, of course."

Smiling, Domingo handed over the sheet. "And a description of the suspect. The post offices are closed for the day, but I'll go out again bright and early if you want me to."

"Do so," Sangster commanded, impressed. Domingo reminded him of himself twenty years earlier. It took zeal and initiative to rise to the top. Domingo had both. As the man turned to go, he added, "Well done. This will reflect well when you come up for promotion."

"Thank you, sir." The patrolman went off walking on air.

Sangster read the sheet, folded it and slid it into his shirt pocket. He had promised to keep Eric Mandeville posted. The clock on the wall showed that he had more than an hour to kill before he was supposed to call Kingston, though. So he rose, took his hat from the rack and headed out into the muggy Jamaican night.

It had been a long day. Sangster hadn't bothered to eat since waking up, and he was famished. A few blocks from headquarters was a restaurant he liked. He headed toward it, deep in thought.

Sangster had long cherished the idea of moving up in rank. Since there were so few captains on the force, it would be years before that avenue panned out. A better idea, he believed, was to land a government job. The only hitch was that they were hard to come by unless a person knew someone with influence.

The policeman saw Eric Mandeville as the answer to his prayer. He knew that Mandeville liked him. Uncovering a few important leads might be all it took to convince the man that his talents were being wasted in Savanna la Mar. A few discreet words, and he could soon be living in Kingston.

It wasn't an easy decision for Sangster to make. He loved being a policeman. It was his whole life. He had given up having a wife and children to further his career. He had stuck with it even though the pay was too low and the risks too high. To think of never wearing the uniform again made him too sad for words.

The lieutenant was about halfway to the restaurant when a low groan rose from an alley on his left. It broke his train of thought. Halting, he turned and studied the murky depths. Garbage cans and boxes were lined against one wall. Thirty feet back a figure knelt, arms clasped to its side.

The groan was repeated. This time Sangster could tell it was a woman. He draped his left hand on his revolver and moved slowly toward her. "Miss? I am a police officer. What is the matter with you?"

The woman groaned louder.

Fearing she might have been mugged or worse, Sangster hastened forward and bent to touch her shoulder. Only then did he see the mane of yellow hair partially hidden by a black cap. He started to draw back, but the blonde was quicker. The business end of a sound suppressor hovered close to his cheek.

"Hello, Lieutenant. Remember me?"

"Katya Steiner," Sangster said. "I'm placing you under arrest."

"Not in this life." The blonde uncurled, stripped him of his weapon and pulled him deeper into the alley. "I bet you're surprised to see me still in the country. But my friend and I aren't ready to leave just yet. We need information. And since the newspaper says that you are in charge of the investigation into what went on out at Xaymaca, you might have it."

"I'll tell you nothing."

"Oh, I think you will," Steiner taunted. "You'll reveal all you have uncovered about the man they call the Wizard. And if you do not, you'll die."

Sangster dug in his heels and refused to be budged. If he was going to die, he'd do so with dignity. "Who are you kidding, woman? You intend to kill me no matter what I do." With that, he lunged, trying to swat her pistol aside. As he did, something brushed his forehead, nose and chin in that order. The next moment his breath was abruptly cut off.

With a start, Sangster realized that something long and thin had been clamped around his neck. It was a garrote! Shifting, he sought to grab the man who stood behind him, but the blonde sprang and caught hold of his arms.

As darkness closed in on him, Sangster realized that Belasko had been right all along. It was possible to kill someone so swiftly that they had no time to cry out.

None at all.

CHAPTER SEVENTEEN

Mack Bolan and Jack Grimaldi were seated in a Rockwell OV-10A Bronco aircraft. It was designed for counterinsurgency use and sported a pair of Garrett turboprops, a full array of electronic equipment and twin 7.62 mm machine guns. Short, sleek and fast, the Bronco saw frequent use by CIA operatives.

At close to three hundred miles per hour the aircraft winged over the Gulf of Mexico toward Yucatán. Grimaldi flew at sea level, so they wouldn't be picked up on any radar.

"Another ten minutes, Sarge."

"Let's just hope that strip is still there."

The airstrip Bolan referred to had shown up on early satellite recon photos taken of the peninsula. Records indicated it had been built years earlier by a mining consortium hoping to find minerals in the region. Their effort had been a bust, so the outfit had pulled up stakes and left.

The strip was located high in the rolling tableland that made up the Yucatán Peninsula. Once Bolan set down, he would have to cover another twenty-five miles to reach his destination.

According to the latest Intel from Mexican authorities, Adolpho Garcia was having a virtual fortress built a day's ride from the town of Ticul. Garcia was supposed to be there at that very moment, with all his lieutenants, supervising the construction.

If Bolan had his way, the new drug lord wouldn't live long enough to see the place completed. And this time he was going to insure that the drug ring would be put out of business permanently. The threat to the President would be neutralized.

But Bolan had a hard job cut out for him. The terrain was rough, alternating between steep hills and lowland jungle. Jaguars were common, as were large snakes that could crush a man to pulp.

There were also the Yucatecos, descendants of the Maya Indians. Many made their living by farming. Others hunted. Most were wary of outsiders, and the wilder ones weren't above putting an arrow or spear into the back of an unsuspecting gringo who was where he had no business being.

Bolan spent the next few minutes double-checking his gear. He wore camouflage fatigues crammed with the special tools of his deadly craft. He'd brought along his usual weapons of choice, a Beretta and a Desert Eagle. Instead of an M-16, though, on this mission he had a Weatherby Mark V big-game rifle. A backpack lay at his feet. He had stuffed it with spare ammo, rations, fifteen pounds of C-4 plastic explosive, detonation cord and several radio detonators.

"Thar she blows!" Grimaldi quipped.

Bolan looked up to see the shoreline sweep toward them. They streaked in low and fast over an isolated cove, then veered off across the flatland choked with undergrowth, making for the high green hills beyond.

The pilot had picked their route with care. At no time did they pass anywhere near a town or village. Except for short stretches when they were forced to fly over isolated farms, they saw no sign of human habitation.

Grimaldi avoided all roads, too, except for one. He had no choice. No plane could reach the interior without passing over the highway that bisected the peninsula from west to east.

The Stony Man pilot had picked a point midway between two isolated towns. Should anyone spot them and become suspicious, it would take hours for that party to get to a telephone. By then Bolan would be safely down and Grimaldi would be halfway back across the Gulf.

The unmarked Bronco banked as Grimaldi gained more altitude. The land climbed dramatically. Soon they were over the tableland, the turboprops whining at full power.

Bolan stared down at the landscape, seeking the landmarks he had memorized. He could see the shadow of the aircraft below them, zipping across the foliage. When the confluence of two streams appeared, he quickly consulted a map.

"One minute to the drop-off point."

"Keep your fingers crossed that it's not so overgrown we can't land."

The strip had been built on the flat-topped crown of a hill and ran from east to west. Grimaldi saw it first, reduced air speed and dipped the nose of the aircraft.

Bolan saw a number of structures to the north of the asphalt ribbon. They were supposed to be deserted, but as the aircraft looped to the west to make its approach, he saw a shadowy figure appear in the doorway of one.

"Did you see that, Sarge?"

"Sure did."

"What do we do? Abort?"

The soldier thought fast. He had to avoid whoever was down there, even if they were friendlies. The east end of the strip, he observed, stopped within yards of dense woodland. Pointing that out to Grimaldi, he directed, "Take me as close to the trees as you can. I can lose myself in there before anyone gets too close."

"You're the boss."

The Bronco banked steeply, well into its loop. Grimaldi whistled to himself as he sank steadily lower. "It's looking good," he declared. "But stay strapped in. The landing will be a bit bumpy."

Which proved to be an understatement. The strip was pitted with ruts and cracks. Numerous potholes dotted its length. Grimaldi throttled down and brought the bird in as lightly as a feather. Even so, the wheels were jarred by the rough surface. Exercising skill few possessed, Grimaldi weaved among the pockmarks, avoiding those that threatened to buckle the landing gear.

As the aircraft shot past the buildings, Bolan saw more watchers. He had only a glimpse of them but it was enough to tell him they weren't Indians. Then the brakes squealed and the Bronco slowly came to a halt at the very edge of the runway. Mere feet separated the tip of the right wing from the trees.

"How's this for service?"

Bolan undid the seat restraints, slung on the backpack, grabbed the Weatherby and was ready when the cockpit slid open. He was out and over the side in a flash. His soles stung when his boots smacked the pavement. Shouts arose from the buildings, and several men raced toward the plane. Without delay he melted into the vegetation.

Grimaldi lost no time preparing to take off. In moments the turboprops revved and the nose of the Bronco swung around. Just as the aircraft lurched forward, shots rang out.

Bolan snapped the rifle to his shoulder and pressed his right eye to the telescopic sight. There were six men, all dressed in grungy clothes, all wearing sombreros. They were armed to the proverbial teeth, with bandoliers crisscrossing their chests and revolvers on their hips. A few fired at the Bronco with antiquated rifles.

Whoever they were, they weren't government troops. Bolan was positive of that. His best guess was that they were gunrunners or smugglers who had claimed the strip as their own. Either that or they were ordinary bandits, throwbacks to the days when *bandidos* harried travelers from one end of Mexico to another.

Bolan couldn't let them cripple the Bronco. He worked the bolt of the Weatherby and fed three .378 Weatherby Magnum cartridges into the weapon. The gunman nearest the strip was taking deliberate aim at the cockpit, at Grimaldi. Bolan lined up the cross hairs of his scope on the man's skull. Not pausing to take a breath in order to steady his aim, he stroked the trigger.

The big rifle boomed and bucked the stock against the Executioner's shoulder. At the same instant, the Mexican was blown back into the dirt.

The gunners had stopped firing at the Bronco. They dived prone as it zipped past them and took to the air in a tight power climb. In seconds Grimaldi was safely out of range.

Bolan was about to head out when the gunmen got to their feet and sprinted toward him. They fanned out as they neared the tree line. It looked as if he had an unwanted firefight on his hands. Then he saw the Bronco.

Grimaldi executed a loop and came in over the airstrip from the northwest, both machine guns hammering like pneumatic drills. Twin paths of 7.62 mm slugs converged on the Mexicans. One of them shouted in alarm and they all scattered.

A portly gunner was a shade slow. The rounds chewed into him and he seemed to dance in place, his arms and legs flinging about in a macabre jig. Holes riddled him from chin to toes. As the Bronco screamed overhead and flashed off to the east, the man pitched onto his face.

Bolan cradled the Weatherby and jogged eastward for fifty yards, then cut to the left. He planned to work his way around the airstrip. Once in the clear, he would stick to a southwesterly compass bearing until he reached the vicinity of Adolpho Garcia's stronghold.

It soon became apparent that the gunmen weren't going to let him slip quietly away. He heard voices and, looking back, spotted figures near the spot where he had turned to the north. A thin man in a wide sombrero was bent over his tracks. The man gave a yell and pointed in the new direction Bolan had taken.

The soldier picked up the pace. Burdened as he was with more than fifty pounds of equipment, he couldn't sustain a long chase. It would be wiser to elude them quickly. To that end, he broke off a thin branch heavy with leaves, turned and erased the tracks he made while swiftly backpedaling. It was an old trick and wouldn't fool a competent tracker, since the brush marks were dead giveaways, but it might buy him some time.

After traveling a hundred yards Bolan cast the branch aside and broke into a run. Suddenly, to his left, appeared the buildings that lined the middle of the airstrip. He had half a mind to go over and see what the gunmen were up to, but he pressed on. The mission came first.

Bolan was almost past the buildings when he saw a pair of shapes dart around a corner and plunge into the woods. Their intent was plain. They were trying to head him off.

Stopping behind a tree, Bolan slung the Weatherby over his left shoulder and drew the Beretta. He removed a sound suppressor from a pocket of his fatigue pants and attached it. He went on slowly, avoiding twigs that might snap, leaves that might rustle. The gunners were forty feet in front of him, scouring the woods.

Lowering onto his belly, Bolan snaked along until he saw one of the men clearly. The guy held a repeating rifle, an old Winchester from the looks of it, and was coming toward him. Bolan crawled under a bush and waited.

The bandit had a round face lined with stubble. His eyes darted from side to side as he walked. Often he stopped to listen.

Bolan could hear rustling in the undergrowth to the east. The first group of gunners would soon be there.

He adopted a two-handed grip and slanted the Beretta up through the thin limbs of the bush. The man was ten feet off and closing. Bolan centered the muzzle on the gunman's chest. He could see beads of sweat on the rifleman's brow when he fired, twice.

Soundlessly the gunner crumpled to the ground.

The other one was twenty feet away, moving parallel to his companion. He didn't hear the cough of the sound suppressor or see his friend drop. Bolan let the man go by, then he rose and ran, staying low until he was screened by the vegetation. Shoving the Beretta into its shoulder rig, he sprinted flat out, his hand on the Weatherby's smooth walnut stock to keep the rifle from slipping off his shoulder.

Bolan hoped that the second death would end it. Whoever they were, they wouldn't want to lose more men and were bound to give up the pursuit. That was the logical thing to do. But then he had second thoughts.

As the soldier had learned long ago, when dealing with the vermin against whom he waged an eternal war, it was better to always expect the unexpected. Terrorists, killers, the Mob and thugs of every sort lived by a twisted, violent creed. There was no predicting how they might act in any given situation. They were like sidewinders—one never knew when they would strike or when they would turn tail and slink off.

In another minute a bellow of rage told him the body had been found. Bolan moved on, settling into a ground-eating dogtrot.

He had traveled more than a quarter of a mile when the sharp crack of a breaking twig confirmed the bandits were still on his trail. Pausing, he checked but saw no one. As yet.

The mission had gotten off to a bad start and wasn't improving. Somehow Bolan had to shake them, and soon. He couldn't make much headway while having to dodge a pack of cutthroats every step of the way.

Another factor was the time constraint Bolan was under. He had only three days in which to terminate Garcia and reach the site where he was to rendezvous with Grimaldi, a spot along a secondary road five miles west of Ticul. They wouldn't use the airstrip twice. As a safety measure, it was wise never to rely on the same site for both insertion and retrieval.

So Bolan had to end it soon. For the next quarter hour he pushed himself to his limit to gain a greater lead. Then he stopped in the shelter of a stand of saplings to study a topographical map he had brought along. It not only showed the elevations of all the surrounding hills, but the precise geographic contours.

After a couple of minutes of study Bolan folded the map and slipped it back into a fatigue pocket. Instead of heading southwest as he was supposed to, he angled to the northwest. Soon he reached the side of the hill and descended the steep slope.

The next hill rose several hundred yards to a flat bench, and from there climbed sharply to an isolated pinnacle. It was the pinnacle that interested Bolan. A sniper always went for the high ground when there was any to be found.

The climb was arduous. The angle was such that Bolan had to dig in his heels and often grabbed handy vegetation for purchase. It slowed him considerably, which wasn't a problem because it would also slow the gunners. When they reached the benchland, they would be exhausted, which would make them that much easier to take out.

Halfway up, a fissure abruptly barred his path. It was over sixty feet deep but only five feet across. Backing up a dozen yards, Bolan took a short, quick breaths to oxygenate his lungs, then sped forward. At the very brink he hurtled into the air, his legs spread wide, bent slightly at the waist so he wouldn't lose his balance when he landed.

He came down well clear of the rim. Or so he assumed, when suddenly the earth gave way under him and he started to toppled backward. He threw his body forward and tried to find solid footing but loose dirt spewed out from under his combat boots.

The yawning fissure was about to swallow the Executioner whole. As a last resort, he flung himself flat and dug his fingers into the soil, catching hold of grass and bushes. He clung there, listening to the rattle of the dirt and stones that cascaded from under his waist and legs. For several harrowing seconds it appeared he would follow the shower down to the rocky bottom and be smashed to death on jagged boulders.

Then the shower ceased. Bolan drew up his knees until they were on firm ground and cautiously crawled away from the fissure. When convinced it was safe to do so, he stood and looked back. A sizeable portion of the rim had buckled. Another few inches and he wouldn't have made it.

Bolan adjusted the straps of his backpack and the rifle's sling, then went on. The close call wasn't unique. He wouldn't give it a second thought.

The bench was eighty yards across, dotted with tress and brush. Above it towered the pinnacle. Bolan stood at the base and studied the many cracks and clefts that laced the surface from bottom to top. About thirty feet up there appeared to be a suitable roost, but he wouldn't be able to tell until he climbed that high.

First Bolan removed the backpack and the rifle. The latter he reslung across his back so that it slanted between his shoulder blades. The former he slid on over the rifle to hold it in place for the climb.

When he was ready, he stepped to the pinnacle and began his ascent. He had to cram his fingers into the cracks, then pull himself high enough to do the same with his toes. It was an arduous process. By the time he had climbed fifteen feet he was slick with sweat.

Bolan finally reached the roost, a coffin-size cavity into which he crawled. After unslinging the rifle, he took a box of cartridges, opened it and spread ten of them out in front of him. Two were in the magazine and one went into the chamber. Now all he could do was count the minutes until the bandits showed up.

The Executioner spotted them from a long way off. They were descending the first hill, moving swiftly, obviously accustomed to the terrain.

In the lead was a swarthy man who had to be a Yucateco. He had the features of an Indian and carried himself differently than the rest. His movements were graceful, with no wasted effort. This was a man at home in the highlands, not a city dweller out of his element. Of them all, he was the most dangerous.

Bolan lost sight of the band once they passed below the rim of the bench. He could hear them from time to time, though, as they scaled the steep slope below it.

Unfastening a shirt pocket, he pulled out a small plastic case that contained several screwdrivers. He knew just which one he needed.

Before leaving the States, Bolan had sighted the Weatherby for dead-on accuracy at 150 yards. That was about the average range for the shots he expected to make over roughly level terrain. But now he had to take into account that he would be firing at a sharp angle from an elevation of thirty feet.

Bolan leaned close to the telescopic sight. He adjusted the elevation screw with the utmost care, raising his head several times to gauge the proper setting. When he was satisfied, he returned the screwdriver to his pocket.

Bolan held the rifle back so the sun wouldn't glint off the barrel and give him away. He fixed his eyes on the bench. It wasn't long before the first bandit appeared. He thought it would be the Indian, but it was a scarecrow whose sombrero hung from his scrawny neck by a leather strap.

Bolan inched deeper into the cavity.

One by one the cutthroats climbed into view. There were five, all told. The Yucateco was the last man, and the first thing he did was move to the shelter of a tree and survey the pinnacle. One of the others gestured for him to move on but he shook his head and said something that made the rest scurry for cover.

Bolan wasn't too worried about being spotted; the groove wasn't obvious unless a person stood almost directly below it. He knew the cutthroats would advance sooner or later if they wanted him badly enough. Time was on his side.

In due course the scarecrow pumped an arm and the five men headed across the bench. They darted from cover to cover, the Yucateco blending into the vegetation so well that at times he was invisible.

Bolan let them get halfway across. Then he edged forward, pressed the recoil pad to his shoulder and slowly extended the rifle. The Yucateco was nowhere in sight, but the other four were. He sighted on the scarecrow, the evident leader.

The skinny gunman darted out from behind some bushes and headed for a tree. He never made it. A heavy Magnum slug cored his head from brow to spine and dropped him in his tracks.

The others went to ground so he held his fire. Once they started shooting back, he would pick them off one by one. Seconds went by, then a full minute. He couldn't understand why they were content to lie low until he glimpsed a hefty bandit through a cluster of trees. The man was speaking into a walkie-talkie.

Moments later a helicopter swooped over the crown of the first hill, heading straight for the pinnacle.

CHAPTER EIGHTEEN

The aircraft was an old Hughes Model 269A, a single-rotor job painted a dusky green. The skids had been modified to carry long wooden crates. Bolan had a fair idea of what was in the pair he saw, but he had no time to dwell on it. The chopper was almost on him.

Two men were in the cockpit. The soldier saw the off-side door swing wide, and the passenger swiveled toward the pinnacle, holding a Heckler & Koch MP-5.

Bolan went prone as the man triggered a burst. Parabellum rounds gouged holes and dug furrows all around the cavity. Some hit inside, striking within a hair's breadth of Bolan. He didn't dare to return fire. It would be certain suicide.

Then the firestorm ended and the Executioner heard the copter seek altitude. He rose on his elbows. The gunners below were barreling toward the bottom of the pinnacle. Automatically he dropped one. The rest sought cover as he worked the bolt. Before he could fire again, the chopper angled out of the sky on his left, and the passenger unleashed another burst.

Only a bottom lip rising several inches above the floor of the niche kept Bolan from being drilled repeatedly. Lead blistered the opening. Rounds rattled around, one nicking his shoulder. It was a miracle that he wasn't slain before the subgun's magazine ran dry and the chopper zipped for cover.

Bolan was effectively trapped. He couldn't leave to find shelter elsewhere because the gunners would pick him off the moment he showed himself. By the same token, he couldn't stay there much longer since it was only a matter of minutes before the guy in the copter scored.

Peering down, Bolan saw two of the three gunmen creeping through the brush. He pegged one with a shot through the torso, then quickly inserted two more cartridges. As he did, a shadow fell across the opening.

The helicopter angled for position. The man with the subgun motioned for the pilot to move in closer, but the pilot prudently balked.

All Bolan could see of both men was their heads and shoulders. But that was enough for the tactic he had in mind. He lined up the passenger in his cross hairs but didn't squeeze the trigger. Taking a calculated gamble, he held stock-still as the aircraft drifted a few yards to the right. Then came the moment he had been waiting for, when the head of the pilot was directly behind the head of the passenger and both were in a direct line with the muzzle of his rifle. Bolan fired.

The Executioner's Weatherby was one of the most powerful rifles in existence. For decades the name had meant the ultimate in stopping power. A single shot was enough to bring down a rampaging bull elephant or a charging rhino. When used on a human being, the internal damage a slug caused was devastating.

Part of the reason had to do with the Weatherby's penetrating power. A Weatherby Magnum cartridge, in whatever caliber, boasted a muzzle velocity few other brands could rival.

In Bolan's case, he preferred the Weatherby .378. When he fired at the men in the copter, the slug was propelled from his barrel at a velocity of 3180 feet per second.

The bullet reached the men before either heard the blast of the shot. It caught the machine gunner above the bridge of his nose, tearing through the bone of his cranium and his brain as if both didn't exist, then exited his skull, leaving a hole large enough to insert a fist.

Still traveling at well over twenty-five hundred feet per second, the slug then struck the pilot in the right temple, drilling completely through his frontal lobes. It burst out the left side of his head, taking a good portion of his brain with it.

Bolan saw both men slump simultaneously. The passenger sagged forward and toppled out the open door while the pilot fell back against the seat. The chopper promptly dropped like a rock.

A wavering scream rose from the bench, which was snuffed out by a tremendous crash. Bolan moved to the opening in time to see that the helicopter had smashed down on top of one of the gunmen, crushing the man to a pulp. The fuel tank ignited and the aircraft went up in a ball of flames and dark smoke. Shards of twisted metal struck the pinnacle, some so close to Bolan's perch that he ducked back.

He stayed put in case there was a secondary explosion. An acrid odor tinged with the distinctive smell of burning flesh filled his nostrils. He breathed shallowly until the worst was over.

Bolan edged to the lip. By his reckoning there was only one gunman left, and if he was right, it was the Yucateco, the most dangerous of the bunch. He looked but couldn't spot the man, who was probably waiting for him to show himself.

The soldier wasn't going anywhere for a while. He noticed that the two crates had shattered on impact, scattering their contents over the bench. As he had guessed, dozens of carbines and rifles lay glittering in the glow from the burning wreckage. Inadvertently he had stumbled on a gang of gunrunners who had been using the abandoned airstrip to funnel guns in and out of the country.

What were the odds? Bolan mused as he lowered his right eye to the sight. Try as he might, he still couldn't find the Indian, even aided by the magnification of the scope.

The sun was well on its westward arc. Bolan rested his chin on his forearms and didn't take his eyes off the bench and the neighboring hill until twilight claimed the high tableland and a brisk wind picked up.

The Executioner took a vial of camouflage cosmetics from a pocket and applied it to his face in wide black bands. When he was done he looked like a Sioux warrior about to go on the warpath.

It was now so dark that Bolan could barely see his hand at arm's length. He had stayed there as long as he was going to. Any longer, and he risked missing the rendezvous with Grimaldi. So, slinging the rifle under the backpack as he had done on the climb up, he inched to the lip and contemplated the climb down.

The fire had dwindled to smoldering embers and plumes of gray smoke. Occasionally there would be a loud snap or crackle. The wind carried the smoke away from the pinnacle, which was too bad. Bolan could have used the cover.

He gripped the lip with both hands and slowly swung his body over the edge. It took a moment for his right foot to find purchase. When it did, he eased himself down. No shots greeted his appearance.

Against the backdrop of the pinnacle, Bolan's fatigues would be awfully hard to spot. He hoped. Dropping his left foot lower, he probed until he gained a toehold and dipped downward. In this painstaking manner he carefully descended until he was close enough to the ground to jump.

As Bolan let go, he drew the Desert Eagle. He landed in a combat crouch, primed to answer a muzzle-flash, but none flared in the night. Slanting to the right, he gained the cover of the brush. He listened for the longest while yet heard nothing out of the ordinary. If the Yucateco was still out there, the man wasn't advertising it.

Bolan worked his way in a half circle to the end of the bench. Not once did he spot movement or hear a stealthy tread. The obvious conclusion was that the Yucateco had gone, but he wasn't about to take it for granted.

Taking out his compass, Bolan checked the illuminated needle. Once he had the proper course fixed in his head, he climbed to the bottom of the hill and struck a southwesterly heading.

The delay had set Bolan's timetable back by at least six hours. That didn't seem like much, but being the tactician that he was, he had his schedule worked out to the minute. And while he had allowed himself some leeway, six hours was more than he had allowed for, almost more then he could hope to make up. He had to push himself until the wee hours of the morning if he wanted to make good the time.

A couple of hours went by. Bolan alternated between jogging for long stretches and walking to rest and conserve his energy. He came to the first valley along his route and followed a winding gully to the valley floor. Around him, the vegetation subtly changed. The trees grew bigger and closer together, the plant growth more profuse. Underfoot, the ground became soft and spongy. Animals were everywhere, their roars, squeals and guttural coughs a constant chorus.

Bolan knew the sights and sounds well. He was now in lowland jungle, the environment that had in large measure molded him into the man he was during his tours in Southeast Asia. He had to stay on his toes every step of the way.

In the jungle there were no second chances. Every creature lived every minute in expectation of being attacked. Reflexes were honed to razor sharpness. Senses were more acute. It was an environment in which only the strongest and the fastest creatures survived.

One of those creatures now snarled a few dozen yards to the south. Bolan halted. The Weatherby was in his hands once again. He would need it, too, if the jaguar that had apparently caught his scent decided that it was hungry.

Jaguars were much more formidable than mountain lions. Dubbed the tigers of the Americas, they were feline killing machines. A grown male could weigh more than three hundred pounds and might reach eight feet in length from nose to tail.

Bolan wasn't about to take the big cat lightly. He forged on, remembering to scour the trees ahead as he went. Jaguars were notorious for pouncing on prey from roosts in low limbs.

The rain-forest canopy blocked off the sky. Only now and then did Bolan catch sight of the stars. Twice he stopped and palmed the compass to verify he hadn't strayed off course.

He walked to the south, seeking a shallow spot to ford, and went forty feet without finding one. Reversing himself, he traveled northward for twice that distance and came on a short gravel bar that jutted a third of the way into the stream.

Taking a broken branch from the ground, Bolan poked it into the water flowing past the bar. It looked to be only two feet deep for the most part, but there might be deeper pools scattering the length of the waterway in which large animals could lurk.

Bolan firmed his grip on the rifle and made for the other side. He watched the surface closely for telltale ripples. When he was more than halfway across, there was a splash to his left and a large creature came up close to the top, but not close enough for him to make out what it was.

The thing floated there, watching him.

Bolan didn't break stride. He covered the animal as he finished crossing and stepped onto the low bank. The creature paddled a few feet closer but still not near enough for him to tell what it was. He slowly backed away, water dripping from his fatigues. Just as he came to the jungle, the creature vanished as abruptly as it had appeared.

The soldier broke into a dogtrot. It was two miles or better to the opposite side of the valley and another series of high hills that he wanted to reach before midnight.

He had traveled approximately half that distance when the breeze brought to his ears the faint hum of voices. Halting, he cocked his head from side to side to determine what direction the voices came from. Whoever was out there lay straight ahead.

Rather than swing wide to avoid them and lose more time in the bargain, Bolan warily advanced. Soon he saw pinpoints of light that grew into a handful of flickering torches. Shadowy forms moved near them. As he drew close enough to note details, he discovered more than twenty robust Indians dressed either in loincloths or nothing at all.

All were men. Their slick black hair had been cropped short, and most had painted their faces and chests. Their weapons consisted of machetes, spears, bows and a few knives. They were ringed around a man wearing a bizarre mask. Quite plainly they were in the middle of a ceremony.

It was common knowledge that some of the tribes in the Yucatán, as in many Central American countries, still believed in the old ways, practicing rituals handed down by their forefathers. They didn't care that the government frowned on such practices, nor did it matter that their beliefs were branded as quaint superstitions by the people who sometimes came to study them.

Bolan didn't know if the tribe was friendly or not. In any event, he wasn't going to show himself. That they saw fit to hold their ceremony in the dead of night deep in the jungle told him that it had to be a special, secret affair, not meant to be witnessed by outsiders. If they were to catch him spying on them, they might kill him on general principle.

So the soldier crept around to the north to skirt the camp.

Another jaguar roared close by, but Bolan reached the end of the valley without incident. Once he had climbed above the rain-forest canopy, he paused to rest and eat a small portion of his rations. He was making good time, but he'd have to push harder to make up for the hours he had lost.

The highland was cooler, less humid. Other than a rare bird cry or the chirp of insects, the animal sounds died off.

When formulating his strategy back in Miami, Bolan had allotted himself thirty-six hours to reach Garcia's stronghold. Subtracting four hours for sleep, it meant he had to cover almost a mile every hour.

A small distance, until one took into account the perils of the jungle, the steepness of the highlands and dozens of other obstacles that could crop up.

Such as the gunrunners. In order for Bolan to be back on schedule by sunrise, he now figured that he had to put more than a mile behind him each hour. So far the soldier had held to a fairly steady pace. The next series of hills slowed him, however, as they were much steeper than the map had led him to believe.

But then, even the best of maps often proved unreliable where remote wilderness was concerned. Few people realized that vast stretches of all the continents were seldom visited by humans. The far jungles, the deep swamps, isolated mountain ranges, they were all listed on maps, sure. But the mapmakers, out of necessity, had to rely on aerial surveys. Mistakes were bound to crop up.

Bolan's legs began to tire. Shutting the discomfort from his mind, he willed himself to keep going. The hills became higher, the last one so high that it gave the illusion he could reach up and touch the stars.

It was shortly after three in the morning when Bolan stopped on a grassy slope. Below lay another tract of rain forest. From its depths came the cough of a prowling cat.

Bolan had done the best he could do. With a little more effort the next day, he should be where he wanted to be sometime around midnight. What he needed most now was rest.

A thicket of broad-leafed plants drew Bolan's attention. Getting on his hands and knees, he wound among them, always on the alert for snakes. At the center of the cluster he knelt, took out the Ka-bar knife, and cut down enough of the plants to make room for him to sleep.

After shrugging out of the backpack, Bolan sat awhile massaging his sore shoulders. He opened a small can of peaches and ate them with his fingers. His hunger abated, he curled up on his right side with the Weatherby tucked between his legs, the barrel resting on his left arm.

Long ago the Executioner had learned the knack of falling asleep instantly when he had to. It came in handy. In the field he didn't always have the luxury of picking when and where he would sleep. He had to make do as events warranted.

The wind soughed through the leaves as Bolan closed his eyes and let himself drift off. He didn't need to set an alarm to awaken. So superb was his conditioning that he awoke when he wanted, just as the blazing crown of the sun cleared the eastern horizon.

CHAPTER NINETEEN

The morning was cool and crisp for the first hour. Bolan made good progress. Since most predators were abroad at night, he had little to worry about in that regard except for snakes, which were easy to spot in broad daylight. He saw only one, a ten-foot boa perched on a thick limb over the game trail he was following at the time. He skirted the tree. The boa hissed and flicked its long tongue but didn't attack.

More hills awaited Bolan once he had the valley behind him. These were the highest yet, but they weren't quite as steep. He made such excellent time that at noon he took a fifteen-minute breather and ate some of the rations in his pack.

Not long after that Bolan came to a shallow stream. He drank his fill, stripped off his fatigue shirt and splashed water on his shoulders, chest and back.

The afternoon passed quickly. Bolan was back on schedule and confident he'd reach his goal in the time he had allotted himself.

Then the soldiers appeared.

Bolan had just passed over the crown of a lushly wooded hill. He spied a line of figures dressed in uniforms on the facing slope and flattened before they spotted him. When he was sure they hadn't, he sat up and studied them through the telescopic sight.

It was an army patrol led by a captain. They were hiking in single file down a clearly defined path that turned due north at the bottom.

The path wasn't marked on any map. Where it led was anyone's guess. Bolan was at a loss to explain the presence of the troops. It was unlikely they were on a routine patrol, since there were no army posts within fifty miles of that spot. He guessed it might be one of the special tactical squads set up by the Mexican government to seek out drug growers and put them out of business.

No matter why they were there, Bolan couldn't let them see him. He was in the country covertly. If caught, the U.S. government would deny any knowledge of him.

So he was content to stay where he was until they disappeared along the fork to the north. But that wasn't to be. When the patrol reached the bottom, the captain barked orders and the patrol left the path and went up the hill toward him.

Bolan looked around for the best place to hide. Not far off lay a fallen forest giant. The log was partly rotted, and there was an opening at one end. He hurried to it. The cavity was empty. By backing in and tucking his knees tight to his chest, he was able to squeeze in far enough so that he wouldn't be seen by anyone walking by unless they were right next to the log and happened to lean down.

Bolan soon heard the tramp of heavy boots plodding uphill. Two of the soldiers were talking. From their conversation, it had to be the officer and a noncom.

"—not wait until we're out of this miserable country, sir. If the mosquitoes don't eat us alive, the snakes will."

"Sometimes you complain too much, Sergeant."

"I mean no disrespect, sir. I know we have a job to do. But if you ask me, we have as much chance of catching a tiger by the tail as we do of catching these stinking gunrunners."

"I admit we have little information to go on, Jorge. But we'll find them. Time is on our side."

By then the voices were at their loudest. Bolan held himself still. The patrol was passing by no more than a dozen feet from the log.

"Yes, Captain. But you must forgive me. I'm from the city. I don't like jungles, I don't like bugs, I don't like snakes. Most of all, I don't like snakes big enough to eat me. Call me strange if you wish."

The officer laughed. "If you think the snakes in the Yucatán are big, you should see the ones in Brazil. I was there once and went on a boat trip up the Amazon. An anaconda I saw was a third the length of a soccer field."

There was more banter as the patrol wound on up the hill and down the other side. Bolan didn't crawl into the open until they were long gone. Descending, he took the path to the southwest. It was risky, since he might run into someone, but it enabled him to make up for lost time, and he was determined not to fall behind again.

The trees thinned. The ground became more open. Bolan passed a plot of tilled soil and saw a small shack in the distance. He realized he was coming into a farming district that wasn't noted on his map. Which was hardly surprising. At the rate the human population was growing and spilling into the countryside, no mapmaker in the world could keep up with the ever-expanding boundaries.

Bolan entered brush on the right. For several miles he paralleled the path. He passed more small farms, some of the dwellings little better than hovels. He saw men and women working the fields. A variety of crops were being grown—corn, cacao, cotton, tobacco.

Toward the middle of the afternoon he rested again and rechecked the grid coordinates. As he was bent over the map, a dog yipped. Bolan glanced at the path and beheld a family of four. The man and two sons were dressed in plain cotton shirts and trousers. The mother wore a long, loose white dress. With them was a mongrel puppy that stood near the brush, sniffing. It knew that Bolan was there.

The Executioner wasn't about to shoot an innocent family and their pet. He could only hope they moved on.

The puppy started into the vegetation, but the man spoke sharply and the older boy grabbed hold of the mongrel by the scruff of the neck.

Whining in protest, the pup was hauled off.

For the rest of the day Bolan was on the watch for dogs. Those he saw were always at a safe distance. By evening another belt of forest replaced the farmland. He could move freely again and doubled his pace until it was too dark to do so safely.

Repeatedly Bolan consulted the compass. He was within a few miles of the site and couldn't afford to stray off course. Confirmation that he was right where he should be came in the form of a pale glow seen from a high ridge. It was exactly where Ticul should be.

Much closer was a narrow valley. From a bordering hill Bolan surveyed it from one end to the other. According to the Intel provided by reliable Mexican sources, this was where the hub of Adolpho Garcia's drug empire would be based.

Lights shone at the north end of the valley. Bolan spent more than an hour moving along the ridge to a basin. He had to climb down a cliff, then cross a basin and scale a low bluff. A warm wind fanned his face and hair as he reached the top.

The rim overlooked the construction site. He had arrived two hours early.

Bolan sat cross-legged and opened his backpack. While the scope was ideal for targeting, it lacked the wide field of view and the higher magnification factor he now needed.

From the bottom of the pack he pulled out a pair of midnight black binoculars. They were compact for easy use and waterproof to withstand heavy rain. More importantly, they boasted a computer-designed optical system, minibionics to boost the clarity and a built-in reticle system for gauging the height and width of distant objects.

Once the Executioner raised the binoculars to his eyes, the entire setup below came into crystal-clear focus. He counted three bulldozers, a backhoe and other heavy equipment within a fifteen-foot-high wall that enclosed roughly ten acres. A number of buildings had already been built, and others were in the process of being put up. One of those was the main house, about two-thirds complete.

Parked close to the west wall were four cars, two Jeeps and a pickup. A black limo sat near the house.

Half of the front gate had been installed. The other half had been propped against the wall and would probably be erected the next day.

Plenty of lights were lit, both within and outside the buildings. Since there were no power lines to the property that Bolan could see, generators had to be supplying the electricity. He pegged a metal shed against the north wall as the likely place to find them.

Men were everywhere. Construction crews were working late. From the house came hammering and the rasp of a saw. A man was using an arc welder in a building the size of a warehouse.

Gunners patrolled in plain sight, subguns slung over their shoulders. Others stood in groups, talking and smoking. Bolan counted twenty-three, but he was certain there were more he couldn't see.

Garcia had a small army at his disposal.

Try as Bolan might, he saw no sign of the big man himself. He concentrated on the windows in the main house. On the ground floor several women in short dresses were seated at a bar. On the second floor workmen were nailing together the frame for a wall.

It was nearly midnight when Bolan shoved the binoculars into the backpack and slid out a green folding shovel. Unfolding the handle, he aligned the spade and locked it in place. Then he knelt and started to dig. When he had dug a shallow trench long enough to lie in, he carried most of the dirt a dozen yards and scattered it widely in high grass.

His next step was to go around pulling waist-high weeds and brush out of the ground. That left circles of fresh earth, which he covered with bits of grass and limbs. As for the plants he had gathered, he carried them to the trench, where he dug a hole for each and inserted the roots. It took a while to pack enough earth down on every one to keep them standing upright. When he was done, the trench was ringed by vegetation.

Bolan lay in it on his stomach. The plants in front of him were spaced so that he could see the stronghold clearly, yet no one would be able to spot him.

On his right sat all that remained of the loose earth, on his left a handful of slender branches. Both were being saved for later use.

The Executioner was about as ready as he'd ever be. Before turning in, he had something to do. Taking the backpack, he headed to the northeast. According to the map, there was a stream just over the rise.

Bolan found it readily enough. He drank and washed the dirt from his hands and forearms. Then, with the Weatherby at his side, he crept toward the high walls. Faint laughter and rowdy voices came from the other side.

It seemed to Bolan that Adolpho Garcia was overrated. Yes, the man was a stone-cold killer, but he didn't have much going for him between the ears or he would have posted guards on the ramparts. Bolan hadn't seen a trace of any while studying the grounds.

Still, he was wary as he approached the southeast corner. He halted a hundred feet out, behind the last of the trees. Garcia wasn't a complete dummy; he'd had the bulldozers clear all vegetation away from the walls. In the light of day Bolan would never be able to do what he was about to do now. He sprinted toward the estate.

Even though the Executioner knew the place was still under construction, he kept expecting a floodlight to pierce the night or shouts to break out. Neither happened and he reached the corner undetected.

Squatting, Bolan removed the C-4, det cord and remote triggering devices from the backpack. Digging down a few inches, he placed the first charge and wired it. A light dusting of dirt sufficed to hide the explosive.

Bolan padded toward the gate. A spotlight had been erected on the arch above it. The beam illuminated a long stretch of dirt road but left the sides of the gate plunged in gloom.

The soldier had no problem slipping inside. With his back to the inner wall, he noted the positions of everyone in sight. Little had changed since he spied on them from the bluff. No one was near the vehicles, and they were his next stop. Slipping from shadow to shadow, he came to the wall behind the cars.

Once again he dug down a few inches and placed the plastique. He used more than before so it took longer. As he finished and was layering dirt over his surprise package, he heard a cough.

Flattening, Bolan peered under the closest car and saw two pairs of shoes coming toward him. He put a hand on the Beretta but had no need to draw it. The gunners had changed direction and were strolling toward the gate. To hear them joking and laughing, it was apparent they didn't have a care in the world.

As their footsteps faded, Bolan clamped a hand on the backpack and headed for the metal shed.

When still a ways off, Bolan nodded. The muffled rumble of generators was audible. He didn't go to the door, above which hung a solitary bulb, but around to the back, where there was a four-foot gap between the rear of the building and the high wall. There he set enough explosive to blow the shed sky high and disable the generators.

So far everything had gone off without a hitch. Bolan had enough C-4 left for one more charge, but this one would be the hardest to put in place. Propping the rifle against the wall, he set the backpack next to it and took with him just the materials he needed. A peek around the corner verified none of the gunners or workers had strayed in his direction.

Bolan boldly headed for the front of the main house. He held the explosive, det cord and remote detonator close to his leg. Through a window he had a better look at the women. They weren't women at all, but teenagers of fifteen or sixteen.

Suddenly a construction worker carrying a roll of wire and a hammer came around the front corner.

Bolan was only twenty feet away, but he was shrouded in darkness. When the worker waved, he did the same. The man went about his business and in another few moments Bolan was near the circle of light that bathed the black limousine.

Pausing, he tried to see through the tinted windows. There might be a driver inside, or a bodyguard. He had to know, so he leaned down and groped the ground until he located a small stone. He tossed it against the windshield. No one jumped out to see what had made the noise, but he still wasn't convinced. He threw another stone. When nothing happened, he sidled closer while scanning the grounds. No one called out or took a shot at him.

The instant his hip brushed the fender, Bolan dropped onto his back and scooted underneath the vehicle, positioning himself directly under the engine block.

Bolan knew the fuel tank would make a more spectacular blast, but he wanted to drive the block back into the body of the limo. That way, if the explosion didn't do the job, the immensely heavy engine would. He placed the C-4 at the front of the block, on a metal rim above the water pump. Working swiftly, he attached the detonator. He had just finished and reached for the bumper to pull himself out when the front door of the house opened and several men emerged. They walked down the steps and did the one thing Bolan didn't want them to do—which was to walk over to the limo.

CHAPTER TWENTY

The Executioner watched as the feet of the three men drew closer to the vehicle. He heard three doors open and the men slide in. The added weight caused the limo to sink an inch lower, and the bottom of the oil pan brushed his thighs.

The doors slammed shut. Bolan started to pull himself forward so he could dart into the darkness before they drove off, but a raspy shout from the porch thwarted him. Whoever was up there might see him.

"Juan, one moment."

A power window whined as the glass came down. "Yes, Mr. Garcia?" the driver responded.

Bolan twisted. He could see a heavyset man standing next to a pillar. It had to be the new drug lord.

Adolpho Garcia had on an undershirt smudged with food stains and pants a size too big. His pudgy chin was covered with stubble. Whereas Luis Terrazas had tried to come across as slick and refined, the new drug lord was nothing more than a venomous slob. But being a slob didn't make him stupid. Behind Garcia stood three alert gunners.

"Don't take no for an answer," Garcia said. "I don't care how late it is. Wake up every shopkeeper in Ticul and find me some beer. Lots of it. We're going to celebrate."

"Yes, sir."

"And hurry back. I'm a thirsty man."

To the Executioner's consternation, the drug lord stood there with the bodyguards instead of going back inside.

There was a loud click and the limo's engine turned over with a roar. A blast of air hit Bolan in the face as the fan surged to life. Its whirring blades were right above his forehead. In sheer reflex he recoiled against the ground. Then he heard the transmission engage.

Bolan had intended to just lie there and let the limo drive off. He couldn't now, though, not with Garcia and the hardmen thirty feet away. There was only one thing he could do, which was take a firmer grip on the front bumper and brace himself as the limo rolled into motion.

With a jerk, the warrior was dragged along the dirt drive toward the front gate. Dust spewed from under the tires and got into his eyes and nose. He was lucky that the driver didn't go over fifteen miles per hour. But he had to crane his neck and keep watch for bumps that might mash him up against the block or the fan.

A piece of rock he hadn't noticed suddenly gouged Bolan hard in the back. He nearly lost his grip. Gritting his teeth, he held on as the vehicle took a gradual curve and braked at the south wall.

Bolan clung there as the front passenger door opened and a gunner climbed out. The man walked to the part of the wrought-iron gate that had been installed and swung it open. Bolan quickly let go of the bumper to wriggle farther under the limo before the gunner turned around.

The man came back. The door slammed. Bolan lay there with his arms at his sides as the vehicle rolled on over him. He flinched when a blast of intense heat from the muffler nearly blistered his cheek. Then he was in the clear, shrouded by darkness. He immediately rolled to the left to get out of the driveway.

Again the limousine stopped. The same gunner got out to close the gate. Moments later the vehicle vanished into the night.

Bolan rose slowly into a crouch. He brushed dirt from his face and hair, then pivoted to go to the generator building. He froze on spying a pair of figures twenty feet away. The orange dot of a cigarette flared as a man took a puff. It had to be the same pair of gunners he had seen over by the vehicles.

Had they spotted him? Bolan wondered, tensing. In the red glow of the limo's taillights he would have been briefly visible. They had to have, because they walked toward him. Going prone, he unearthed the Beretta and took aim.

"I didn't see anything," one of the men was saying.

"Well, I did, I tell you," the other replied. "Just for a second there."

Those were the last words either hardman would ever utter. The Berretta coughed twice in swift succession and the gunners dropped in their tracks.

Bolan didn't move until he was positive no one else had seen. Easing the 93-R into its shoulder rig, he hurriedly hauled the two bodies to the base of the wall, where they were less likely to be stumbled on until daylight.

It didn't take long for the soldier to retrieve the Weatherby and the backpack. The only person he encountered was a workman carrying two-by-fours toward the house, and the man didn't give him a second glance.

Bolan finally reached the trees. He had done all he could do. His plan would either work or it wouldn't. It was as simple as that.

A cool breeze stirred the foliage at the top of the bluff. Bolan set the backpack beside the trench, then eased into it, facing the estate. He sprinkled his back and legs with the loose dirt he had left piled for that purpose, then covered his head and the rifle with the small branches.

The Executioner was tired. It had been a long day. Within seconds of placing his chin on his folded forearms, he was sound asleep. He woke up twice, briefly. Once when a large animal crossed the bluff behind him, rumbling deep in its chest. He knew without looking that it was a puma or jaguar. When it stopped and sniffed, he put his hands on the rifle and shifted. He caught sight of a tawny blur as the cat loped off rather than attacked.

The second time was in the middle of the night when the limousine returned, the growl of its engine so distinct from the normal sounds of the night that it woke him up when it was still a mile away. He stared at the headlights a few moments, then closed his eyes. Morning wasn't that far off and he had to be well rested.

Before the day was done, all hell would bust loose.

A HALF HOUR BEFORE DAWN the hawk-faced driver nudged the woman sleeping beside him.

Katya Steiner instantly came awake. She rubbed her eyes, stared at the gloomy woodland on both sides of the narrow road and scowled. "Are we there yet?" she asked in German.

"If the directions the man at the gas station gave us are right, we should be there soon," Gunther replied.

The woman opened her purse and took out a compact. She scrunched up her face on seeing her reflection and ran a hand through her tousled hair. "I liked being a blonde much better than I like being a brunette. Brunettes are so dull."

"It's only for a while," Gunther told her. "Once we've delivered this Wizard to Reutlingen, you can color your hair any way you like. Maybe dye it purple and shape it into spikes like those young ones in Munich do."

"And walk around looking like a refugee from a circus? I would rather be shot dead." Katya snapped the compact shut and stuffed it into her handbag. "I just hope this pans out. I don't mind telling you that I'm eager to get this over with."

"That makes two of us." Gunther shifted to relieve a cramp. "This damn leg keeps acting up. I've never been shot before. It's is not an experience I recommend."

"I wonder who he was."

"Certainly not a Jamaican. Did you see the way he moved? How fast he was?" Gunther slowed to take a turn. "And did you notice that there was no mention of him in the news reports? Not a single word. They gave that policeman all the credit."

"CIA, I would guess."

"Whatever, I don't want to run into him again."

The woman laughed and poked him in the ribs. "Why, Gunther, can it be that you have finally met your match?"

"Don't make fun of me," Gunther said sternly. He was going to say more but an isolated mailbox loomed in the dark beside a dirt drive that wound off between long rows of maples and willows toward a farmhouse half a mile away. Stopping their sedan, he rolled down his window. "That must be it."

Katya bent down to see better. The farmhouse was dark except for a single outside light. To the west of the house reared a large barn capped by a weather vane. To the east stood a smaller building. "Why here, do you think?"

Gunther shrugged. "Who can say? He must have several retreats scattered around the globe. Perhaps he felt this one would be the safest."

A pale glow lined the eastern horizon. Katya pursed her lips and said, "It'll soon be daylight. Let's go back to that motel we passed and take a room. I can use a bath and a good sleep."

Gunther pressed his foot on the accelerator. "Good idea. I'll practice with my garrote on a pillow. You never know. The Wizard might not be alone in there."

Smirking, Katya patted him on the cheek. "That's one of the things I like about you, darling. Your mind never strays off your work." She gestured at the farm. "But there's no rush. We'll spend a day or so scouting the area. It wouldn't do to rush in blindly. A man like the Wizard is bound to have taken certain precautions."

"He can set all the traps he wants. It won't stop us. Two days from now he'll be on his way to Germany. And Reutlingen will make us richer than we ever thought we would be."

Katya leaned back in the seat dreamily. "I wonder what Switzerland is like at this time of the year?"

THE SUN HAD JUST crested, and a haze hung over the tableland. Snatches of fog drifted in the valley. Only part of the estate could be seen. The workers were still busy, working in shifts around the clock to complete the construction.

Bolan had brought a few pieces of beef jerky along. They were his breakfast, along with the last of his wafers. The fog had dissipated by the time he was done, so he roved his binoculars over the entire valley floor. He saw no other dwellings.

Adolpho Garcia had the valley all to himself. It was probably one of the reasons the drug lord had picked it—that and the fact it was relatively close to Ticul. Mérida itself, the biggest city in the Yucatán, was only an hour away.

Bolan lowered his right eye to the telescopic sight to monitor the activity below. Just as he did, strident shouts broke out. He guessed that someone had discovered the two bodies.

Gunners converged from all directions. In another minute the corpses were carted to the front porch.

The soldier couldn't see what was going on because of the porch roof. He imagined that Garcia had come out. Shortly the drug lord's small army scattered across the grounds and conducted a thorough search. They looked in every building, in every vehicle. They poked into bushes and checked the limbs of trees. But they didn't find the C-4.

The sun slowly climbed. Bolan kept the rifle's sights fixed on the steps leading up to the front porch, since that was where Garcia would most likely appear.

Toward the middle of the morning there was a new development, one Bolan watched closely. Twelve gunners headed for the gate. Beyond the walls, they split into two six-man patrols and fanned out to make a complete sweep of the perimeter.

At the same time, a man appeared on the south wall. He opened a case and took out a parabolic mike and headphones. For the next half hour the man swept the large white dish back and forth.

Bolan had to smile when the man suddenly pointed the mike at a cluster of trees hundreds of yards away and barked at the gunners. The hardmen jogged to the stand, surrounded it and advanced with their weapons leveled.

The soldier's smile died when two does burst from cover and fled in long leaps. Several of the gunners automatically cut loose, mowing down the deer in mid-jump. Riddled with bullets, the animals convulsed for a while before dying. Some of the hardmen laughed and clapped one another on the back, taking it as a grand joke.

They hiked back to the estate. The man on the wall stored the mike in the case and disappeared.

Nothing else of note happened until shortly after noon. A gunner with a slung Uzi left the house and walked to the limo. Bolan thought that maybe the man was going somewhere, but the gunner walked around to the front of the vehicle and popped the hood. It was then that Bolan saw the cloth the man held.

Bolan fixed the scope on the gunner's face. If the man found the charge, the Executioner had to set his plan into effect right away.

The gunner leaned low over the engine, searched around a moment, then found the dipstick and pulled it out. After wiping it clean on the cloth, he stuck it back in, waited a few moments and checked the level.

Apparently satisfied, he replaced the stick again and took a step to the left.

From where the gunner was standing, Bolan knew the guy would see the C-4 if he looked straight down. The soldier continued to watch as the hardman opened the radiator cap and stuck a finger in the radiator. The finger came out coated with green coolant. Nodding, the man put the cap back on, reached up to close the hood and hesitated.

The gunner was looking at something on the block, Bolan knew. He lowered a hand to his pocket to take out the radio detonator but stopped when the gunner bent to remove the air cleaner cover. After checking the filter, the man banged down the hood and went into the house.

Now what was that all about? Bolan wondered. Did it mean Garcia was about to take a long ride? His hunch was borne out fifteen minutes later when the same gunner reappeared carrying a pair of suitcases that he placed in the trunk.

The drug lord wasn't going anywhere, not if Bolan could help it, not with the life of the President at stake.

Figuring that Garcia would soon show himself, Bolan placed the radio detonator in front of him and verified the frequency selector dial was set to the frequency of the explosive charge he had set along the outer wall.

Unlike conventional detonators, which were set to a specific frequency, the state-of-the-art unit whipped up for him by the specialists at Stony Man Farm allowed for a variable range. That way he could plant up to a dozen charges and set them off one by one simply by varying the frequency of each.

No one else came out of the house for more than an hour, and Bolan questioned if perhaps it had been a false alarm and Garcia had changed his mind.

Time dragged by. Bolan checked his watch. He had to meet Grimaldi at the extraction point in five hours. He could no longer wait for the drug lord to show himself. He had to take the fight to Adolpho Garcia.

The Executioner flicked the radio's mode switch to Test and pressed the red button. As it should, the VU needle pegged, which told him the batteries were at full power. He flicked the switch back, glanced down at the southeast corner of the wall and pressed the red button again.

This time there was a booming blast. A wide section of wall went up in a billowing cloud of dust and debris.

Men came from everywhere to see what had happened. The construction workers hung back in alarm while many of the gunners raced to the gaping hole.

More hardmen poured out of the house, and Bolan revised his earlier estimate—there had to be close to fifty in total. He ignored them all and focused on the porch steps. Sooner or later Garcia had to appear, and he was going to be ready.

One voice rose above all the rest. The gunners swiveled toward the house and listened. It was Garcia, but, just like the last time, he didn't step out from under the overhang. His private army galvanized into action. Some hastened to the wall. Some made for the vehicles. Others surrounded the main house to protect their boss.

Bolan let them climb into the cars, trucks and pickups. When every last vehicle was crammed with hardmen and several of the engines had turned over, he rotated the dial to the second frequency and activated the detonator.

This explosion dwarfed the first. Vehicles were lifted off their tires and flung through the air as if they were made of cardboard instead of tons of steel, chrome and plastic. One of the trucks rolled over and over and came to rest a crumpled wreck. A car landed on its roof, which flattened like a pancake on the heads of those inside. Screams and curses added to the bedlam.

As the explosion died away, a swirling cloud of smoke engulfed the scene. Some of those who had been in the vehicles staggered into the open, their clothes torn and bloody. Gunners at the wall and house ran to help, but shouted instructions from Garcia halted them.

It was plain that many of the hardmen were close to panic. They were looking right and left in fear of another blast.

Bolan was all too willing to oblige. Once more he adjusted the setting, once more his finger stabbed the red button.

This time the generator building went up in a fiery display of electrical pyrotechnics. Flames, smoke and vivid arcs of electricity shot high into the sky. Even after the remains of the building smashed down, wild, gleaming bolts danced a crackling jig.

It was too much for some of the gunners. They broke, racing for the gate and presumed safety.

Their boss had the same idea. Bolan saw Garcia bolt down the steps. He shifted the Weatherby and almost had the drug lord lined up in the cross hairs when Garcia ducked into the limousine.

Several hardmen spilled in after him. The driver peeled out and tore down the driveway. He lost control. The limo slid into a knot of fleeing men, bowling them over. Garcia never had the car stop to see how his men had fared. It sped on to the gate and smashed the closed half aside.

Bolan shifted the rifle to cover the stretch of road below the bluff. One last time he reset the frequency. He waited until the limo was due west of his position, then hit the button.

There was no explosion.

The Executioner hit the button again with the same result. He realized that somehow one of the wires or the det cord had been jiggled loose, either on the ride into Ticul the previous night or when the gunner slammed the hood. Instantly he brought the Weatherby to bear.

Bolan's first shot punctured the front tire on the passenger side. The limo went into a slide, and just as the driver brought it under control, the soldier shot out the rear tire. Crippled but still able to run, the car kept going.

Aware that Garcia might escape unless he did something drastic, Bolan worked the bolt and sent a high-velocity slug into the engine. Twice he did so, and on the second shot the limousine spat smoke from the exhaust. A horrendous rattling and pinging marked the engine's death throes.

The limousine abruptly stopped in a spray of dust.

Reloading quickly, Bolan elevated the barrel and waited for those inside to get out. But no one did. Evidently Garcia figured he was safer inside. Bolan decided to prove the man wrong. His next shot punctured the center of the front window.

Three of the doors were shoved wide open and out bolted Garcia and a trio of gunners. They sprinted madly for the walls, the gunners ringing their boss, who huffed and puffed after only a few steps. He was miserably out of shape.

Bolan sighted on the foremost gunner and fired. The man flung out his arms as if impaled, then did a slow melt to the soil. The other two hardmen turned toward the bluff. One had a pistol, the other an SMG. They cut loose, but their rounds fell short of the rim, as Bolan had expected. The soldier first dropped the underling with the SMG. The man with the pistol tried to flee but managed only four steps.

Garcia never slowed. His face was red as he pumped his arms and legs. He screamed for gunners to come to his aid but none of them could hear him over the confused bedlam.

The Executioner lined up the drug lord's head squarely in his sights. At that magnification every bead of sweat stood out in stark relief. Garcia glanced up at the bluff and mouthed an oath.

Bolan held himself perfectly still. He applied light pressure to the trigger and saw the top of Garcia's head dissolve in a crimson mist. A second shot wasn't needed.

Swiftly Bolan rose and grabbed the backpack. A few of the hardmen at the estate were pointing at the bluff. By the time they regrouped and rushed out after him, he'd be long gone.

The soldier whirled and hurried off. He had a rendezvous to keep.

CHAPTER TWENTY-ONE

Mack Bolan and Jack Grimaldi were halfway to Miami when they received a coded transmission rerouting them to Stony Man Farm. Nestled among the rolling green hills of Virginia, Stony Man was the secret nerve center of the government's antiterrorism effort.

The Farm was also the nearest thing to a home Mack Bolan had. It was where he went between missions to enjoy rare moments of peace and relaxation. It was one of the few places on Earth where he could let himself unwind without risk.

But not this time. Hardly had Grimaldi sat down than a blacksuit whisked Bolan to the War Room in the farmhouse. Both Brognola and John Kissinger were on hand to greet him.

"Congratulations, Striker," the big Fed said, offering his hand. "Jack sent word that everything went off without a hitch."

"Nothing to speak of," Bolan said dryly. He nodded at Stony Man's resident weaponsmith and slid into a chair. "What's the latest?"

Brognola sat down. He had a cup of coffee in front of him, which he sipped before speaking. "Now that you've neutralized Garcia, the heat is off the President and we can concentrate on the Wizard. As luck would have it, we've had a few breaks since you left for the Yucatán."

"What kind of breaks?"

"First, Interpol came through on the blonde and her friend. They're free-lance pros, Germans who hire themselves out for top dollar. The names they went under in Jamaica, Katya Steiner and Gunther Merzig, are aliases. They've used several from time to time. Their true identities are unknown as yet."

"Any idea why they're after Trask?"

Brognola leaned on his elbows. "No clue as yet, but here's the interesting part. Interpol says that Steiner and Merzig will do anything provided the money is right. Contract hits, a little smuggling, kidnapping, you name it. Once they abducted an Italian businessman for a rival and forced him to sign over his company under the threat of having his family murdered. The man later went to the authorities. He thought the police would protect them."

"The threat was carried out?"

"Was it ever. Steiner and Merzig killed his wife, two sons and a five-year-old daughter. They made him watch. He told the police that the woman would laugh when each one died."

Bolan had been digesting the information and now voiced his conclusion. "So it could be that these two don't intend to kill Trask at all. They might have been hired to kidnap him."

"It's a very real possibility. Trask's know-how would be worth millions on the armaments market."

"Do we know where the Germans are at this moment?"

"Not exactly, but we do have a strong lead." Brognola's features clouded. "Before we go on, I have to tell you that Eric Mandeville contacted me while you were in Mexico. He thought you'd want to know that a policeman you worked with on the case has been murdered. Garroted in an alley."

"Thomas Sangster?"

Brognola nodded. "There's no rhyme or reason to it. Maybe they wanted revenge because they thought his interference spoiled their plans. Or maybe they wanted to learn what the police department had uncovered. It's all speculation at this point."

Bolan hadn't known Sangster all that well, but well enough to like the man and respect his dedication. A bitter taste came into his mouth at the thought of the sterling officer having his life snuffed out as callously as if he were no more than a bothersome insect.

"Mandeville believes that Steiner and Merzig slipped out of Jamaica on a passenger plane bound for the States. They used forged documents and had changed their appearances."

"I wish we knew where to find them."

"We might be able to shed some light on that." Brognola nodded at the armorer. "Cowboy, if you would."

Kissinger flipped open a manila folder. "I'm not much of a detective, but with the help of Kurtzman and the computers, I was able to come up with something."

He was referring to Aaron Kurtzman, Stony Man's resident computer specialist.

Bolan raised his head to listen. It would do no good to let Sangster's fate get to him.

"Not that many manufacturers deal in high-tech components that can be used in missiles and bombs," Kissinger said. "It's not as if you can walk into your local hardware store and buy an infrared sensor. And retail electronics and computer outlets only carry run-of-the-mill stuff.

"But the Wizard has to be buying components from somewhere. No matter how good he is, he can't whip up a circuit board from scratch. Acting on that idea, I picked the six companies the Wizard was most likely to buy from, then Aaron and I ran a computerized comparison check of their purchasing orders. We concentrated on individual buyers rather than companies and came up with a few names."

"But what if Trask has set up dummy corporations as fronts?" Bolan asked.

"To do that he'd need to hire a lawyer and file mountains of paperwork. He'd lose his anonymity. I seriously doubt he'd go to all the trouble and run the risk."

"Point taken."

"So anyway, we ran an ID check on these names and found several that were phony. At the same time I was asking around, calling contacts of mine. One of them mentioned a whiz kid at Berkeley who had shown a lot of promise but wound up in prison for embezzlement.

After he got out, he vanished into thin air and no one has heard from him since."

"This whiz kid have a name?"

"Tasse. Mark J. Tasse." Kissinger grinned and looked at Bolan as if expecting him to do the same.

"Should that mean something to me?"

The weaponsmith glanced at Brognola, then shook his head. "I suppose not. I guess you weren't much of a Scrabble player when you were a kid." He took a pen and wrote the name James Trask on the front of the folder in bold print. "There are ten letters. Now let's scramble them and watch what we come up with." One by one Kissinger checked off a letter and added it to a new name below. When he was done, he had spelled out Mark J. Tasse.

"It's an anagram."

"Exactly." Kissinger grinned. "Just the sort of thing a genius like Tasse or Trask or whatever he's calling himself now would go in for. It was the same with the names Kurtzman and I came up with. They were all anagrams."

"But does it tell us where to find this warped mastermind?" Bolan pressed the point most crucial to him.

"I'm getting to that," Kissinger said patiently. "We traced the ordered parts to several locations. One in California, another in Arizona and a third in Pennsylvania."

"It all fits," Brognola stated. "Eric Mandeville told me that the Savanna la Mar police had a lead. A man who used the name James Trask sent some boxes from

Jamaica to the States." He leaned forward. "To an address in Pennsylvania."

"Then we have him," Bolan said, beginning to rise.

"That's not all, though," Brognola added quickly. "Sangster was given the address by an officer who saw him put it in his pocket just a few minutes before Sangster left the station and was killed. You know what that means, don't you?"

"Steiner and Merzig have it, too."

"And they'll kill anyone who gets in their way."

The Executioner stood, his face a grim mask. "Well, they better make their first shot count."

Pennsylvania

THREE HOURS LATER Bolan was behind the wheel of a jeep winding along a country road in the Keystone State. Several miles to the southwest lay the quaint town of Ephrata. For the past half hour he had passed only neatly tilled fields and tidy farms.

Bolan was in the heart of Amish country. Already he had seen a number of horse-drawn wagons bearing stout bearded men in black and women wearing long dresses and bonnets. It was like being in another world, one where people treated one another as neighbors and always had a friendly word of greeting. It was so different from the world of deceit and death in which he lived.

A series of rolling hills brought Bolan to a rise overlooking several more farms. At the next turnoff he took a left. There were more trees in the area, and the farm to his left showed evidence of neglect. He came to a lone mailbox perched on a cracked wooden post and slowed to read the faded numbers painted on the side.

This was the place.

The glimpse Bolan had of the run-down farmhouse revealed nothing. No lights were on and no vehicles were parked in the driveway. The Wizard might be there; he might not. There was only one way to find out, but Bolan was going to wait for the cover of darkness before he moved in. He still had four hours to kill.

Bolan drove on to a secondary road that ran parallel to the north property line. He searched for surveillance equipment or for any trace of the kind of hardware he had gone up against in Jamaica. There was none that he could see.

To all intents and purposes the farm was just like any other, except that the fields hadn't been tilled. There was an apple orchard due north of the farmhouse and a hedge on the west side of the house. The only sign of life consisted of a flock of pigeons roosting on top of the barn silo.

Bolan glanced over a shoulder at his duffel bag in the back seat. He had brought all the gear he would need, including a few devices cooked up for him by Cowboy that might save his hide if the property had a computer-controlled defense system like the one on Xaymaca.

Soon the soldier came to another fork and took a right. It wouldn't do to go back the way he had come and draw attention to himself, so he cruised the countryside for the next quarter hour. Eventually he found his way to the highway that had brought him from Ephrata and he headed for town.

As Bolan passed the turnoff to the Wizard's farm, he spotted an Amish wagon up ahead, on the shoulder of the highway. The farmer, his wife and a strapping son had climbed out. The wagon tilted to one side thanks to a busted wheel. Bolan couldn't say what prompted him to brake and pull over next to them. "Can you use a hand?"

The farmer fixed kindly eyes on him. "We thank you, friend, but there is no need to trouble yourself. I have all the tools I need in the wagon. We will be on our way in no time, the Lord willing."

Nodding, Bolan drove on. At Ephrata he parked on the main street and entered a restaurant. He took a seat by the front window so he could keep a lookout for the Germans.

The menu listed only Pennsylvania Dutch dishes. Bolan ordered pot pie, thinking he would get a small pie in a metal dish. Instead, the waitress brought a heaping plate of boiled beef, potatoes and onions covered by thick squares of dough.

Any other time, and Bolan would have eaten every last morsel. But he had a job to do soon, a job he couldn't do well if he were sluggish from being too full. He ate a third of the plate, then had to assure the waitress that nothing was wrong with the food, he just wasn't hungry.

The sun had set when Bolan slid into the Jeep and fastened his seat belt. There had been no sign of the blonde and her friend. He wondered if perhaps he was too late, if maybe Steiner and Merzig had already gotten their hands on the Wizard and flown the coop.

Traffic was sparse. A full moon had risen, and it bathed the fields in its bright glow.

Bolan was almost to the turnoff when he remembered the Amish family with the broken wheel. He glanced at the shoulder and was surprised to see the busted wheel lying on the gravel. Even more surprising was the wooden toolbox next to it.

On an impulse Bolan made a U-turn and got out. The toolbox contained a wide assortment of well-maintained tools worth more than a hundred dollars. It wasn't the sort of thing a man would thoughtlessly leave behind. Especially not someone who relied on his tools every single day.

Bolan gazed down the highway but saw no sign of the farmer and his family. He debated leaving the toolbox there, but the odds were that someone else would come along and steal it. So he put the box in the back beside his duffel bag. Once the mission was done with, he intended to turn it over to the police in Ephrata. They should be able to track down the owner.

Getting back in, Bolan rode to the dirt turnoff. He made the turn slowly, passing a cluster of maples bordering the road, and was about to speed up when out of the corner of his eye he saw a pale form lying well in among the trees. His foot seemed to slam on the brake pedal of its own accord.

Bolan threw the jeep into Reverse and backed up. He stopped across from the maples, killed the engine and opened the door feeling distinctly uneasy. Loosening the Beretta under his jacket, he crossed the road.

As he drew nearer, he saw it was a woman in a long white slip. He knew who it would be before he stopped at her side. It was the farmer's wife. Her dress and bonnet were gone.

A cold rage flared within him. Normally he kept his emotions tightly in check. He had to, if he wanted to survive. But this brutal murder of a total innocent shook him to his core. He forced himself to squat and examine the corpse. The woman's skin was warm to the touch, showing that she hadn't been dead long. The cause was a knife wound through the rib cage. She had been stabbed in the heart by someone who knew exactly where to bury the blade.

The husband and the boy were a few yards away. A garrote had disposed of the farmer. From the blood on his fingertips and his broken nails it was apparent the man had struggled mightily, to no avail. Like the woman, his outer clothes and hat were gone.

Mechanically Bolan faced the youngster, who was still clothed. The boy had been stabbed in the back, and from the way the overalls and shirt were torn, Bolan guessed that he had been fleeing when death overtook him.

There was nothing Bolan could do about the bodies until later. He did close the woman's eyelids before jogging to the Jeep. Hoping that if he hurried he would catch the wagon, Bolan gunned the engine and raced along the road.

But the Amish wagon never appeared. Soon Bolan drew near enough to the farm to have to shut off his headlights. He slowed to a crawl, and when he was abreast of the Wizard's property he veered to the right and parked in high weeds far from the road. The car would be safe from prying eyes.

Bolan slipped a penlight from a pocket, switched it on and set it on the dash, pointed at the back seat. He stripped off his jacket, then opened the duffel bag.

Before leaving Stony Man Farm Bolan had stripped down the M-16 and cleaned it. So the rifle would fit in the bag, he had reassembled the upper receiver group and the lower receiver group but hadn't joined them together. He did so now.

Since the soldier counted on the Wizard putting up a fight, he had attached an M-203 grenade launcher. This time he wasn't going to be outgunned if he could help it.

Bolan had brought along a camouflage fatigue shirt, which he pulled on over his cotton shirt. He left it unbuttoned for quick access to the Beretta and the Desert Eagle. His slacks were black and would do just fine.

He then pulled out the special devices he had brought along. The first was a scrambler designed to jam electronic signals. The second was a modified NVEC 800, a night-vision unit shaped like binoculars. It fit around his temples and left his hands free for combat.

Finally Bolan palmed a small device shaped like an ordinary hearing aid, which picked up sound much more crisply than any commercial model. This he affixed to his left ear. When he pressed a tiny button, it was as if he could hear for the very first time. Every sound he heard was amplified sharply. The wind, the rustle of nearby leaves and the chorus of crickets were so loud that he tweaked the gain so he could hear himself think.

The warrior was ready. He slid out and quietly closed the door. Moving to the edge of the road, he knelt and turned on the night-vision device. The unit magnified the ambient light of the moon to such a degree that he could see everything clearly.

The NVEC also did something else. It was able to register heat sources, such as the natural body heat of a hidden gunner or the artificial heat of an infrared source such as those used in laser alarm systems.

Bolan crept to the road. The field and the farmhouse beyond were as quiet as a graveyard. No lights were on in the house, but an outside bulb lit up the front door.

Crouching in tall grass that bordered the wire fence, Bolan paused. The fence looked just like every other one he had seen that day. But if there was one thing he had learned in Jamaica, it was to never underestimate his adversary.

Many fences like the one in front of him were electrified with low voltage to keep cows from straying. Since there were no cattle on Tasse's property, it made no sense for the fence to be on. But it was. Bolan could hear the hum clearly, and when he boosted the volume the microphone made the current crackle like a thing alive.

Bolan guessed that one touch and he would be fried to a crisp. He hadn't brought wire cutters and rubber gloves, so he had to find another way in. Or over. He moved along the fence, toward the mailbox.

If it hadn't been for the NVEC, Bolan might have missed spotting a stump between the road and the fence. It was half-covered by grass. The tree had been cut down long ago, and the wood was partially rotted out. But it supported his weight without crumbling when he stepped up and faced the electrified fence.

The log was about two feet high and close enough that Bolan could make it over the top wire in one jump. It would be close, though. Almost too close for comfort. To increase his chances he had to lighten his load.

The soldier stepped as close to the fence as he dared, held out the M-16 and let the rifle drop. It hit stock first and toppled into a patch of grass. He also dropped over the scrambler and the night-vision goggles.

Backing up past the stump to the middle of the road, Bolan blocked everything from his mind except what he had to do. The fence was barely visible, but that didn't deter him. He tensed, focused on the stump to the exclusion of all else and exploded into motion.

At his top speed Bolan sprang up onto the stump and leaped for all he was worth. He held his arms out to either side as if he were doing a swan dive into a pool. Bending and kicking his legs upward, he hurdled over and dipped into a shoulder roll. On landing, he swept up into a crouch. The Desert Eagle was in his hand and cocked, but no targets showed themselves.

The Executioner lost no time rearming himself with the M-16 and reclaiming the two devices. Hunched behind some weeds, he turned up the ear mike as far as it would go. Insect noises formed a constant buzz. Off to the left he heard a crackling like the frying of bacon in an open pan. In the green glow of the goggles he saw a rabbit sneaking away through a patch of dry brush.

Bolan also heard something else. It was an electronic hum different in pitch from that of the fence, and it came from the middle of the field, not the perimeter.

He wanted to take Mark Tasse by surprise. To do so, he had to avoid all the traps and sensors the genius had installed. So rather than cross the field and maybe activate one of the farm's defenses, he moved parallel with the fence toward the dark shapes of the trees that lined the driveway.

Bolan's reasoning was that the Wizard wouldn't install anything close to the fence because the high voltage would probably cause interference. But he erred. He had gone only a short distance when he skirted a clod of earth and happened to glance down. The glow of an electronic eye gleamed up at him.

Almost immediately the bionic ear registered a peculiar grinding noise somewhere in the field. It was followed by the growl of an engine turning over. A strange clanking noise ensued, growing rapidly louder.

Dropping low, Bolan wedged the M-16 to his shoulder. He had no idea what to expect, but he certainly didn't expect what appeared at the limits of the NVEC's range.

It was a robot. One of those remote-controlled mobile units used by SWAT teams and other law enforcement agencies. It had treads like a tank, and it was covered with armor plating. And mounted on top was what looked like a GE M-214 multibarreled minigun, which could unleash up to six thousand rounds a minute.

Worst of all, it was bearing right down on him.

CHAPTER TWENTY-TWO

Even as Mack Bolan set eyes on the mechanized killing machine, he flung himself to the right. It was none too soon. The minigun whined into operation, spewing a 5.56 mm hailstorm no living creature could withstand. If it were to strike him, he would be chewed to ribbons in the blink of an eye.

The ground erupted in hundreds of tiny geysers that followed Bolan as he rolled. He couldn't pause to fire because that brief instant would be all the robot's tracking sensor needed to lock on to his body-heat signature and nail him. So he went on rolling. He had no idea of what might lie in front of him and could only hope he didn't roll over a mine or some other equally lethal device.

Unexpectedly the firing ceased.

Bolan rolled onto his stomach and stopped. The robot's treads were digging into the earth as it backed up and swiveled its front end around to get another shot at him. In a flash he realized that the minigun had a ninety-degree field of fire, a flaw he might be able to exploit.

Shoving to his feet, Bolan spun and ran. The robot was much too close for him to try using a grenade; he'd be caught in the blast radius. He needed distance, just enough to put him at the limit of the kill zone.

Weaving wildly to throw off the robot's tracking system, Bolan covered twenty yards. It was far enough, he judged. He dug in his heels and whirled to see the armored monster barreling toward him. The minigun was swiveling to a dead-on lock.

The soldier worked the pump action of the grenade launcher. He didn't take the time to use the leaf sights, but simply pointed the M-203 and found the trigger. The moment he squeezed, he dropped flat.

The blast was everything Bolan expected it to be. The concussion buffeted him with the force of a physical blow. His ears throbbed with terrible pain. Fortunately the bionic ear had an automatic cutoff circuit that activated at a certain decibel level. His eardrum would have been ruptured had the mike not shut down just as the pain became almost too great to bear.

The sound of the explosion rippled off across the farm. So much for the element of surprise, Bolan mused. If by some fluke the Wizard hadn't known he was there before, the man most definitely did now.

A swirling cloud of dust hid the robot. Bolan worked the pump again but didn't rise. He waited for the cloud to settle, poised to fire. It seemed to take forever. But at last he glimpsed the robot, motionless, a small jagged hole in the plating of its underbelly.

Bolan glanced at the minigun, which drooped like a broken arm with its multiple barrels pointed straight down at the robot itself. He rose slowly. Evidently the thing hadn't been as tough as it looked.

No lights had blinked on at the farmhouse, which was disturbing. Bolan recalled Jamaica, and how the island's defensive systems had all been computer-controlled. Maybe it was the same here. Tasse might be elsewhere.

There was only one way to find out. Bolan went warily on, amazed at how quiet the night had become. The insects had fallen silent and even the wind had died.

Bolan scanned the pasture. In the distance a few fireflies sparkled. Otherwise he appeared to be totally alone. But he knew better. His gut instinct told him that unseen eyes were on him. And since he didn't like being out in the open—a virtual sitting duck for whatever tricks his enemies had up their sleeves—he dropped into a combat crouch and raced toward the cover of the maples and willows lining the driveway.

Halfway there, Bolan drew up in midstride. The tiny mike had detected a mechanical cough and sputter. He strained to hear more, and did. A servomotor kicked over, gears ratcheted and treads dug into the turf.

The robot was back on-line.

Bolan saw the glint of moonlight off metal. The mechanical killer was moving slowly in the direction of the farmhouse, not the trees. It made him suspect that its sensors had lost track of him and it was hunting him down.

The warrior gauged the distance to the trees. He was safe for the moment, but it was only a matter of time before the robot pinpointed him. Another grenade might take it out of commission, yet the robot had just as good a chance of nailing him first as long as he stayed out in the open.

Keeping low, Bolan bolted. He relied on the bionic ear to let him know if the robot locked on to him. For ten yards all went well, then he heard the robot speed up, heard the grind of the treads grow steadily louder. A glance showed it to be thirty yards from him and closing fast. Much too fast. It would overtake him long before he reached the trees.

Stopping on the head of a pin, Bolan whirled and let fly another grenade. He didn't stick around to see it hit. Legs flying, he continued toward the driveway. The blast wasn't as loud as the previous one. The concussion barely fazed him. He looked back and saw the front end of the robot materialize out of the cloud like a tank clanking out of dense fog.

One of the armor plates on top of the thing was partially buckled. Otherwise it hadn't been affected. The minigun kept swiveling back and forth as if the sensors were eager for target acquisition.

Bolan pushed himself to his limit. The night-vision goggles bounced with every stride, threatening to come loose and fall, but he couldn't spare the few seconds it would take to tighten them.

Seconds later the bionic ear warned him that the robot had increased its speed.

A hasty glance revealed it had locked on to him and was closing in for the kill. The minigun no longer swiveled but pointed right at him.

Bolan was still too far from cover. He had to stand and fight. But at the very moment he decided to stop and turn, a godsend presented itself in the form of an irrigation ditch a few yards in front of him.

It was shallow, no more than four feet deep. It hadn't been used in ages, and thistles lined the bottom and sides. But it was just what Bolan needed. Without hesitation he flung himself into it.

As the Executioner dived, the minigun burped to life, churning the soil under his flying body. The firing stopped, though, once he cleared the rim. He landed prone with the M-16 half under him and started to twist onto his side so he could use the weapon if necessary.

Suddenly the robot was there, looming out of the night like a metallic gray rhino. It braked a yard from the ditch, the whir of internal parts audible from the hole the first grenade had made.

Bolan didn't move a muscle. For all he knew, the unit was fit with motion sensors, as well as heat sensors. From the way the minigun pivoted back and forth, it was plain the thing had lost track of him.

Standard sensors in police and military robots were calibrated for a specific range. Usually they picked up targets from ground level to a preset height.

Aware of that, Bolan had dropped *below* ground level. To the robot, it was as if he had abruptly vanished. He had a perfect shot at the robot's underbelly, but he was much too close to even think of firing.

The thing's treads lurched into motion and it swung to the right, then to the left.

Bolan studied it, seeking a weak point. A large square box behind the minigun held the ammo belt, which threaded through a slit at the top and fed into the gun at a controlled rate. A smaller box at the rear gave no clues to its purpose, but Bolan doubted it had anything to do with the sensor arrays.

He stopped trying to find a weak point. The Wizard had been clever enough to conceal the sensors so no one could cripple the robot without a fight. He would have to find another way.

After several more seconds the sophisticated remote-controlled assassin moved off, conducting a grid sweep of the adjacent area.

Bolan slid the M-16 from under him and knelt. He tempted fate by raising his eyes above the top of the ditch. The robot was working its way back over the ground he had covered and had its rear end to him. It was like an engraved invitation.

Taking careful aim, Bolan fired a third grenade. He ducked as it detonated and was on his feet before the crashing boom died out. Smoke and dust hid the robot from him. They also hid him from it. He pivoted and leaped up out of the ditch, then made for the trees as if his heels were on fire.

The ruse almost worked. Bolan was a dozen steps shy of a string of maples when a jarring crash drew his attention.

The robot had locked on to him. It had to have been traveling at well over twenty miles per hour when it came to the irrigation ditch. The front end had tilted down and smashed onto the opposite rim, at which point the perpetual forward thrust of the treads had thrown the front half into the air.

As the soldier watched, the robot pancaked, hitting the ground so hard that it swerved wildly from side to side before the guidance system brought it under control. He darted to the right a fraction before the minigun cut loose. Lead smacked into a trunk in front of him. Before the robot's brain could compensate, he reached the maples.

Bolan squatted at the base of a trunk and fed another grenade into the launcher. He had done enough running. Sighting carefully, he went to fire when the minigun opened up with a blustering firestorm. Bolan had to jerk back as the tree shielding him was blistered. So was the next tree, and the next. One by one the robot was going down the row, trying to drive him into the open.

The Executioner lunged to the left and landed on his shoulder with the M-16 extended. The launcher coughed. A deafening explosion rocked the robot, and the metal beast swung back toward him. Quickly Bolan pumped in yet another grenade. He fired at the very moment the robot did, then had to flip behind the maple again as rounds kicked up dirt almost at his side.

A rending of metal heralded abrupt silence. Bolan cautiously edged around the trunk. This time he had scored. The explosion had torn the minigun from its housing and left it lying in twisted ruin on the ground. In addition, plates under and around the housing had buckled and tendrils of smoke wafted skyward.

Bolan figured the robot had been disabled. He rose and turned toward the farmhouse, and as he did, the mechanical predator proved him wrong by growling to life one more time. To his surprise, it lurched forward, gaining speed swiftly, making straight for him. Its intent was unmistakable. Since it couldn't gun him down, it was going to try to run him down.

Rather than waste another grenade, Bolan held his ground until the thing was almost upon him, then threw himself behind the tree to his right. The robot shot past, out onto the dirt driveway. Its treads locked and it began to slow, to turn.

Bolan wasn't going to be there when it did. He headed for the next tree. Suddenly part of the driveway went up like a volcano. He heard rather than saw the blast, but he did feel the invisible hand that picked him up as if he were a rag doll, casting him ten feet out into the field. He landed on his back and lay there, stunned but still conscious, with his eyes closed.

The robot had struck a mine, Bolan realized. His head hurt and his back was sore, but that was all. He was lucky to be alive, since the explosion would have killed him had the robot not borne the brunt of it.

Gritting his teeth, Bolan opened his eyes, then frowned. The night was black now instead of neon green. He had lost the goggles. And as if that weren't bad enough, the ear mike was crackling like a radio with a short. It had been rendered useless, its circuitry blown.

Bolan sat up, removed the bionic ear and stuck it into a pocket. Rising, he saw the M-16 a few feet away. He examined it carefully to confirm it would still work, then headed for the trees. Halfway there his left foot bumped something and he looked down to find the NVEC 800. The right lens had been shattered and the device was slightly bent, but he tried it on.

In the green glow of the left half, Bolan saw the crumpled wreckage of the robot at one side of the driveway. The mine had nearly torn its body in two. Strands of wire had burst out like the intestines of some wild beast and lay strewed across the drive.

Since stealth was no longer required, Bolan made for the house at a trot. He stayed close to the trees and kept his gaze to the ground, alert for more mines. Because he had his head bent, he nearly missed seeing the network of pencil-thin beams.

They crisscrossed the driveway and extended out into the field as far as the Executioner could see. They formed a barrier that no unaided human eye could detect. It was the ultimate alarm system, one more in keeping with the high-tech wizardry employed at Stony

Man than the pastoral simplicity of Pennsylvania Dutch country.

The beams themselves weren't dangerous. But once Bolan broke one, Tasse would know exactly where he was and would be bound to attack. Bolan wanted to avoid that if he could.

But how? he asked himself. The laser fence rose to a height of seven feet, and there was no way he could jump over it. Nor was there enough space to crawl under the lowest beam. It seemed the system was foolproof.

Then Bolan saw the small black box that stuck a few inches out of the soil. Kneeling, he determined that it was some sort of relay device, just one of many that controlled the beams of light. Breaking it would defeat his purpose. But what would happen if he used the scrambler? Bolan wondered.

Taking the unit out, Bolan pressed the On button and felt a tingle in his palm. He watched the power meter as he had been instructed, and when it reached one hundred percent he held the scrambler down close to the signal amplifier and pressed another button.

Immediately the section of laser light fence generated by the black box disappeared. Its circuitry had been momentarily disrupted.

Bolan stepped past the fence and waited the few seconds it took for the black box to reactivate. If all had gone well, the Wizard's monitoring system had registered the blackout as a simple electronic glitch, similar to static on a radio. Tasse wouldn't think twice about it. With any luck.

The Executioner was now sixty feet from the farmhouse. Still no lights had come on, and there was no sign that anyone was home. Hating to think that he had gone to all that trouble for nothing, Bolan glided nearer, the M-16 leveled.

Bolan reached the last of the trees, a weeping willow with branches so low the leaves brushed the ground as he walked into the open. The next moment the light over the front door winked out. He squatted and trained the rifle on the entrance, unsure of what to expect.

There was movement, but not at the door. A shutter beside a corner window swung out, revealing a hole about the size of a tennis ball. A rounded metal cone began to ease outward.

Bolan was reminded of the missile launcher at Xaymaca. This had to be a small missile similar to those, probably a heat-seeker that would be triggered once the miniature thruster was clear of the house.

Whipping out the scrambler, Bolan turned it on and watched impatiently as the power meter climbed. He glanced again at the launcher. Six inches had emerged, and it was still sliding out. Whirling, he ran to the willow and hastily wedged the scrambler in the fork of a limb. Then he sprinted farther down the drive, passing three more trees. At the fourth he darted behind the trunk.

There was no guarantee the tactic would work, but it was the only card Bolan had to play. The heat-seeker would probably home in on the scrambler and blow it to smithereens instead of him. He peered around the trunk, and suddenly the goggles hissed and went completely dead.

As if on cue, the driveway was lit up by an incendiary blast. A blaze of white light engulfed the willow. A fireball seared the branches that held the scrambler, and one of them crashed to earth.

If not for the NVEC, Bolan would have been briefly blinded. He set down the useless goggles and ran to the willow. The trunk was on fire, but the flames were small and would soon die down.

It didn't take a genius to know that a sensor planted between the trees and the porch had activated the missile. And there were bound to be more. Once Bolan stepped out from under the willow, he would be fair game.

But there might be a way for him to beat Tasse at the man's own game. He couldn't help but notice that there had been a time lag between the tripping of the sensor and the firing of the missile. If he was right, it meant he had four or five seconds to reach the front door before the next defensive device was activated.

If he was wrong, he'd be dead before he traveled ten feet.

The Executioner raised the M-16 and sprinted toward the porch. He ran in long, loping strides, avoiding bumps that might be mines, on the lookout for trip wires. Unharmed, he reached the bottom step, but as he went to climb, a panel to the left of the door swung open and the muzzle of a machine gun slid out.

Bolan dropped onto the steps as .45-caliber slugs whizzed overhead. He still had two grenades left, and he triggered one now. It not only destroyed the machine gun but blew a jagged hole in the wall big enough for him to walk through. It gave him an idea.

Since the door was more than likely booby-trapped, Bolan went through the hole with his senses primed. Smoke and dust hung in the air. He was in a living room. Some of the furniture had been torn apart by the explosion and a bookshelf had toppled over. It hadn't held books, though. Broken electronic equipment lay in ruin.

But what interested Bolan the most was that an overhead light was on, and another burned in a hallway. A quick check of the nearest window showed why all of them had appeared as black as pitch from the outside. Someone had coated the panes with black paint.

The house was quiet. Bolan crossed to the doorway and poked his head out. To his right the hall passed several rooms. To his left, at the end of the hall, was a kitchen. A table and part of an old-fashioned potbellied stove were framed by the jamb.

Bolan bore to the right. He had learned his lesson well in Jamaica and scoured the walls, floor and ceiling for hidden sensors and pressure plates. The first room he came to contained a dusty piano, chairs and a settee. Venturing on, he stopped cold when he spotted a surveillance camera mounted close to the ceiling at the far end. It was fixed on him, and a red indicator light below the lens blazed brightly.

The Wizard was watching his every move.

Automatically Bolan fired a short burst into the camera. Sparks shot from the casing as it broke apart and fell in pieces to the hardwood floor. Bolan flattened against the wall and braced for Tasse's response, but the house stayed quiet. It seemed to be added proof that the warped weapons maker wasn't there, that once again Bolan had been up against a computer instead of a human foe.

The next door was closed. Bolan gingerly tested the black metal latch. It lifted easily, so he carefully eased the door inward far enough to see behind it. No trip wires were attached. Instead, a flight of wooden stairs led down to a brightly lit basement. Banks of equipment lined the walls, and the hum of a computer was audible.

It had to be the Wizard's control center.

Bolan eased onto the first step. The wood appeared solid enough but he knew how cleverly pressure plates could be concealed. He didn't want to get halfway down and have the stairs blow up under him.

Taking them two at a time and staying close to the edge, where there was less chance of triggering an explosive, Bolan safely reached the bottom.

The basement had to have been little more than a root cellar at one time. Tasse had enlarged it immensely. Half of the floor was a workshop, while the rest was filled with computer equipment. But none of it was of any interest to Bolan. For seated in a swivel chair was a lean man in casual clothes. He was unconscious, and he had been bound hand and foot. His chin rested on his chest, while his body tilted to one side, on the verge of sliding off the edge of the seat.

Bolan took a few steps nearer. He bent to see the man's face and recognized Mark Tasse from the mug shots Brognola had shown him before he left Stony Man Farm. How could that be? he mused. Who had tied the man up? As soon as his mind formed the question, Bolan had the answer—the Germans.

Almost too late, Bolan sensed someone come up behind him. Instantly he straightened and began to turn. As he did, a long, thin wire slipped over his head.

CHAPTER TWENTY-THREE

Rarely was the Executioner taken by surprise. His combat senses were too razor sharp, his reflexes too lightning quick, for anyone to get the better of him.

In this instance the loud hum of the computer and other equipment drowned out what little noise Gunther Merzig made as the man crept up on him. And for a few seconds Bolan had been so intent on the bound man in the chair that he hadn't stayed fully alert.

Now, as the garrote swept over the Executioner's head, only one thing saved his life. As he had bent to examine the Wizard, he had held the M-16 close to his chest. The barrel was near his neck, so near that the sweeping wire snagged it.

Bolan steeled his arms and surged forward to throw Merzig off-balance. The rifle's barrel kept the garrote from closing on his throat, although the wire did bite into the flesh on either side of his neck.

At that very moment Katya Steiner stepped into the open. She had changed her hair from blond to brunette and had on the long dress worn by the Amish farmer's wife. She also wore a mocking smile that evaporated when she saw Gunther stumble and nearly lose his grip.

Uttering a curse in German, Katya sprang to grab the big man in the fatigue shirt and hold him still so Gunther could finish the job. She had done the same to many others since teaming with Gunther. How she liked watching their faces change color, their eyes bulge and their tongues loll out! It gave her a thrill so intense she was almost giddy.

Bolan saw the woman rush forward as he struggled to keep the garrote from wrapping tight around him. Her hands swept up and he guessed her intent before she grabbed hold. Suddenly shifting, he delivered a snap kick to her right leg, trying to hit her knee. There was no loud snap, as there would have been had the kneecap shattered, but Steiner still cried out and staggered against the computer.

It enraged Gunther Merzig, who growled deep in his throat like a wild animal and drove his own knee into the back of the soldier's leg.

Almost buckling under the blow, Bolan righted himself at the last moment and threw all his weight to the right, then the left. It was critical that he keep Merzig from planting his feet and getting a firm grip.

To her credit, Katya recovered swiftly. Her face a mask of raw blood lust, she clawed her fingers and leaped.

Bolan was between the woman and the man. Once she clamped her hands on him and held him fast, Merzig would be able to set himself. It would all be over in moments. Bolan wasn't about to let that happen. He threw everything he had into bending at the waist while at the same instant he whipped to the right. It had the desired effect.

Gunther Merzig hadn't been able to set himself. He had dug in his heels time and again only to be thrown off stride by the soldier's constant motion. Now, as if catapulted from a cannon, he was hurled through the air, straight into Katya. For the first time ever, Gunther lost his grip on his garrote as the two of them tumbled to the floor.

The same move that saved Bolan sent him to his knees. His neck throbbed with pain, and blood trickled down the right side. Reaching up, he tore the limp wire from his throat and cast it to the floor. Then he spun to confront the pair of professionals.

As Bolan started to bring up the M-16, he caught sight of the Wizard. The man had to have faked being unconscious because he was on his feet, madly hopping toward the stairs like an oversize rabbit. For the moment Bolan had to let him go. He had his hands full.

Merzig was already in a crouch. From under a sleeve he had produced a knife, which he held ready to thrust. Snarling, he lunged.

The M-16 became an extension of Bolan's own arms as he parried the knife with the barrel and then whipped a vertical butt stroke to the chin that sent Merzig flying into a console. Bolan twisted and brought the rifle up to shoot the German in the chest, but as he did a shoulder slammed into him from the rear and he was knocked onto his side. Slim fingers closed on the barrel and tried to wrest the M-16 from his grasp.

Katya Steiner was beside herself with rage at being balked and seeing her lover bested. She yanked on the rifle with all her might while trying to kick the Executioner in the head. Hampered by the long white dress, her blows lacked power. Bolan shrugged them off, hooked an arm behind her left ankle and heaved. She toppled. In doing so, she finally managed to tear the rifle free and it fell with her.

As Bolan pushed up off the floor, he was dimly aware of a peculiar thumping sound and realized it had to be Tasse going up the cellar stairs. He didn't think the man would get very far trussed up, so he dismissed the man as he made a grab for the Beretta.

Steiner was sitting up, a grin of triumph lighting her face, her finger on the trigger of the M-16 as she brought the rifle to bear. She believed that she had her adversary dead to rights. She was wrong.

The sound suppressor coughed three times, the shots spaced so closely that there was scarcely a break between them. As each slug cored her head, Steiner jolted to the impact. Three holes blossomed in a cluster squarely in the center of her forehead. She wore a look of utter astonishment as she flopped backward and lay with her wide eyes fixed on the ceiling. Her body spasmed and her finger closed on the trigger. A volley ripped into the acoustic tiles. Bits and pieces rained to the floor, covering her flawless features with a layer of fine white dust.

Bolan had already started to turn toward Merzig when the M-16 went off. Automatically he ducked, thinking that the woman had fired at him. When he saw that she hadn't, he went to finish his turn. But it was too late. Merzig had recovered.

The German drove the knife at the soldier's chest while grabbing hold of his right wrist. Bolan seized Gunther's own wrist to block the blade. Locked together, they strained against each other. Gunther was on his feet, Bolan on his knees. It gave the assassin an edge, and he began to bend his opponent backward.

Bolan used that to his advantage. He went with the flow and threw himself to the rear. Merzig was yanked off his feet. As the German fell toward him, the Executioner rammed both feet into Merzig's gut, rolled onto his shoulders and kicked.

Gunther smashed into a table, which upended. Both crashed down, the table pinning Merzig's knife arm. In falling, the German's flailing legs hit a tall rack laden with heavy test equipment. The whole rack fell on top of him as he was trying to lift off the table. The thud of its impact was lost in the raucous smash of breaking components.

Bolan had the Beretta trained, ready to fire when Merzig rose. But the killer lay unmoving, his head and chest under the rack. The Executioner got to his feet and stepped closer.

Gunther Merzig was out cold. A wide gash on his temple bled freely, and his lower lip had been pulped. In addition, his left arm had been broken below the elbow. Pale bone gleamed through ruptured flesh.

Bolan tried to lift the rack, but it weighed well over two hundred pounds and was much too bulky to handle easily. Confident that the German wouldn't be going anywhere anytime soon, he sprinted to the steps. He had to catch the Wizard.

He paused at the top. He heard a faint sound from the kitchen, or beyond it, so he headed in that direction. On the kitchen floor below an open drawer he spotted the cut pieces of rope used to bind Tasse, and a butcher knife.

The outside door hung half-open. Bolan slammed out into the cool night air.

The Amish farmer's wagon stood on the grass. The horse pricked its ears at him, then lowered its head to graze.

Bolan guessed that the Germans had disguised themselves to get safely onto the property. Tasse would hardly have been rash enough to slay a friendly farmer and his wife, since the last thing he wanted was to have police swarming over the area. The man had probably deactivated his security systems and let the pair drive right up to the house. It was ironic that one of the most notorious criminal geniuses alive had been outsmarted by one of the oldest tricks in the book.

A loud noise from a large shed across the lawn attracted Bolan's attention. The wide double doors weren't quite closed, and through them he spied the dull gleam of metal. It looked like chrome.

An engine roared to life. The double doors were flung wide as a brand-new pickup truck shot out of the shed and angled toward the driveway.

Bolan was right in its path, caught in the glare of its headlights. He barely had time to raise the Beretta and fire before the vehicle was on him. He missed the Wizard by a hair. Then the truck's grille loomed in front of his face and he leaped to the right to avoid being run down.

As the pickup flashed by, the soldier jumped and caught hold of the side of the bed. Yanked off his feet, he clung tight. He tried to pull himself up but the pickup suddenly swerved. He nearly lost his grip. He did lose the Beretta, which skittered off across the bed.

Another swerve sent Bolan swinging wildly outward. It was all he could do to stay on. He saw that the Wizard was making a beeline for the pasture instead of the driveway. It had to be because Tasse didn't care to risk hitting a mine.

Bolan arced his right leg up onto the side and was about to slide over onto the bed when the vehicle roared out to the field doing fifty miles per hour. It hit a rut. The whole truck bounced off the ground and landed with a bone-jarring thud. The Executioner was almost thrown off. His leg slipped and he fell, and he held on by the tips of his fingers as his legs were dragged along dangerously close to the rear wheel.

The Wizard looked in the side mirror and smirked.

Again the truck swerved. Bolan bunched his shoulder muscles but felt himself slowly slipping. Another bump was all it would take to dislodge him. Without a moment to spare he pushed upward and swung an elbow over the side. It was all that saved him when the vehicle hit a dip that bucked the tail end into the air. He swayed but didn't fall. Then the wheels crashed down and his chin smashed against the side panel so hard that for a few seconds his vision swam.

The impact did something else. Unexpectedly it flipped Bolan into the bed. He grabbed at the side for support and struggled to sit up as his head cleared.

Tasse was hunched over the wheel and had the gas pedal floored. He was heading right for the electrified fence at seventy miles per hour.

Bolan swooped his hand to the Desert Eagle. As he started to draw, the Wizard spun the steering wheel and he was pitched against the side. He tried to steady himself, to rise and shoot, but the truck fishtailed again and he was thrown onto his back.

Pushing to his knees, Bolan saw that he had run out of time. They were almost to the fence. He shoved to his feet so his rubber soles would insulate him from the massive voltage, but as he did, the truck was jarred by yet another bump. Before he could catch himself, Bolan was hurled clear of the bed. In midair he saw the pickup ram into the fence. Vivid arcs of electricity lit up the night. Then the truck was through to the other side, leaving in its wake the stench of burnt paint and charred rubber.

He took all this in as he smacked down on his back. A rocky knob bruised his shoulder and sent fingers of pain shooting up his arm, but otherwise he was unhurt. Springing erect, he raced toward the road and tried to fix a bead on Tasse as the pickup flew toward the main highway. It was hopeless.

The man was getting away.

Bolan sprinted through the gap in the fence. He plunged a hand into a pocket and pulled out the keys to the jeep as he crossed the road.

Tasse was only a few hundred yards off when he plowed the vehicle through the wall of vegetation and gave chase. Bolan pressed the pedal flat, and the speedometer rapidly climbed from forty to eighty.

As fast as Bolan was going, it wasn't fast enough. He didn't gain any ground. The engine in the pickup was more powerful than the jeep's. All he could do was try to keep Tasse in view.

No other vehicles were in sight, not even when they reached the highway. The Wizard took the turn at a reckless speed and the pickup swerved sharply, nearly out of control. Bolan hoped it would roll, but no such luck. Tires screaming, Tasse headed toward Ephrata.

Bolan took the turn on the inside corner. He came within a hand's width of clipping a fence post. Then the tires caught on the asphalt and he floored it, zeroing in on the pickup's taillights.

For the next several minutes the two vehicles flashed through the night, the pickup gradually widening its lead. Bolan could only sit and watch in growing frustration as yet another chance to bring the Wizard to bay fizzled. He had the speedometer buried but it did no good. Jeeps were built to handle rugged terrain, not for setting speed records.

The pickup swept over a rise. To Bolan it seemed as if the jeep crawled to the top. Once there, he was disturbed to see the pickup's lead had increased even more. It was hopeless.

Just then a small gray cloud appeared in the middle of the lane. Bolan passed through it and smelled a strong odor that brought to mind hot engine oil. He came to a second cloud, then a third.

Bolan hoped that they came from the pickup. Its undercarriage had been viciously battered when it crossed the pasture. Maybe, just maybe, some serious damage had been done. He might still catch his quarry.

A low hill came between them. On cresting it, Bolan saw that the taillights were closer than they had been before. Ever so slowly, he gained.

The jeep barreled through more and more tiny clouds. Bolan took out the Desert Eagle and placed it on the console beside him. He saw the pickup shimmy and belch black smoke. And then he spotted something in front of the pickup.

It was another Amish wagon, hugging the shoulder so that motorized vehicles could pass. An elderly farmer was handling the reins. He glanced back and beckoned so Tasse would swing on around. But the Wizard did no such thing. The pickup cut in front of the wagon and braked, causing the horse to rear in fright. The farmer had his hands full trying to prevent the animal from bolting. And as the Amish man struggled with the reins, Tasse vaulted out of the truck, ran up to the wagon and at point-blank range shot the farmer in the head.

There was nothing Bolan could do. He was still several hundred feet away when the Wizard pulled the body from the wagon seat and took its place. With a flick of the reins, Tasse lashed the horse into a trot and made off across the adjacent field.

Bolan figured the man had lost his senses. There was no way on earth a horse and wagon could outrun a jeep. Then he saw a dark wall of trees at the end of the field and knew that Tasse intended to lose him in the woods. He left the road, bounced over a ditch and attempted to head the man off.

In seconds the jeep was a stone's throw from the back of the wagon. Bolan slanted to the right to come up alongside of it. His window was down. All he had to do was point the big .44 and squeeze off a few rounds.

Suddenly the Wizard slid to the edge of the wagon seat. He glared at the onrushing jeep, took one hand from the reins and reached into a pants pocket. A small, circular shiny object was in his palm when he pulled the hand out.

Bolan didn't like the mocking sneer that creased Tasse's face. He liked it even less when the Wizard twisted and heaved the small object at the jeep. Arms churning, he spun the steering wheel to put more distance between them.

The metal sphere hit the ground twenty feet away. A brilliant burst of blinding light lit up the darkness. It was so bright that Bolan had to throw a hand in front of his eyes in order not to be blinded. He tramped on the brakes. The jeep slid to a lurching stop, and he blinked to dispel the white dots that seemed to swirl in front of him.

The wagon had clattered to the very edge of the trees.

Bolan drove on. He was forty yards back when Tasse leaped from the seat and darted into the undergrowth. Leery of being lured into a trap, Bolan stopped well short of the wagon, turned off the lights and killed the engine. He made a point of pocketing the keys in case the Wizard planned to circle around him and escape in his vehicle.

Taking the Desert Eagle, Bolan ran toward the spot where Tasse had entered the woods. He slowed to listen but heard no crunch of fleeing footsteps. The Wizard was too smart for that.

The horse harnessed to the wagon made it hard for the warrior to hear. Rattled by the gunshot, the scent of blood and the race across the field, it nervously pranced and snorted.

Bolan veered to the right. He skirted a thicket of blackberry bushes and crouched behind an oak tree. Other than the flutter of leaves overhead and the antics of the horse, the woods were still. Tasse was either a skilled woodsman or the man was waiting for Bolan to show himself.

Way off to the south a train whistled. To the east an owl voiced its eternal question.

The minutes dragged by. Bolan leaned a shoulder on the trunk and probed the shadows. Several stones were close to his feet. Picking one up, he chose a point where the brush was thickest and threw it.

The crackle of limbs provoked no reaction at all.

Bolan stared deep into the forest. He figured that he would loop around to the west to try to outflank Tasse. As he rose, the horse let out a strident whinny. Bolan turned and glimpsed a figure moving near the animal.

The Executioner sprinted back past the thicket in time to see a vague form duck behind the wagon. Certain that he had Tasse dead to rights, he bore to the left to better see the rear of the wagon, where the Wizard was likely to reappear.

Bolan adopted a Weaver stance and lined up the sights. A whisper of air above him made him look up. Arcing down toward him was a spinning metal sphere. He brought up his right hand to cover his eyes, but he was a shade too slow.

The blaze of white light was like the sun going nova. Bolan staggered back, blinking in a vain bid to clear his vision. All he could see was a pale haze. He had to get out of there, had to find cover before the Wizard put a dozen bullets into him. But as he turned, his right foot caught on a clump of grass. Before he could stop himself, he pitched onto his stomach. In the process he pinned his own arm under his chest and could feel the pistol poking his ribs.

Bolan put his left hand flat to brace himself as he rose. The scuff of a shoe on the ground told him that he was no longer alone. A gun barrel touched his temple, and he tensed for the shot to come.

"You should have known this would be the result," the Wizard declared smugly. "Whoever you are, you're no match for a man of my intellect. No one is."

The voice came from above Bolan and to the right. To stall, and to pinpoint the man's exact position, he said, "You're not so smart, Tasse. Or didn't you know I have a partner?"

"You do not," the Wizard said, but his tone lacked total conviction.

Bolan could tell that the man had looked up to scan the area. He still couldn't see well, yet that didn't stop him from suddenly twisting and swinging at Tasse's pistol even as he jerked the Desert Eagle out from under him and fired again and again at the spot where he believed the Wizard to be standing. He heard the man's gun go off, heard the soft thud of slugs striking home.

Then with a scream, Tasse crashed on top of him. Bolan rolled out from under the corpse and confirmed the kill. It was over.

EPILOGUE

The Executioner was honing his marksmanship at the indoor firing range at Stony Man Farm when Hal Brognola approached. Bolan ran a finger over the one-inch cluster of shots that he had put into a target at a range of one hundred yards, then turned.

"Not bad," the big Fed said, nodding.

"What's up?" Bolan asked as he ejected the spent magazine and inserted another.

"Gunther Merzig sang like a dove to avoid being extradited. He wants to do his time in this country instead of in Germany." Brognola paused. "It's a sad state of affairs when our prison system has a reputation for being one of the easiest on criminals of any on the planet. But that's life, I guess."

"Did he say who hired him?"

"An industrialist by the name of Reutlingen. German authorities have taken him into custody and expect to charge him with half a dozen crimes, including several counts of being an accessory to murder."

"Then that's that." Bolan pressed the button that would send the target sliding back to the far end of the range, where it would be replaced by a new one.

The Executioner would spend a few days at the Farm, recharging his batteries, relishing seventy-two hours' respite from his War Everlasting. Then the phone call would come and he'd be off again, heading into the hellgrounds. But until then, Mack Bolan was standing down.

A global war is about to begin. There is one chance for peace...

Satan missiles, the world's most powerful nuclear warheads, are being sold on the Moscow black market. The Stony Man warriors must act with swift and deadly force if they're going to keep the missiles from reaching terrorist launching pads.

Look for it in March, wherever Gold Eagle books are sold.

Or order your copy now by sending your name, address, zip or postal code along with a check or money order (please do not send cash) for $4.99 for each book ordered ($5.50 in Canada), plus 75¢ postage and handling ($1.00 in Canada), payable to Gold Eagle Books, to:

In the U.S.
Gold Eagle Books
3010 Walden Avenue
P.O. Box 9077
Buffalo, NY 14269-9077

In Canada
Gold Eagle Books
P.O. Box 636
Fort Erie, Ontario
L2A 5X3

Please specify book title with your order.
Canadian residents add applicable federal and provincial taxes.

SM21

It's the ultimate battle between
good and bad—Made in Mexico

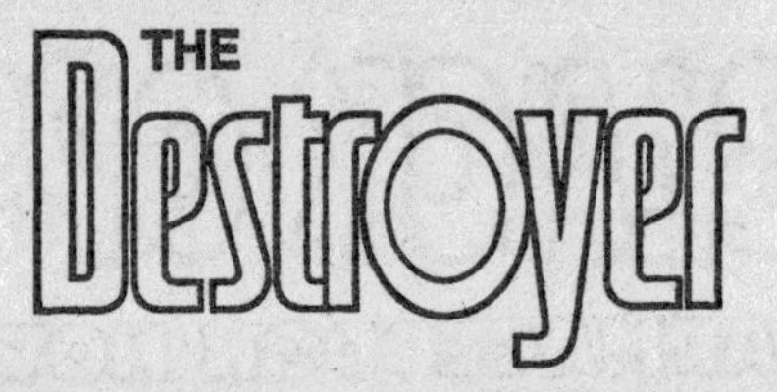

#102 Unite and Conquer

**Created by
WARREN MURPHY
and RICHARD SAPIR**

Not that things were so hot before, but when a huge earthquake guts Mexico, nobody wants to hang around, especially with all sorts of demonic doings by the barbaric gods of old Mexico, released from hell when the earth ruptured. It's god versus god, with the human race helpless trophies for the victor.

Look for it in March, wherever Gold Eagle books are sold.

Or order your copy now by sending your name, address, zip or postal code, along with a check or money order (please do not send cash) for $4.99 for each book ordered ($5.50 in Canada), plus 75¢ postage and handling ($1.00 in Canada), payable to Gold Eagle Books, to:

In the U.S.
Gold Eagle Books
3010 Walden Ave.
P. O. Box 9077
Buffalo, NY 14269-9077

In Canada
Gold Eagle Books
P. O. Box 636
Fort Erie, Ontario
L2A 5X3

Please specify book title with order.
Canadian residents add applicable federal and provincial taxes.

DEST102

A flare-up of hatred and violence threatens to engulf America

BLACK OPS #2

ARMAGEDDON NOW

created by MICHAEL KASNER

The Black Ops team goes where the law can't—to avenge acts of terror directed against Americans around the world. But now the carnage is the bloody handiwork of Americans as Los Angeles turns into a powder keg in a sweeping interracial war. Deployed to infiltrate the gangs, the Black Ops commandos uncover a trail of diabolical horror leading to a gruesome vision of social engineering....

Available in May at your favorite retail outlet or order your copy now by sending your name, address, zip or postal code, along with a check or money order (please do not send cash) for $4.99 ($5.50 in Canada) for each book ordered, plus 75¢ postage and handling ($1.00 in Canada), payable to Gold Eagle Books, to:

In the U.S.
Gold Eagle Books
3010 Walden Ave.
P.O. Box 9077
Buffalo, NY 14269-9077

In Canada
Gold Eagle Books
P.O. Box 636
Fort Erie, Ontario
L2A 5X3

Please specify book title with your order.
Canadian residents add applicable federal and provincial taxes.

BO2